Beyond the Law

Beyond the Law

F. M. Kahren

6-5-14

To Dr V. Tang with
Very Best Wishes.

J. M. Kahren

Copyright © 2014 by F.M. Kahren

Beyond the Law

Cover, Book Design, and Editing by Jo Kahren

Beyond the Law is a work of fiction. Although many of the places referenced in the book are real, some characteristics have been changed to fit the story. Some real historical characters and events have been mentioned to enhance the story. However, all names, characters, businesses, places, organizations, historical events, and incidents are the product of the author's imagination, used fictitiously, and not to be confused with fact. Any resemblance to events, locals, organizations, and persons, living or dead, is entirely coincidental.

Product names, brands, and other trademarks referred to within this book are the property of their respective trademark holders. Unless otherwise specified, no association between the author and any trademark holder is expressed or implied. Use of a term in this book should not be regarded as affecting the validity of any trademark, registered trademark, or service mark.

Library of Congress Control Number: 2014906848

ISBN-13: 978-0-9720269-4-9
Paperback

First Edition, April 2014
24681097531

Published by F.M. Kahren
Danville, CA

Beyond the Law is also available in:

Kindle ISBN-13: 978-0-9720269-3-2
Large Print Paperback ISBN-13: 978-0-9720269-5-6

Printed in the United States of America

Books by F.M. Kahren
Brand Loyalty
Beyond the Law

To Thomas L. Gatten, who served, and well.

Contents

Acknowledgments

I would like to thank Cheryl Andersen, Ron and Paulette Avery, Sue Bunch, Chris Igo, Carol Nuesslein, and Michael Tanner for their intelligence, diligence, and attention to detail in reading the manuscript.

Also, much appreciated are those generous souls who read and enjoyed my first novel, *Brand Loyalty*, and wanted more.

I would also like to thank former Correctional Officer Michael Davis for sharing some of his experiences at San Quentin State Prison.

For the final edits, cover art, and all of the endless, brute-force work involved in bringing *Beyond the Law* to market: I owe everything to my loving wife, Jo.

Beyond this, I alone am responsible for this absolutely and completely fictitious account.

Beyond the Law

1

Before the Great Storm

You need what you need when you need it. Weapons, ammunition, food, shelter, medical supplies. Amateurs talk strategy, professionals talk logistics. For a military enterprise, logistical failure means scarcity: not enough food, not enough mobility, not enough firepower. Scarcity can mean defeat, and defeat is unacceptable. So, there has to be a place to store the equipment and supplies needed for victory, and such treasure requires protection. The best protection involves a location so undesirable that even the prospect of valuable military loot fades in comparison to the prospect of enduring such a miserable environment. One possibility: a sweltering California wasteland baking in the central valley sun. Barstow, California—where double-wide trailers go to die.

USMC Logistics Base, Yermo Annex, Barstow, California: Close to town, far from anywhere, and the home of the only horse-mounted color guard in the corps. On this day, the focus was not on horses but on the small base theater. Here, for a dollar, off-duty personnel could see the films that cable TV had grown tired of showing. Thanks to the magic of air conditioning, the base theater was also a prime location for awards and decorations and retirement ceremonies. Today was something special, a real changing of the guard. Gunnery Sergeant Darren Feith would become the depot's new senior noncommissioned officer, or NCO, but it was the departing senior NCO that everyone was coming to see, a real slice of the old corps, a near legendary hard-charger with an incredible forty-eight years of service.

The only child of an alcoholic couple, Michael Patrick Gilhooley cared for his parents practically from the time he was a toddler—dodging the old man's backhand, lifting enough money from his wallet to buy food and pay the rent. Gilhooley had despised his father as a drunk, but cherished and cared for his mother as the victim of a terrible disease even though they suffered from the same disease.

One day, shortly after his fourteenth birthday, his parents were out on the town celebrating payday. The lovely spring evening must have felt wonderful as they stood swaying at the top of the long, tall, steep concrete stairway that looked over the city lights sparkling on the river. Moments later, they were ex-alcoholics and Michael was an orphan. Within the week, Michael Patrick Gilhooley had lied about his age, enlisted in the United States Marine Corps, and was on his way to Camp Lejeune.

Forty-eight years later, from the stage of the base theater, Master Gunnery Sergeant Gilhooley looked out on the audience, on his beloved corps. Physically, he was a smaller man than his successor. Over his more than four decades of service, Gilhooley's beloved corps had grown bigger, faster, stronger, smarter. Feith and Gilhooley in their olive-green service uniforms—both men fit, commanding. But Gilhooley possessed a fire. A man of boundless energy and imagination, Gilhooley still radiated an intensity that sustained him right up to his sixty-second birthday and mandatory retirement. His was a physically destructive profession. NCOs are leaders, and leaders must do so from the front. As a senior NCO, Gilhooley inflicted an endless mix of tours of the obstacle course, forced marches, and pugil stick exercises that exhausted everyone involved. These were unusual events for a logistics base. Like every zealot, Master Gunnery Sergeant Gilhooley could be a pain.

The ceremony of succession should have been simple. Feith would accept the mantle of senior status on the base, praise and honor his predecessor, and then allow the Master Gunnery Sergeant to make his valedictory address. Feith had other plans.

"I see twelve service stripes on the sleeve of my predecessor," Feith began. "I see awards for valor and gallantry. I also see an old man, a remnant of an unsophisticated corps whose time has passed. In fact, it passed long ago. Our modern corps must turn to the future, an intellectually and technically demanding future, a future where America has no permanent friends, or even permanent values, only permanent interests. The profession of arms is becoming one that demands a high degree of proficiency and one which, for some, will offer a high degree of compensation, particularly in the private sector."

With that, Master Gunnery Sergeant Gilhooley executed an about-face and exited the rear of the theater. Feith smiled out at his stunned audience. "The truth is a hard thing to face. For some, facing change can be even harder. But we are here to face the future, its challenges as well as its rewards." Feith heard the rear door click open. *So, the old man had come back.* Feith turned slowly to smile down on the smaller, older man. A flash of white streaked into his peripheral vision. Sparks exploded inside his head as Feith collapsed to the stage floor.

The entire theater seemed to snap to attention as three hundred pairs of eyes focused on the two players on stage. The big man was out cold, but he was breathing. On any given day in the corps, someone could get well-and-truly clocked. Nearly always, such an event was the result of a training exercise. Two men don helmets, brandish pugil sticks, and step into the pit. During the exercise, one combatant could seize upon the mistake of his adversary. A ferocious buttstroke could send the hapless foe unconscious into the gravel. No one in the theater moved. Truth be known, the Marine Corps has a special place in its heart for violent men, and, over the decades, Gilhooley had cultivated a reputation as a man who managed to stay just this side of the nuthouse. The silence was absolute and intense.

Master Gunnery Sergeant Gilhooley held a large whitewashed stone over his head. He turned it so that everyone could see the blood smeared across it. He called out in a booming, imperious voice that shook the walls. "Behold this rock. The mark one rock! When the Hittites were trawling the ancient desert in search of Babylonian pussy, this rock was old technology. But it still works."

"Vietnam. Grenada. Panama. Kuwait. I have served with the men and women who have fought our country's battles. The weapons changed. The tactics changed. The honor and valor and sacrifice of my beloved corps—that has never changed, and it never will. We fight. We die. That's what we're made for. But the corps never dies, and while the corps lives, we live through the corps."

"I leave you now with one last lesson from my long career. I have known two kinds of people during my years of service: shit-talkers and killers. Remember this—never talk shit to a killer." The theater erupted in a roar. Gilhooley waved and turned to go. He paused, looked down at Feith, and said one last thing to the audience, "Somebody take out the garbage." Five noncoms immediately left the theater. Two went to find the duty officer who would call the MPs. Two went to find a corpsman; an ambulance seemed to be in order. One went to find the only chance Gilhooley had of staying out of the brig: Lieutenant Colonel Matt Rommel.

∝⟩∽

In less than twenty minutes, LTC Rommel was in sick bay, towering over the bed of the injured Feith as the corpsman examined the wound. It was a beaut. The bleeding was controlled, but more than a few stitches were required. Given the probability of a concussion, an overnight stay was also in order.

• • •

Feith looked up at Rommel. The colonel had the scars, the bearing, and the unmistakable look of a killer, but the word was that Rommel had failed in the Balkans, and this tour in Barstow, a punishment tour, would be his last. The word was that Gilhooley had something on Rommel, and that was why the old man had been allowed to run rampant with endless drills and TO- and E-checks over the last two years. At sixty-two, the old lifer's career had been allowed to continue for far too long. The last two years had been Gilhooley's almost desperate effort to impart everything he knew about organized violence to those who would carry on *in his beloved corps.*

What Feith had done was deliberate. Feith knew this small ceremony would be important to Gilhooley. He intended to humiliate the old man and emphasize to the enlisted personnel that he was not only the new NCOIC, but that the world had changed. Feith was going to be a part of the future. Feith had underestimated the old man, but everything was not lost. Gilhooley was guilty of a number of infractions. Some of them, like attempted murder, were serious. Feith would press charges. There could be no cover-up. The MPs would have to arrest Gilhooley. There would almost certainly be a court-martial. Gilhooley might not only see time in the brig, the old man might lose his pension.

Colonel Rommel's presence in sick bay troubled Feith. For the past two years, Rommel had backed Gilhooley's every decision. Rommel would have pointed out the obvious: Noncommissioned officers are the first line of supervision and the absolute backbone of the corps. When it came to noncoms, there were only two things you could do with them: find the good ones and support them, find the bad ones and run them out of the service. Still, there was something between Lieutenant Colonel Rommel and Master Gunnery Sergeant Gilhooley. Scuttlebutt was that it went back to Bosnia. Rommel had cratered his career. Gilhooley was there when it happened. It was obvious that Gilhooley knew something, and the brass knew, but no one was talking. Some even said that the two had stolen and hidden millions in gold bullion. Whatever it was, it all tracked back to a small village in Bosnia.

"I'm not letting this slide," Feith said. "I want to file a complaint. I'm pressing charges." Feith intended to be provocative.

"Are you talking to me, Sergeant?" Rommel leaned over the table, close enough to Feith so that no one else could hear. "Did we suddenly become asshole buddies?" Rommel's deep low voice rumbled into Feith's skull. Feith looked into the dead eyes of a killer.

"No, sir," Feith said. The word was that Rommel was practically a renegade. There was no percentage in setting him off.

Rommel straightened up, "Officer of the day!"

"Yes, sir!" The first lieutenant snapped to.

"There is reason to believe that Master Gunnery Sergeant Gilhooley assaulted this man. Find Gilhooley immediately. Place him under arrest and have him brought here," Rommel barked.

"Yes, sir!" The officer of the day hesitated. "Sir, shouldn't Sergeant Gilhooley be conducted to the brig?"

"Under normal circumstances, yes. Given his age and what may be a fragile emotional state, I want him here."

The OD responded, "We can put him on suicide watch in the brig, sir."

"Were those my orders, Lieutenant?"

"No, sir!"

"Do you intend to obey me?"

"Yes, sir. I just thought—"

"Obey me, Lieutenant. Carry out my orders with a will. That is your safest course of action. I want Master Gunnery Sergeant Gilhooley in custody and right here, in a rack, right next to this man for the next twenty-four hours," Rommel roared. Feith's eyes grew large as he contemplated the possibilities.

"Yes, sir!" the OD responded, turning smartly and heading for the door.

"Halt, Lieutenant," Rommel barked. He looked at Feith. "Is there a problem, gunny?"

"You're going to put him right here, sir?" Feith said.

"He's an old man, gunny. I don't want anything to happen to him. There's no problem, is there? Hell, you're twice his size," Rommel said.

"I just don't think he belongs here, sir."

"I wouldn't worry about that, gunny. I'm sure Sergeant Gilhooley just had a momentary lapse in judgment. He's probably stricken with remorse. I wouldn't be surprised if he busts out crying," Rommel said.

"Sir, I respectfully disagree. I think he may be dangerous. I'm certain that this is the wrong place for him," Feith said.

Rommel slowly shook his head. "I'll take that under advisement, gunny. If I'm wrong, I will waste no time apologizing to any and all of your next of kin." Rommel paused, shook his head. "I can see your point, gunny. Master Gunnery Sergeant Gilhooley is the meanest man I know. He's a battered old goblin. He fears nothing and feels no pain. Forty-eight years of hard service, and, to this day, all he wants to do is close and kill. Of all the dangerous people I know, he might be the worst. Still, we can't have him process out and leave the base for civilian life. You need to see him brought to justice. Think how good it's going to feel to see him brought in, under arrest, right here before you. You can look at him all night. Come to think of it, you might want to do that."

This was a complication Feith hadn't counted on. As NCOIC, Feith was coming into a position of power, power over the day-to-day operations at the depot's Nebo annex: eight square kilometers of storage and industrial facilities that had just become his personal playground. He'd already worked out a deal with one of the nation's premier security firms for a discreet cooperative relationship that wouldn't cost the corps a nickel and would put him on the fast track to a lucrative corporate gig when he retired in a few years. Gilhooley was all but gone, and Rommel would be leaving before long. Feith understood that he had only a moment to turn the situation around. "Colonel, he's a sad, old man. Let him go."

"If you say so." Rommel turned toward the OD. "Belay those orders, Lieutenant. Return to your duties."

"Yes, sir." The OD turned and left.

"If I see that old man again, I'll pull him apart like a chicken," Feith said.

"Sure you will, gunny. Good night."

Feith watched Lieutenant Colonel Rommel leave the sick bay. That old burn-out was no one to lecture on obeying orders. He hadn't done so well in Bosnia. Not unless the scuttlebutt was true, and he and that malignant dwarf really had scored a fortune in Slavic gold. It didn't matter. Rommel's day was over. Whatever reasons the brass had for not court-martialing Rommel, he was still paying a price. Command had already canceled Rommel's line number to full colonel, so he'd lost his chance at promotion. Further, when Rommel did retire from this assignment, he would officially be retired at the last rank he had completed satisfactorily. Since Rommel had been a lieutenant colonel when disaster hit, the corps would retire Rommel as a major. It served him right.

The future belonged to professional warriors—skilled men who brought special value to the marketplace. Men who would be handsomely rewarded for the services they offered.

Someday, Rommel and that sad old bastard Gilhooley would face a reckoning.

2

New Orleans –
After the Great Storm

It seemed as if the perfect storm had a perfect sociological storm of its own. Race, class, geography: When these factors presented themselves altogether, all at once, it never seemed to be for the good. Alethea considered this and a dozen other things as she walked along the roadside, breathing in the thick Louisiana air. Years of congressional thieving had stripped nearly half a billion dollars in flood-control projects from the Corps of Engineers, an agency too docile to protest. Its levee defenses inadequate, neglected, corroded: the lower Mississippi lie naked before the inevitable—the long predicted, much prophesied storm of the century. Black water swept the Ninth Ward driving the doomed before it. The bodies of the dead, floating along, twisted and indifferent, making their way to the gulf while corporate-controlled news focused on the true outrage: survivors foraging among the spoiled stock of devastated supermarkets.

Alethea's little band passed a television camera crew operating out of a nice new van. Would it be possible for the crew to take one of the elders and perhaps one or two of the younger children with them when the crew returned to clean sheets and fresh water at the end of the day? The crew ignored them, following instead the progress of a thick, lifeless figure being carried along by the dark water—dingy sundress hiked up over lifeless thighs—cruising unassisted, unmolested, unrescued under the small footbridge. What had this dead woman's thoughts been as a child? Fame? Stardom? What child doesn't guard such thoughts deep within? Now, as an old woman, she was both famous and anonymous. Around the world, thousands of times, she and her blue print housedress passed under that bridge, face turned away, looking into the murk, into the random death reserved for the powerless. A compassionate world watched her pass under that bridge and grieved. An indifferent world watched her pass within easy reach, too busy to pull her to shore, to return her to her family. She was one of thousands. She was a photo op.

Despite the repeated warnings of the engineers, warnings unworthy of news coverage, this was a disaster Washington claimed no one could have foreseen. Now that push had come to shove, FEMA, the Federal Emergency Management Agency, proved as stunned and feckless as the rest of the nation. No one could relieve the suffering or shelter the homeless or evacuate the survivors. Heck of a job, Brownie.

Alethea and the contingent from the Bethel Baptist Church walked on. The day had gone from bad to worse. A ten-hour walk out of the city only to be turned back on the bridge by the constable, protecting the small town between them and the interstate from the trespass of a few women, some children, and a couple of old men. Worse, the law had stolen their water. Confiscated it. If they couldn't enter his town, how could he have the jurisdiction to steal their water? They had the guns. The contingent from Bethel Baptist Church was no match for men with guns. They walked on in the gathering darkness. The older children carrying the babies. The stronger supporting the weaker. They walked.

The neighborhood got nicer. Much nicer. Even in the approaching darkness they could see that. The ground was higher. The streets were broader and cleaner. Set back, off the road and well apart from each other—the houses were grand. Some were even lit. How was it they had electricity? And there were no cops. No small-town police to rob and bully them. It was just the Bethel Baptist Ladies Society and these fine homes and those two SUVs roaring down the road toward them.

The large, black SUVs screeched to a halt twenty yards in front of them. Men in bloused boots and black canvas uniforms, carrying large black rifles formed a skirmish line. The Bethel Baptist Ladies Society, outgunned once again, stood and waited and listened to the crackle of radio traffic. Alethea could see the lights of four, no, five more vehicles through the row of trees, tearing down a side road toward the street on which they stood. The tires squealed around the corner and roared toward them. They stopped abruptly behind the original two vehicles. A single tall man with close-cropped hair stepped out of the SUV, strode through the skirmish line, and approached them.

"Who's in charge here?" the man demanded.

"I guess I am," Alethea said.

"Why are you here?"

"Have you heard anything about a hurricane and some flooding?" Alethea said, gently.

"That's why *we're* here," he said, seeming almost reasonable.

"Us, too. We're trying to find shelter and transportation out of the area." They had the hurricane in common. Alethea thought it might be their uniting factor.

The man turned, stepped back, talking into his handheld radio. He paused, listening, and then returned to her. "How many of you are there?" he asked, his tone moderate, intelligent, almost human.

"Eighteen," she said. When you lead people, you have to know how many you have. Her father had taught her that. She fingered the Force Recon badge she sometimes wore as a broach. It brought her luck and strength.

The man pointed at the row of black SUVs. "Your group will ride in those vehicles down that road to our CP."

"You're not the police?" Alethea asked.

"No, ma'am. The police were required to leave."

This puzzled Alethea. "Who required the police to leave?"

"We did."

"Why?"

"To prevent looting," he said.

"Are you government troops?"

"No, ma'am."

"Then who are you?" Alethea asked.

"Ma'am, please get your people into the vehicles. All of your questions will be answered at the CP."

"Command Post, right?" Alethea said, hoping to establish some sort of connection.

"Get in the vehicles."

3

Bad Dog

good dog brings slippers. A bad dog brings trouble. Chesty took the slack out of the leash and began to pull. Alive, intent, her claws made short, rough scratches against the pavement. Matt Rommel clutched the end of the leash in his big fist, pretending that his one-eyed gargoyle wasn't hard to control.

Everyone brings at least one gift into the world with them. Matt Rommel's was the gift of noble sentiment gone sideways. Having a rescue pet is fashionable. Walking into a dogfighting ring, beating three men senseless, cramming them into dog cages, and expropriating the establishment's canine inventory is not. Had he chosen to discuss it, Rommel would have pointed out that anonymous calls to animal control had gone ignored. Besides, doing it Rommel's way lets you have your pick. Rommel's pick was Chesty, a former practice dog of indeterminate lineage. Some retriever, some rottweiler, who could say? Too female and too small to long survive the ring, Chesty and the other practice dogs were used to build the confidence and ferocity of the true fighting dogs. As an industry practice, it was their lot to fight, to be mauled, and to die. Only, for those particular

● ● ●

15

dogs on that night, it was their lot to be saved by a man far more dangerous than the men who had controlled and terrorized them. Chesty emerged one-eyed and deeply scarred around her head and shoulders, scars that shone like stripes through her lustrous black fur. As far as Rommel could tell, Chesty's scars, both physical and emotional, were pretty well on the mend.

They rounded the corner just two blocks from the small apartment Rommel kept over Vince's, the Mission District bar in which he had a small holding. Chesty could see Annie setting up camp behind a two-story wood-frame house. The high wooden gate at the rear of the house was open, revealing a patio extending from the house to the back fence. Nearly all backyards in San Francisco are small. Some of them have delightful gardens. Some are cement pads ideal for ad hoc auto maintenance or for a homeless woman's evening encampment.

Annie lived in a charmed world. Everywhere she looked, she saw reminders of a gentile girlhood filled with gentle adventures and characters pulled from any of the Jane Austin novels she kept tucked in a plastic bag at the bottom of her shopping cart. It was a girlhood Rommel understood to be fictitious. A girlhood carved from sixty years of disappointment and hard living. A girlhood created in adversity and defended against an increasingly savage age. It was resolutely secured against any eventuality because it was her one anchor. It was easier to believe that once things had been beautiful, that she had been beautiful, that there had been a successful father, a happy family, beaus to choose among. All had existed before the misfortunes of the present. It was the wonderful past that kept the ugly present at bay. A wonderful past that would, one day, reassert itself and deliver her into a better, kinder future.

Chesty strained against the leash, her nails stabbing at the pavement, her stub of a tail vibrating wildly as she approached the gentle, old woman. The lop-eared Chesty with her single crazy eye didn't frighten the old woman. Across the street, there would be praise. Loving hands would map her head. Rheumy eyes would adore her, while the thin sweet voice praised her. Chesty had only ever wanted to be loved and praised. Each loving touch drove the cruelty of the fighting ring further into the mists of her canine psyche.

"Babe! Come here, sweet baby! You brought Mr. Bunyan with you," she warbled. "How are you, Mr. Bunyan?"

Rommel gave what passed for a smile and nodded. In his life, he had been called many things, and after all, Annie lived in a world of her own. The people she met in the Mission were named from the fantastic stories of her youth. Of course, the Pendleton plaid shirts that he wore against the evening cold, the blue denim jeans, and the steel-toed boots had almost certainly provoked her imagination. Big, grizzled man. Big, grizzled dog. Paul Bunyan and Babe, the blue ox.

"A lovely night, Miss Annie. Even so, wouldn't it be nice to stay in the shelter? It's just a few blocks away and Ch— Babe and I would be pleased to walk with you."

"No, thank you. That place is far too crowded, and, just between us, some of the people aren't very nice." She smiled and began unfolding a blue plastic tarp that she had removed from her cart. "And as you said, it is a lovely night. Ever since I was a girl, I have just loved camping out in the backyard. I mean, here we are, out in the wilderness, and, at the same time, there's the safety of the house."

Rommel wondered if she understood that it wasn't her house, that help wasn't just a few feet away. On some level, she must have known because she unpacked quietly and kept her soft voice lowered.

"I wish I had a fine big friend like Babe. When I was a child, we had Duke. He was huge! Sometimes, we girls would dress him up. He put up with so much!" She laughed. "Perhaps, when things are better, we'll all get together again, and we shall have room for a fine big dog."

Not for the first time, Rommel was at a loss. "Sounds nice. But for tonight, wouldn't you like to spend the night at the shelter?"

"No, this is just perfect, thank you."

Rommel said good-bye as Chesty was indulging in one last round of affectionate petting. He quietly pulled the gate shut.

چچ

Rommel could hear the muffled bass of the jukebox from the bar below. He sat in the gray twill lounge chair staring at the wall, letting the tensions of the day leach away. He took a pull at the Balvenie, watching the shimmering waves of rich amber liquor tumble over the melting ice within the stolid squared glass. Behind him, Chesty was on the march, pacing about the apartment. He could hear the nails and strong paws padding down the hall toward the front door. Then, the muscular dog would turn and trot back toward the kitchen. Chesty repeated the trip down the hall, each time her thudding steps took on a slightly greater sense of urgency. Down the hall, into the kitchen, and the back door that led down to the bar. Back again toward the front door. Rommel could sense Chesty looking toward the front door, looking toward the big man. Rommel ignored her. Down and back again. Down and back. Building intensity. Building toward some canine purpose.

"You've been out. Knock it off," Rommel called to the agitated animal.

Back down the hall. Back to the door. A searching gaze at Rommel. Back down the hall. Back to the door.

"Knock it off, meathead."

Chesty approached the chair, staring at the big man with a single searching eye. Rommel ignored her. The walk was over. The day was over. Scotch time. Rommel took another quiet pull, studiously ignoring the dog. Chesty approached closer, less than an inch from contact.

"BOOF!!!" The single bark boomed through the flat, shaking the walls. From the bar below, surprised laughter. Rommel was half out of his chair. The animal was agitated.

• • •

18

"What the hell is your problem? You want out AGAIN?" The dog strutted toward the door.

"Hold on." Rommel went for the leash.

༚༚

Chesty strained against the leash, turning at the corner, pulling toward Annie's campsite, pulling toward a crowd of men who appeared to be in various states of personal, moral, and physical decay. The crowd surrounded the wooden gate, giving up a collective rumbling that was at once excited, agitated, uncertain, and aroused.

From across the street, Rommel released the leash. Chesty barreled forward, crashing into the crowd at knee level, knocking two unwary men to the ground. Immediately, an uproar of startled, angry shouts and frantic agitated barking boomed from the small, crowded patio. Perhaps the people in the house would call the police.

Rommel had a few decisions to make and no time to make them. He could plow to the front of the mob and fight them all, or he could begin his attack from the rear of the crowd and sucker-punch as many of the filthy pencil-necks as possible. It made sense to him that the crowd at the back would be less committed to the attack on the old woman. The little patio area was packed. For the wretches in the rear of the crowd, it was all they could do to sneak a peek at the action. It occurred to Rommel that a real man would push to the front and make a fair fight of it. Screw that. Rommel knew he would be overmatched soon enough. As he began to thin the crowd from behind, Rommel wondered, *How long would it take San Francisco's finest to respond in force to a riot of homeless men behind a shack in the Mission? Forty-five minutes? A week? Who's up for a pitched battle with desperate, drug-addled men who have nothing to lose? Let's go, boys! We have to save the slum!*

Attacking from behind, it took almost no time to disperse a large portion of the mob at the rear. They were the ones with little commitment to the action at hand. They weren't even lookouts. They were onlookers. Rommel drove into them with fists and boots and a roaring fury, holding back just a bit, avoiding the crippling blows for those uncommitted who valued the better part of valor. In handfuls, they scattered up and down and across the street into the opposite alley. That left only the determined filthy clutch, perhaps a dozen, packed into the little patio surrounded by the wooden fence.

Where he could, Rommel crashed his big boot down on the available calf behind the unguarded knee, crashing them to the pavement, breaking what he could. Those he could not cripple on the way in, he would have to fight on the way out. The pandemonium at the front masked much of the tumult from the rear. Rommel pushed forward, grabbing a smaller man at the neck and belted waist, and hoisting him over the fence, letting him clatter upon the garbage cans on the other side. Finally, he reached the front where half-naked men were held at bay by a muscular dog who swept an arc before a partially stripped, bleeding old woman—cowering, jabbering in terror. Annie. No gentile, bemused pretensions, just rheumy faded eyes, skinned knees and elbows, tattered clothes, long deep scratches, blood, and the swollen, battered face. Rommel turned on what was left of the mob, Chesty behind him, Annie behind Chesty.

"You need to leave, old man. We're here to party, and we're not done." It took no time to size him up. This would be the leader. He was bigger, younger, healthier, and probably nuts. "Get out! There are more than enough of us to kill you and that dog."

It occurred to Rommel that this was way too much talk. Too much for a gang rape, too much for a battle. He knew what he was going to do. He should just start in. But he had been a civilian too long. He just had to give the filthy wretch some sort of warning.

"Save your ass. Do it now," Rommel growled.

That was all it took. The wretch buried his knife into Rommel's left bicep. In that instant, Rommel was crushing the wretch's collarbone with his right fist. The mob surged forward, Rommel pushed back into them, grabbing an arm with one hand, pulling it aside, and crushing his opponent's collarbone with the big clenched fist.

Visually, a broken collarbone is a horrendous injury. The clavicle supports the arm and the shoulder on each side. When the collarbone is completely fractured, the entire side of the body seems to fall away uselessly. For men impaired by drink or drugs, flailing away in the night, it is a terrifying injury that alters both the assailant's capability and intent.

The small battleground allowed Rommel to keep the enemy in front. No one could flank the big man with that ferocious animal swerving back and forth looking for someone to bite.

From Chesty's point of view, the fight was still undecided. She could smell the man-avalanche of bum flesh. They were getting closer. She had to act. A big denim haunch was being pushed toward her. Chesty launched forward, taking the denim buttock into her fierce jaws and delivering a savage, crushing bite. Well, this wasn't right. These jeans feel new and smell clean. If anything, this butt smells a lot like—

Rommel roared. It was a sound like no one in the Mission had ever heard. It was stunningly loud, laced with surprise and alarm. For an instant, that roar was the only thing there was. It filled the small place of battle. It surged through the few remaining combatants, filling them with pure terror. This tortured cry seemed the very essence of violent death. It bathed the remaining mob in the last shining moment of clarity most of them would ever know. They must flee. It was the one universal thought. It dominated them all. In that moment, that roar made manifest that they must flee or be immediately destroyed. The collective force of that shared terror swept them out, into, and through the street like dried leaves before the cyclone. They disappeared just as the distant sirens could be heard. Rommel knelt before Annie. Her unreasoning eyes were still wide with terror, but it seemed to Rommel that she could hear the approaching sirens. Help was on the way. Before her were a few of her tormentors, the bodies of partially broken men trying to crawl or drag themselves away. Rommel seized the nearest man, hoisting him over the wooden fence and onto a clattering of garbage cans. With that, the rest fled in panic.

● ● ●

Rommel surveyed the ad hoc battleground. Even for the Mission, this was a massive breach of the peace. Soon the cops would come, and someone would have to ride in the back of the squad car. As a rule, Rommel understood that if you're going to have a riot, someone has to go to jail, if only for appearances. A certain one-eyed dog would be taken by animal control. If that one-eyed dog had bitten any one, as was likely, she would have to be destroyed. Again, if only for appearances. There would be hell to pay. If Rommel stayed, there would certainly be hell to pay.

4

The Wheels of Justice

Lieutenant Carmichael surveyed the bull pen, studying the newest member of her team. She hadn't picked him. She didn't trust him. Trust was a subordinate's virtue. Three years from motorcycle cop to detective was fast tracking for someone with no political patronage. His evaluations were good enough. He did his job. He was even-tempered and fearless. Other cops trusted him—that word again. His educational background was nothing special: Bachelor's degree, night school. Still, that worked in his favor, no pretensions. None of the bizarre behavior you get from the climbers, "Look at me! I'm a cop *and* a lawyer!" Long ago, she had tired of the careerists who pursued jobs they considered beneath them, so they could strive for higher positions they also considered beneath them.

No, detective Garcia was here because he single-handedly broke the biggest case the city had seen in twenty-five years. Two arrests in the dead of night, in the middle of a city landmark, closing a string of homicides including a cop killing. Citation, promotion, publicity: all because he had answered the phone. All because of the problematical Matt Rommel.

Rommel didn't have a job; he didn't need one. It wasn't the Marine Corps' pension or the one from the California Department of Corrections that made him financially independent. It was the stock ownership of the country's largest manufacturer of Internet bridgers and routers. Ownership in a company whose stock had split two-for-one, like clockwork, for a single decade. The stock market had boomed with Rommel and busted without him.

That he owned a house in Sea Cliff overlooking the Pacific Ocean and the Golden Gate, yet chose to spend many of his nights in a tiny apartment over a bar in the Mission. *That* was suspicious. A tiny apartment only a few blocks from "The 14th Street Massacre." Typical of the newspapers. No one had been killed or even gravely injured, but, somehow, it was supposed to be a massacre. What was true was that a parade of ambulances had dumped the better part of a dozen homeless men onto the always chaotic emergency room at Mission Memorial Hospital. It was bedlam, and it was damned expensive, with the city footing the bill. For the city and for the San Francisco police—who were tasked with maintaining order while, simultaneously, allowing everyone in the city to do as they pleased—it had been a long, ugly, and expensive night. The DA's objective: order without enforcement.

"Garcia." Vince looked over at Lieutenant Carmichael, his new boss. "Anything on that melee in the Mission?"

"Not much. One witness: elderly, homeless, female. It appears to be a dispute."

"Over what?"

"Gang rape."

"A dispute over gang rape. Care to explain yourself, detective?"

"An unspecified number of homeless men had apparently decided to rape the elderly homeless woman. She and another party disagreed with the men, and an altercation ensued."

"Do we have a description of the other party involved?"

"Yes, and a name to go with it."

"Good. Who's our suspect?"

"One Paul Bunyan, according to the woman. He was in the company of a blue ox she called Babe. We believe the witness to be unreliable."

"What about the victims?"

"The who?"

"The homeless men who were injured."

"The consensus among them is that they were minding their own business, organizing a social event with the woman in question as the guest of honor, when they were attacked by a large, well-organized group of men."

"Any mention of an ox?"

"None, although some of the vigilantes had dogs."

"Any descriptions?"

"Plenty, none of them consistent. They claimed to have been attacked by white, black, Hispanic, and Asian men, all of them of large stature."

"Any other witnesses?"

"Not yet. The *Comical* claims to have a lead. They say it was probably someone from the Castro taking his dog for a long walk. They're calling him the *Gay Avenger*.

"Oh, God, how do they figure that?"

"Paul Bunyan. Lumberjack. He was probably wearing a plaid flannel shirt, jeans, and boots. Short hair, physically fit. They claim one or more gay men, walking a dog or dogs, were attacked by the homeless band of men, possibly in a robbery attempt or attempted gay bashing which would make it a case of self-defense. I don't know if it fits what little we know, but it makes more sense than Paul Bunyan coming to the defense of an old homeless woman," Garcia said.

Lieutenant Carmichael eyed the young detective. "So you don't see rape as a factor in this?"

"Not really."

"Why?"

"The homeless are all around us. There isn't a week that goes by that we don't find one or more of them dead, either on the street, in a shelter, or in a flop."

"Residential hotel," the lieutenant corrected.

"The point is, there hasn't been a serious attempt to control them since Matrix. They rob each other. They rape each other. They occasionally kill each other. It doesn't seem to be a municipal priority. Rape, as a factor in this case, means that there is someone in this city that would attack a mob of up to two dozen men to protect an old homeless woman. Tactically, it makes sense that one very fit, highly skilled man could take two or even three men in a fight. Even if you double that, it's only six guys down. I think there were two or more men, and I don't think they were trying to save a bag lady."

"So you think the *Comical* is right?"

"I think the *Comical* makes more sense than the story coming from the bag lady."

"Go down to the Castro and see what you can find out." Carmichael paused. "Your pal Rommel has a dog." She eyed him closely.

"He's more a friend of the family. What's your point, Lieutenant?"

"You don't like him for this?" she asked.

Garcia shook his head. "The crime occurred two or three blocks from his apartment. In a city at night, three blocks is a long way to wander for no reason, particularly late at night, particularly in the Mission. He's a big man, but he's in his fifties, and the dog only has one eye."

Carmichael nodded. She seemed unconvinced, but she nodded and walked away. Cops are always unconvinced of innocence and not without reason.

Vince Garcia pretended to read one of the victim's statements. Carmichael should know better. Single-handedly attacking a mob is suicide; even she had to accept that. At the core of her theory was the idea that, somewhere in this city, there was a man with the personal combat skills to engage and defeat a mob and that this person would willingly lay down his life for a defenseless old woman. One guy. For a stranger. For less than no reason. Who would do that? Detective Garcia stared into and through his paperwork. A tiny smile crept onto his face.

"Goddamn you, Uncle Matt."

5

—

Post-Traumatic Stress

Heart pounding, sweat trickling along the rib beneath her breast, Carolyn clawed her way back to consciousness, staring wide-eyed into the mindless predawn gray. It was the time of day with no memory and no sense of the future. A time that absorbed terror and hope with equal indifference.

The nightmare was still with her, though recurring less often now. Each time, she stood in her own kitchen, bathed in gentle sunlight, stood at her center island counter. She was grinding spices with a mortar and pestle, looking out through the living room window at the bay and the distant Golden Gate. The rose-colored salt would not grind. According to the recipe, everything must be reduced to a fine powder. She applied more pressure, raising her elbow, grinding harder. The grains would not yield, seeming more like quartz than salt. She began to pound the pestle into the mortar.

The day dimmed, shadows growing longer. The pestle grew larger, the mortar too, becoming a great bone-colored bowl. She pounded with two hands. Furiously. No longer in her kitchen, she was standing on a terrazzo landing between stone flights of stairs. The pestle was a fire extinguisher. She pounded as if her life depended on it. Bits of rose-tinted salt stuck to her clothes, to her skin. The bits were warm and moist. She was back in the mausoleum, pounding the heavy fire extinguisher into the skulls of her two attackers. She couldn't let them up. They would kill her if they got up. She pounded savagely, both skulls long since stove-in, gobbets of gore and hair and bone. She would suddenly feel trapped within the vast, shadowy mausoleum. Damned to it. She had to fight her way out. She had to claw her way back to the light. Each time, Carolyn fought her way to consciousness, fought her way into the cold, gray predawn.

It was Sunday morning, much too early to be up. On the other hand, she dared not return to sleep and risk a return to the mausoleum. Carolyn sat up, turned on the lamp and sat on the edge of the bed. Minutes passed as her mind cleared, waiting for some plan of action to suggest itself. Nothing. There was always work. Carolyn got up and headed for the shower.

For Carolyn, there were only two things. There was work, and there was her daughter Aubrey. Seven-year-old Aubrey was at a sleepover. With luck, Carolyn could be in the office before seven, put in a couple of hours and be back to pick up Aubrey in plenty of time.

By the time Carolyn's SLK had reached the Bay Bridge, the sun was well up, and the morning chill was falling away. She had traded the old flaming copper SLK in for the even more gorgeous new model. Yes, in this regard, she was spoiling herself, but, after all, work was not just work. Her ad agency, Brand Loyalty, was the eighth largest independent agency in the San Francisco Bay Area. She employed over a hundred people and, even in the dreadfully slow belly of this business cycle, they were getting by. That was the thing about advertising, your inventory consisted only of ideas. Tomorrow, better ideas could put you out of business, leaving you with nothing unless you made a regular habit of stashing your cash.

Advertising was a young person's game, and Brand Loyalty had lots of bright, energetic, imaginative people.

They laughed, played, hooked-up, unhooked, or whatever and poured their youth into the firm probably because they didn't know what else to do with it. Keeping them on a more or less even keel was a handful of older men and women. In the advertising wilderness that was Brand Loyalty, the young ones were the demented flock, the few managers were the shepherds, Carolyn—the boss lady, and then there was Denni—the rampaging cougar.

Brand Loyalty Associates had begun with three partners. After a series of attempts on Carolyn's life, one partner left to pursue opportunities in the California penal system. One partner, Carolyn, oversaw the creative end of the business and that left Carolyn's college roommate and friend, Denni, to run the day-to-day requirements of the office. By virtue of her partnership in the firm, Denni del Grecco was, possibly, one of the wealthiest office managers in the country.

For the past few months, Denni's life had been fraught with more drama than usual. Carolyn's response was to allow more latitude.

As a young woman, Denni had wanted a family in the worst way. Out of college, her relationships had been a series of disasters. Then came Bill, twenty years her senior with two failed marriages behind him. Well, as the joke went, at least he wasn't afraid to make a commitment. Together they raised three sons. After Bill's retirement, the two of them tried their hand at running two businesses: a video store that gradually failed and a rent-a-guard firm that could not succeed and would not die. Year after year, the security firm lingered, earning just enough to keep the doors open. During that time, Bill began to fade. Much like his business, Bill lingered. As Denni was entering the Indian summer of her sexuality, Bill was ambling toward his dotage. An undercurrent of discontent set in, a discontent whose symptoms Denni occasionally relieved with anonymous, intimate, and meaningless adventures, but whose underlying cause continued.

• • •

Denni came to fear a single thing: becoming Bill's nurse—tending him through an inexorable decline. Sometime during Brand Loyalty's second year in business, Bill was diagnosed with cancer of the colon. It had been a February, and after two courses of chemotherapy, which resulted in one weak remission, Bill died in his sleep. For Denni, it was like an endless sleepwalk through a dream where nothing worked as it should. Early detection should have greatly improved the odds of survival. But not for Bill. Recent advances in chemotherapy were much easier to tolerate and were resulting in much better outcomes. But not for Bill. Even for patients who succumbed to the cancer, lifespans were much improved. But not for Bill. For Denni, the chores and the fatigue seemed endless. At the last of it, there were hospice nurses who showed up daily. Carolyn dedicated the better part of two days per week watching over Bill so that Denni could rest, but the life-sapping process took all Denni had. Then, in the predawn of that inevitable Wednesday, Bill was gone. There were final arrangements, dealing with the endless condolences of friends and family, task after task, and an unrelenting demand that Denni felt to present a dignified front to the world.

One day, it was all over. Bill's ashes were scattered off the Marin headlands. The bills were paid. Probate was settled. At that moment, Denni asked herself what she wanted, what she wanted to do. The answer was as clear as anything she had ever encountered. Denni wanted to be alive. Denni wanted adventure. Denni wanted romance. Denni wanted sex, a lot of sex. Denni wanted a lot of vibrant, adventurous, fulfilling sex with men she would choose, use, and excuse.

❧❧

Carolyn's SLK slid down the Fremont exit into the city, bounced across the trolley tracks, crossed Market Street, turned right on California, left onto Montgomery, and left again into the parking structure beneath her building. Parking was ruinously expensive, but business was good, and Brand Loyalty Associates reserved half a dozen spaces.

Carolyn had made up her mind. If she was going to work late, as she often did, she was going to do it in safety. She rode the art deco elevator up to the fifteenth floor. Today should be a quiet day. A few hours on a Sunday helped her stay on top of the workload. She would organize things for the next week and then see a certain someone about her night terrors.

As soon as Carolyn unlocked the front door, she could hear them. There was shouting and taunting laughter, and angry tear-choked screaming all at once. Her first instinct was to leave the door, run for the elevator, and get help. She heard Denni shouting, "Stop it, you morons! Armando, shut up. That goes for you, too, Jim."

If Denni was in trouble, Carolyn would have to help. She reached into her purse for her pepper spray and crept past the front desk toward the open work area and the offices that ringed it. She crouched down, keeping her head just high enough to look over the low partitions and see what was going on. A shrieking, sobbing, flabby, naked, middle-aged white man was chasing a much younger and also naked, Latino man between the desks and drafting tables. The younger man was cackling and hooting, easily staying ahead of his pursuer. Occasionally, the younger man would stop and face his pursuer. "You got to put some starch in that little thing!" he said, as he flaunted a determined little erection that sprouted from a thatch of pubic hair. The younger man then hooted and sprang easily away from his red-faced, rage-choked pursuer. Denni, partially naked, chased behind them. "Stop it, you assholes."

Carolyn relaxed. Denni was having another of her episodes. *Was this what mourning looked like?* she wondered. Carolyn stood up and reached into her purse for yet another tool, a small high-pressure air horn. She held it high over her head and let loose with one long ear-shattering blast. The two would-be satyrs and Denni, the middle-aged nymph wannabe, froze in their tracks, staring at Carolyn like deer caught in the headlights. "You two!" Carolyn shouted, "I don't care who you are. Get dressed and get the hell out. This is a place of business!"

The younger man faced Carolyn with his bobbing erection. He seemed about to speak. Carolyn roared, "I don't want to hear it. Get your clothes. Get out. Do it now, or I will pepper spray your sorry asses till hell won't have it!" *Hell won't have pepper spray? Did that last part make sense*, Carolyn wondered? She didn't care. These clowns were leaving immediately.

The two men gathered their clothes in silence. The older man seemed detached, as if he were already trying to put an ugly episode behind him. He was the first out the door. The younger man seemed to be looking for some way to salvage the opportunity. He made eye contact with Denni, but was preempted. "Nobody likes a cock-blocker, Armando."

Armando left in silence.

Denni pulled her outfit together and walked to her office. Carolyn followed her. Denni sat. "You'd think that a three-way would be easy to organize, one woman, two horndogs," she said.

"No, I wouldn't think that at all. I would think that something like that could go wrong in about a hundred ways," Carolyn said, staring at Denni.

"You're not mad are you? You're not really all that shocked, are you? It's not like we're a couple of youngsters."

"No, we are not youngsters, but this is our place of business. What were you thinking, and why would you bring them here?" Carolyn said.

"I was thinking that a little adventure would be a good thing, and I certainly didn't want those losers to know where I live."

"No, you just wanted them to know where I work. Even with the rotten economy, we employ nearly a hundred people. What if one of our people had come in this morning? The way these youngsters are, your little escapade would have ended up on YouTube. Your reputation would be worse than it already is and that employee would probably find an excuse to sue us anyway. Beyond that, the advertising community in San Francisco is small. There are no secrets. Brand Loyalty would become the punch line for a thousand drunken ad execs. Something like this could seriously damage our image. Getting and keeping clients is difficult enough." Carolyn took a breath. "I never thought I would have to say this, but *no orgies in the office*. Is that clear? Are we going to have a problem?"

"I don't think you need to talk to me like that. I'm not a child."

"A child wouldn't do something this stupid. Please promise me that you will keep the naked part of your private life away from our office."

Denni shrugged. "I guess that's reasonable."

Carolyn leaned forward. "If you ever start dating better-looking men, we can revisit our decision. Seriously, you're a wealthy woman now. Don't the Chippendales ever come to town?" They both smiled. Carolyn headed for her office. A few hours of work, and then off to the museum to see someone who would understand night terrors.

6

Among the Beaux-Arts

It was a trip she didn't want to make, to visit a man she didn't want to see. She owed him much. She owed him her life, but now she wanted her life back, and that would not happen until the dreams stopped. She had killed to stay alive, and now the dreams would not stop. Matt Rommel would understand. A killer would know how to make the dreams stop. Aside from her business partner serving a life term in Chowchilla, Matt Rommel was the only killer she knew. Carolyn thought of the old punch line to the Eva Perón joke, *I'm still called an admiral, though I gave up the sea long ago.* Matt Rommel had retired from the Marine Corps, had retired from the California Department of Corrections. Now, he spent his days as a docent at the Palace of the Legion of Honor, surrounded by a thousand years of fine art. He lived just down the hill from the museum in Sea Cliff, one of San Francisco's finest neighborhoods, in a house that looked as if it had been designed by Julia Morgan, although the interior was strictly old bachelor, in shades of tan, gold, and brown. He owed it all to the same Internet boom that had ruined Carolyn's life. Matt Rommel had killed. Matt Rommel lived

• • •

37

with it. Matt Rommel would know how to live with the dreams, or better yet, make them go away.

Carolyn turned off Geary, on to 34th, and then into Lincoln Park. *Navigating San Francisco isn't difficult,* Carolyn thought. San Francisco is a city, a county, and a peninsula all in one. If you think of San Francisco as a thumb, Market and Van Ness are avenues that run lengthwise, and Geary crosses the width. Geary takes you from the city center, out past Japan Town, out to the Ocean, to the same blue-green Pacific that the Palace of the Legion of Honor overlooks from the knoll it commands.

Modeled after an eighteenth-century French palace, the Palace of the Legion of Honor was a gift the city of San Francisco had given itself in the 1920s. The human cost of the First World War left citizens across the country dumbstruck. War had changed. It was no longer the splendid little affair the nation had experienced against Spain. War had become a great machine that fed on wave after wave of young men. The Great War was a mechanized war, a war of machines and industrial poisons. Man no longer controlled war. Man burrowed into the mud and cold and disease, as war roared above and around. When it was over, man crawled from the trenches, filthy and dumb, and wondered what had been worth the loss of nearly an entire generation. What was the purpose of so much swift, merciless death and blindness and dismemberment?

The Palace of the Legion of Honor was a partial answer.

The scale of her problem was smaller, but the question was no less real for Carolyn. She had fought to stay alive. She was alive, but where was the peace, the freedom from fear? Matt Rommel would know. He had to.

Parking was an afterthought at the Legion of Honor, a tiny lot in front of the museum, the roadway leading up from Sea Cliff, and a long, ill-defined area on the side. Carolyn found a space, far down along the seaward side of the museum, and began the trek back to the front entrance.

Today was a rare occasion. On any given day, Matt Rommel was a fixture of the medieval gallery, installed across from a Germanic carving of Saint Boniface in the robes and mitre of a medieval bishop and beneath the ornate ceiling that had been rescued from a ruined Spanish castle. A scarred giant in a dark suit, the medieval gallery suited him. But not today. Today found Matt Rommel among the pastels and Beaux-Arts of the impressionists. There, among the water lilies and parasols he stood. His charcoal suit and gray turtleneck showered in diffused white light, a great scarred gargoyle standing amidst the Belle Époque. Carolyn was startled to see him. It seemed to her that he was surprised to see her, too. As she approached, she began to size him up. He was giant and broad across the chest. His massive hands, traced with scars, rested before him in the fig leaf position. As she looked up, she saw that the thickly muscled neck and chiseled head were, likewise, traced with scars—mementos of high-velocity fragments thrown up in the heat of now forgotten firefights. As her then six-year-old daughter, Aubrey, had said, "That's a lot of owies!"

Rommel seemed genuinely pleased. "Hello," he smiled, "nice to see you. Has Aubrey come to visit?"

Carolyn's smile was tempered with the recollection of dark days. She had seen the man's capacity for violent action. The image of Rommel carrying two bound men as if they were luggage came back to her. "No, Aubrey's not here today."

Rommel waited.

"You look almost happy."

"I am happy." Rommel allowed the admission. "To tell you the truth, I'm thinking about closing the house and going to visit the relatives of all this work." He gestured at the paintings around him. "Versailles, the d'Orsay, and, of course, the mother ship—the Louvre. I'm thinking maybe a month. No, six weeks. Strike that, two months—two months of long walks, fine dining, and fine art."

"What about Chesty?"

"She comes along. Dogs are welcome in France. I might take her for a train ride."

"I need to speak with you," Carolyn said.

Rommel nodded toward the rear of the museum. "Step into my office."

The museum café is niched into the southwest corner of the ground floor: its outer walls, floor to ceiling windows looking out at the cypresses, and, through them, the Pacific Ocean. Rommel led Carolyn to the far corner. They sat across the table from each other, bathed in warm light. Rommel waited.

"It's been a while," Carolyn began tentatively. Rommel made the slightest of nods.

"How are you?" she said.

"I'm fine."

"And how's Chesty?"

"Chesty's a troublemaker, but she's fine, too. How's Aubrey?"

"Aubrey's fine."

Rommel looked at Carolyn, paused, then said, "So everyone is fine…"

Carolyn had seen this man at his work. Dark work. Still, she was surprised at how gentle he could be. She thought of Chesty. It took a gentle, patient man to nurse the mauled fighting dog back to health. If what she had heard was true, it took a brutal, dangerous man to rescue Chesty and the other dogs from the fighting ring in the Mission District. Had he really beaten those men until they crawled into the dog cages and willingly called 911 begging for the police? Carolyn had to take a chance. She had to talk to him.

"It's awkward coming to you. I know it's been a while. It isn't…"

Rommel spoke softly, "You think I don't understand? You think it doesn't occur to me that you were almost murdered here in this building? That, somehow, I'm not aware that I am associated with one of the worst parts of your life? I do understand. Take a breath. Relax. When you're ready, tell me what's on your mind."

Carolyn took her moment, felt the sunshine streaming in through the windows and onto her face, watched the cypresses surging gently against the cloudless blue sky. "I'm having dreams," she said.

"OK, tell me about them."

Carolyn did.

"I'm not an expert. You might want to see someone. If business is good, you can probably afford it," Rommel said.

"And?"

"And I don't see anything mysterious. You have a recurring dream where one minute, you are safe and happy, and the next minute, you are fighting for your life, killing with your bare hands."

"Yes."

"Well, that's basically what happened, isn't it? When you could not escape, you fought and killed. Now, part of you thinks it can happen again without warning. You didn't invent these feelings. This knowledge, this dark sense, is part of what it means to be a combat veteran. Across this country, there are tens of thousands of men and women who know what you know and have felt what you feel."

"I'm not a combat veteran."

"Did you fight?"

"I didn't want to…"

"That's eighty percent of the guys going into action," Rommel snapped. "Did you fight?"

"Yes."

"Did you kill?"

"Yes."

"Are you trying to put it behind you?"

"Yes."

Rommel leaned forward across the table. His eyes seemed to gently search her out. "What do you think a

• • •

combat veteran is? You're not a victim of crime. That opportunity passed when you decided that you were going to live and that you would kill to do it. Now, you need to learn to live with it and move on, which is easier said than done."

Carolyn looked around. "And this is how you chose to move on?"

"Do you want to talk about me or about you?" Rommel asked.

"I want to understand. Maybe if I understand a little about you, that will help me."

"Fine. I got this idea from my uncle Ed, sort of. Years ago, Ed died, and I took my mother back to St. Louis for the funeral. We lived in St. Louis when I was a kid. When the funeral was over, we stayed in town for a couple of days to see the old neighborhood, places we used to go.

"We went to the fine arts museum in Forest Park. Forest Park is where they held the 1904 World's Fair. Nice place. I remembered the museum as being huge. I figured, as an adult, it would seem smaller." Rommel nodded. "That wasn't the case. It's still a big place. I remember I approached one of the archways into a gallery. There were two museum guards, one on either side: red blazers, black ties, and gray slacks—a man and a woman. The man was talking as I approached. I couldn't hear what he was saying. I assumed that it would be the usual crap. You know, pointless reminiscences, bragging, maybe he was trying to get a date with her. When I got closer, I could finally hear him. He was talking about how art shapes man's relationship with God. I remember thinking that if they had been working in a burger joint they wouldn't have had that conversation. Man shapes art. Art shapes man.

"You know, I used to be married. The corps didn't ruin that marriage. I ruined that marriage all by myself. I had retired from the corps, but I still needed a job. Working with people is one of the things I'm good at."

Carolyn blanched. She had seen him working with people. It reminded her of the joke about the funeral director who said he took the job because he enjoyed working with people.

"I took a job working as a corrections officer, a prison guard. Twelve hours a day of stink, nonstop bedlam, and serious assholes. There's a reason these convicts are in prison. Not to belabor the point, but they make bad decisions, and they hurt people. They constantly fish for victims. They never switch off. Every minute you are on the job, you are face-to-face with a convict, and you have to figure out what he's really up to. Is he trying to sucker me? Is someone sneaking up behind me? Is this a distraction so his pals can drag some new fish off into a dark corner?

"At the end of the day, when I got home and my wife would try to talk to me, I'd give her the stone face, trying to figure out what she was really up to. The behavior was automatic. I am sorry to say that I listened and talked to her the way I would with a convict. Back then, everything was conflict for me. I had no idea what I was doing until my marriage was over.

"I was like one of those fighting dogs. It was always going to be life or death. Between the corps and San Quentin, I'd had thirty years of that. One day, I made a decision. I wanted what those museum guards had. I wanted the beautiful things I thought I was fighting to protect. I wanted to push away all the ugliness and be a better man."

Carolyn was near tears. "And that worked?"

"Er, after a fashion. There are some people I think God would like to slap the snot out of."

Carolyn looked over Rommel's shoulder toward the entrance. "Were you expecting the police?"

Rommel rolled his eyes. "Not really."

"It looks like that investigator from the night Sara was murdered. Lieutenant…"

"Carmichael?"

"Uh huh."

"Young Latin kid with her?"

● ● ●

"Uh huh."

"Yeah, they might be looking for me." Rommel turned to face the cops at the café entrance and raised an arm in acknowledgment as they approached.

"Have a seat, Lieutenant, detective Garcia."

Lieutenant Sharon Carmichael looked at the big man. "Thanks, we'll stand."

Rommel said nothing. "Aren't you wondering why we're here?" Carmichael said.

"Not really," Rommel said.

"Where were you last night at eleven forty-five?"

"At home, in my apartment on 16th Street."

"Can anyone vouch for you?" Carmichael looked at Carolyn.

"Not really."

"Are you aware of an incident that occurred last night?"

"Again, not really."

"You didn't notice sirens from three squad cars, a fire engine, and a dozen ambulances only three blocks from your apartment?" Carmichael said.

"Sirens are not unusual in the Mission."

"This was a major disturbance. More than a dozen homeless men were badly injured. We have eyewitnesses. The emergency room at Mission General was in a state of near chaos for hours," Carmichael said.

"I don't go near Mission General. It's almost always a madhouse," Rommel said.

Carmichael looked at Carolyn. "What about you? Where were you last night?"

Carolyn's eyes grew wide. Carmichael smiled. Fear: the natural reaction of the average taxpayer to questions from the police. "I was at home with my daughter," Carolyn said. "In Berkeley. What's this about?"

Carmichael turned up the heat. "We're investigating a hate crime. A large number of homeless men were savagely beaten in what we believe was the act of a vigilante."

Carolyn looked at Lieutenant Carmichael. "That thing in the paper. You're talking about the thing that was in the paper? Didn't a couple of gay men walking their dogs prevent a homeless woman from being gang raped?"

"We don't know how many men were involved. We're considering the possibility that it might have been a single man: a single, large man who is prone to violence," Carmichael said. Now, it was her turn to seem uncomfortable.

Lieutenant Carmichael had put Carolyn on the spot with her question. Carolyn's defensive reaction had released just a little adrenaline, edging Carolyn toward a fight-or-flight sensation. Now, it was Carolyn's turn to go on the offensive. "One man attacks a mob in the act of raping a single woman. A dozen men are injured and go to the hospital, and you think there was just one man. This doesn't sound stupid to you, Lieutenant? How many men can *you* take in a fight? Or him," Carolyn said, gesturing at Vince Garcia. "The two of you together, can you beat up a dozen men? Is this your theory? You should be looking for someone in a cape. Don't you have a big spot light on the roof of city hall that you can use to call this guy?"

Carolyn's discourse was interrupted by the approach of a young woman who was trying to get Rommel's attention. "Mr. Rommel?" the young woman ventured. She had to be all of twenty. Rommel tried smiling. Smiling didn't feel natural to him, and it seemed to put everyone else on edge.

"Yes?"

"Mr. Rommel, there's a call for you in the office. I don't know who it is, but they seem very insistent."

Rommel stood. "Thank you. I'll be right there."

Carmichael interjected, "We're not done here."

"If you want, I can forward the call to your cell phone," The young woman offered.

Rommel blushed, as if having a cell phone was some sort of admission. "That would be very kind, Theresa." The young woman smiled, as if at a compliment. The famous ogre of the museum knew who she was, knew her by name. Theresa left the museum café.

"Mr. Rommel, we would like you to come with us," Carmichael said.

"Are you arresting me?"

"We just want to talk to you without distractions." Carmichael looked directly at Carolyn.

"Sorry, I prefer the distractions I have, to whatever you have in mind." A buzzing sound broke into the conversation. Rommel reached into his jacket. "Yes?"

"Major Matthew Rommel?"

Rommel bristled a bit. "Retired. Who is this?"

"This is Robert Holmes. I'm an administrator at the Yountville Veterans Home. I'm afraid we have a bit of a situation. We need your help."

"You're calling me here for a donation?"

"No, you're going to have to come here and pick up your relative."

"You're on the wrong track. I don't have any relatives in Yountville."

"Your uncle."

"Died in Saint Louis, years ago."

"Your Uncle Patrick."

"I don't have an Uncle Patrick."

"Patrick Michael Gilhooley?"

"Goddamn. That old man told you he was my uncle?"

"You are listed as his next of kin."

"Is he dead? Brighten my day. Tell me he's dead and you want me to bury his ass."

"Mr. Gilhooley has assaulted one of the patients at a nearby facility. Then he went on a rampage and has barricaded himself in his quarters. He has to go. You can come down here and get him, or the sheriff is going to send in a SWAT team and take him to jail. No one wants the spectacle of a drunken geriatric veteran being dragged away by the authorities."

"Drunken."

"Drunken and raging."

"That would be Gunny."

"Major Rommel, with you or without you, Mr. Gilhooley is leaving this facility. What will it be?"

Rommel stared into the phone. "I'll be there."

"It has to be tonight."

"I'll be there."

"If we don't see you by seven o'clock, the sheriff will have no alternative: He will have to send in the SWAT team."

"I'll be there."

"You understand, we have no alternative."

Rommel spoke slowly, "You are the one who doesn't understand. That old man is the wreckage of one of the most dangerous men in the history of the United States Marine Corps. If Gilhooley's armed, the sheriff will be lucky if he doesn't lose half his team. If he's not armed, Gilhooley's still a killer. Some people are plumbers. Some people are carpenters. Gunny's a killer and has been since his sixteenth birthday. Make yourselves comfortable, but stay away from that man until I get there. I haven't seen this man in years, but I promise you, if you leave this man with nothing to lose, your next of kin will regret it."

There was a pause. "We will be waiting for you." Robert seemed a more thoughtful man.

Rommel disconnected the call. Carmichael stepped forward. "We have a few more questions, Mr. Rommel. Will you come down for an interview?"

Carolyn stepped forward, standing directly between the two. "Not today, and not without his attorney." Rommel looked at her. Carolyn continued, "This has gone on long enough. I'm sorry someone has spoiled your gang rape and beaten up some of your bums. This man has nothing to do with it. He has a life. You should get one, too. Talk to his lawyer."

"This is not going away," Carmichael said. Carolyn stood toe-to-toe with Lieutenant Carmichael, clearly staking a claim.

"You let women do your fighting for you, Mr. Rommel?" Carmichael taunted.

"Wish I'd thought of it sooner," Rommel said.

"Good afternoon, Lieutenant," Carolyn said.

Carmichael headed for the exit, Vince Garcia uncomfortably in tow.

Rommel looked at Carolyn, preparing to excuse himself. "I don't know what that was about."

"Save it," Carolyn said, as she unclutched his forearm. She held up her wet crimson hand. "You're bleeding."

"Amateur stitching. I'll take care of it." Rommel nodded and moved toward the exit.

Carolyn stared at him. Lieutenant Carmichael had had an excellent reason for seeking Rommel out. But it didn't make sense. Matt Rommel was a dangerous man. A very large, very dangerous man, but this was insanity. No one person could do what the paper said. Maybe Carmichael couldn't make him talk, but now, Carolyn felt that she had a right to some answers. Rommel was turning away. "So, where are you going?" Carolyn asked.

"First, I have to tend to a recent wound. Then I have to see about an old one."

7

The Yountville Veterans Home

Depending on traffic, the Napa Valley lies about an hour north of San Francisco—across the Golden Gate Bridge, through prosperous Marin county, north at Sears Point, and over the gentle hills. At the foot of the valley is the town of Napa. The sides of the valley are traced by the Silverado Trail on the East and Highway 29 on the West. Up Highway 29 from the town of Napa, Yountville is the first village up-valley: a town of boutiques, expensive restaurants, even more expensive homes, and—a holdover from the Army of the Republic—the Yountville Veterans Home.

Founded in 1884, the Yountville Veterans Home is a 250-acre campus of California mission-style structures not unlike those of older military bases. After a stop at the administration facility, Rommel was directed to a white cinder-block structure on the far end of the campus. Three squad cars and a police-services panel van were clustered near the curb. A tall, thin, dark-haired man in his thirties stood on the stoop of one of the units.

"Patrick Michael Gilhooley?" Rommel asked.

"In there."

"So what's the deal?"

"Short or long version?" the thin man said.

"Huh?"

"Mr. Gilhooley had an altercation with one of the patients from the drug rehab facility."

"Drug rehab," Rommel said. "The VA placed a drug rehab facility next to a retirement home?"

"No. Once, this whole campus was for the exclusive use of elderly veterans. There was even a hospital just for the residents. As more people moved into the valley, real estate prices skyrocketed and the demand for all kinds of community services increased. Our campus was used to sponsor art galleries. The locals even put a million dollars toward renovating the old movie theater into a concert hall, something that could be used for cultural events. We have films, concerts, art gallery showings. With the increase in population, this veterans' facility has come to be at the heart of the valley's social scene. It has provided quality entertainment that the residents here can enjoy, along with everyone else. It has also made the old gents guests in their own homes as the surrounding community continues to encroach. One of the less popular intruders has been the rehab facility."

"Rehab?"

"Drugs, alcohol. They have their own facilities as far from the main campus as we can manage."

"OK, so what?"

"Not all of the people admitted to the rehab facility do well in treatment. Some of them continue to use drugs. To do that, sometimes they need money, which they are not allowed to have while in treatment. Sometimes they steal from our veterans. These younger, affluent addicts are not popular with our elderly residents."

Rommel smiled. It was not an attractive smile. "So, one of your dopers robbed old Gunny. Hard to imagine the old vulture getting old and helpless."

"No, the patient was interrupted while robbing Mr. Gilhooley's quarters."

Rommel bristled. "So what's the problem? An old man beats the crap out of a burglar. Take the punk into custody. Case closed."

"It's not that easy. The young man was badly beaten. He has been severely traumatized. Mr. Gilhooley is raging drunk and has gone wild, lashing out at anyone who tries to talk to him."

"So you called me?"

"He has to go. Our regulations are clear. They are not subject to negotiation. Alcohol abuse and violence are not permitted. He has to go."

"This is bullshit. You people put those punks in proximity with these old gentlemen. What did you think would happen?"

"He has to go. He can go with you, or the SWAT team can remove him, but he is going."

"This is bullshit."

Rommel knocked at the door. No answer. Rommel turned the door knob gently. The door opened easily, releasing a fetid stench of sweat, vomit and whiskey.

"Oh, my God," the administrator gasped, "he has to go."

Rommel looked at the sheriff's deputies and the SWAT van. He turned back toward the door and the stench and the darkness within. "Gunny, you in there?" he roared. A weak, confused voice called from the dimness.

"Major?"

"You're being transferred, Gunny. You're coming with me. Are you armed?"

"No, sir."

"If I come in there, are you going to make trouble?"

"No, sir."

Under the circumstances, Rommel decided things could be worse. He turned to the administrator and nodded toward the SWAT van. "We'll be out of here by 0700 tomorrow. Send them home. Get me a bucket, a mop, a stiff bristle brush, a box of Spic and Span, and a bottle of Lysol."

"That won't be necessary. Just take him and go."

"Get me the cleaning gear. These quarters will be clean when we leave."

Rommel moved into the darkened apartment. "You in here, old man?" Rommel roared. "Up on your feet, you old murderer. Time to turn and burn."

From beneath a pile of clothes, an ancient, reptilian arm slithered into the dim light, followed by a long groan. The small bedroom was positioned toward the rear of the apartment, near the small bathroom. Rommel moved past the clutter and stood next to the bed. He stripped the blankets and bed linen and threw them in a heap near the front door. Ten years earlier, the situation would have called for rough treatment that Rommel would have gladly provided. Ten years ago, Gunny would have found himself in a heap, in the bottom of the shower, fully dressed, under a surging stream of cold water. Rommel looked at Gilhooley, still lying helplessly on the floor. Over the last decade, the old man must have lost half of his body mass. He looked like a sea tortoise, stripped of his shell, lying on the beach with nothing left to distinguish him beyond his beak and claws.

Rommel spoke in a moderate tone, "Here's how this is going to work. You are going to lie on your rack until I come for you. I've got a few loads of wash to do, then I'm going to police this facility and stow your gear in my car. I'm taking the clothes you are wearing and leaving you with a fresh set of civvies." Rommel helped the old man gently to his feet. Gilhooley wobbled toward the bed and fell across it, looking away, toward the wall.

"The whole world is going to shit," the old man said.

Rommel began to bundle the clothes strewn about into a large plastic bag. "Smells like it."

8

Are You Eyeballing My Dog?

He didn't smell puke. He didn't taste it. Something was wrong. Gunny was alert. His eyes snapped open. The eyes would be the only thing to spring into action. Gunny hurt. Any part of his body not stabbed with sharp, piercing pain, was suffused with an encompassing ache. Last night must have been something. But had it been enough?

The room was lousy with sunlight. The curtains were pulled back from two oversized windows, which seen from the bed, were filled with blue sky and scattered, brilliantly white clouds. The walls were papered: flowers in yellow, lavender, and green scattered on a field of white. The linen was fresh and cool to the touch. Past the foot of the bed, Gunny could see an alcove with a large mirror and double sink mounted against the far wall. This wasn't an institution, and it sure as hell wasn't jail. Gunny got slowly to his feet, which sank into a thick palomino colored carpet. From a standing position, the blue sky became an ocean panorama flecked with the occasional distant freighter on a misting horizon. "Somebody's got money," he observed to no one.

He took two steps toward the door before he understood he was naked. No socks, no watch, nothing.

Absolutely, completely naked. Gunny looked around. No shoes on the floor. No trousers, shirt, nothing. He looked across the room at the mirror. A withered, gray, naked old man looked back at him. But also in the mirror, he could see a robe hanging from a hook reflected from the back side of the partitioning wall. Gunny walked over and picked it up. Big, fluffy, blue terrycloth robe. On the floor below, slippers. Gunny stepped into the slippers, put on the robe, and looked into the bathroom. Big tub, lots of towels. Who did he know with this kind of money?

Gunny walked back to the door and stepped out into the dark hallway. He felt for a switch. Nothing. Someone was moving around. Gunny moved toward the sound. Halfway down, a large, low, black mass stepped into the hallway, blocking his path. Gunny stopped. The black mass approached slowly. It was a dog: a big, curious, and not entirely happy dog. Gunny thought to call out. As if sensing the impending noise, the dog emitted a low growl. Gunny thought, *OK, don't show fear. What else?* Gunny took a step backward. The dog advanced a step. It was the wrong thing to do. It established the pattern that ended up with the dog walking the old man down the hall and back into his room. Now, Gunny stood in the middle of the room, staring at the dog. Some kind of a rottweiler mix. Gunny could see only one eye. The other looked to be permanently shut. A strip of fur rose along the dog's back, one long canine mohawk. The dog growled more loudly.

A voice boomed from the hallway. "To a dog, staring is a sign of aggression. Are you eyeballing my dog?"

"Is that you, colonel?"

"So, now I'm a colonel. Bosnia, remember? If you must use a rank, and you might as well, it's major."

"My beloved corps does hold its grudges."

"So does the Yountville Veterans Home. Guess who doesn't live there anymore?"

"That was a bum rap," Gunny said.

• • •

54

"Bullshit. Rich junkies are America's most precious resource. How dare you hurt that sensitive young man's feelings?"

"I did more than hurt his feelings."

"Which is why you don't live there anymore. You're lucky they didn't take you off to the jug."

"Where's my gear?"

"Things that need cleaning are at the cleaners. Things that need washing are in the washer. Those things that do not need cleaning or washing are either in the closet or in a corner of the garage."

"So where am I?" Gunny asked.

"You're in a guest room in my house in San Francisco. I assume that you are Zone A on the concept of a guest room. It's a place you visit, not a place you live."

"I understand."

"Why would you list me as next of kin?"

"I had to put something down. I didn't think it would come to this."

"Come to you beating up a drug addict, going on a drunken rampage, and having the Napa County Sheriff's tactical team gear up to drag your drunken ass to jail?"

"I'd like to see them try."

"Precisely the kind of crap they called me to prevent. I expected a weapon, but I didn't find anything but a Ka-Bar and half a pool cue. Unarmed is not your style. What are you up to?"

"We're not allowed to have firearms. It's a dismissal offense. Rents are low. I needed that place. One of the rich junkies from that country club rehab facility breaks into my quarters to rob me. I kick his ass, and I'm the outcast."

"I know you, Gunny, you old alligator. You are long on sneaky, long on mean, and nothing is ever an accident with you. Did you start this?"

Gunny's expression was one of injured innocence. "It's been almost twenty years, Major. I'm not the rampaging ass-kicker that I was. I'm just an old man who needs a quiet place to stay."

"You can start looking for a place tomorrow," Rommel said.

"What's the dog's name?"

"Chesty."

"No kidding?"

"I'll go see if your stuff in the dryer is done. Don't touch the dog." Rommel left the room and walked down the hall.

Gunny listened for a moment to the receding foot-steps, got down on one knee, and gently reached out with both hands. He caressed the dog's head and spoke softly, "Hello, Chesty. My name is Gunny. You and me are gonna be pals. The major doesn't know it, but things are going to happen. Big things."

≈≈

Only a week ago, Gunny had been in Yountville, on campus at the Veterans Home. He was parked on his duff and waiting for a death that was taking forever. He remembered sitting alone in the recreation room one day, alone with a copy of the San Francisco paper. There it was, in the second section, the Gay Avenger. The details were fuzzy, but the story was vivid. A single man walking a dog, fights a mob to protect an old woman in the Mission District. Since the Castro District was less than a mile away from the Mission District and the man—or men—were physically fit, had short haircuts, and wore boots with their flannel shirts and jeans, the speculation was that the man—or men—were gay, hence the Gay Avenger. Gunny read the story, set the paper down, and went for a walk. Lost in thought, Gunny walked off the campus of the veterans' home and under the Highway 29 overpass. As he walked, the story stayed with him. Most news stories were crap: a few facts and a lot of speculation. It occurred to Gunny that with a large gay population in San Francisco, the Gay Avenger slant would sell a lot of papers. There might not have even been a guy or a dog. Even on a good day, bums have a tenuous grip on reality. The mob could have taken to fighting with each other.

There was a nice, old street lady interviewed. She claimed she had been protected by Paul Bunyan and Babe, the blue ox. Well, that was nuts, but even crazy stories have some basis in fact. A big man, a really big man and a big animal. One guy. That would be a hell of a fight. Of course, if these maggots were all facing one way and you attacked from the rear, you could break a lot of heads before a mob of drunken bums knew what was going on.

He could have done it. He would have, too. Forty years ago, Gunny knew he would have put half of them in the hospital and the other half in the morgue. Over the course of his life, Gunny had known a hundred men just this dangerous. Was it possible he knew this man? A huge, violent man who a simpleminded woman would confuse for a beloved character from her childhood. Big, violent, beloved, gentle. Yeah, that would narrow it down quite a bit. Narrow it down to no one. A great big, violent guy who would lay his life down for a nobody. Or a village full of nobodies! With a guy like this, Gunny could have the one thing he needed: Justice. With Justice, Gunny could finally lie down and die in peace. She would be waiting for him. When Gunny thought about her, she was always a gangly child. In his mind, she ran to him, long skinny neck, all knees and elbows and great big teeth. She would run to him, and he would heft her up. They would be together, and they would both know peace.

On that day, Gunny stopped dead in his tracks. There was one last chance after all. He looked up from the road and the gravel and dirt shoulder. Only then did Gunny realize that he had walked all the way across the valley floor to the Silverado Trail.

≈≈≈

The first few days were recon. Gunny discovered all the common areas of the house—including the soundproofed pistol range in the basement. Gunny didn't know arts and crafts architecture, but he knew that the layout of the house pleased him. It was large, but with pleasingly human dimensions. The materials—largely wood, stucco, and slate—created an environment that felt natural, almost old-world European. As much as anything, it reminded him of a house in a fantasy village. Gunny made a point of sleeping late. His eyes might open at four thirty, but he closed them and forced himself to remain in bed until six. Sadly, Gunny observed that Rommel was worse. Often, Rommel did not come downstairs until seven in the morning. What does anyone do in the rack until seven in the morning? After reconnoitering the local health food stores, Gunny took it upon himself to bring in the morning paper and make breakfast for the two of them.

Making breakfast gave Gunny control of a third of Rommel's diet. If Rommel could taste the enzymes and amino acids Gunny added to the eggs and juice, he never mentioned it. He had been training fighting men for the better part of a lifetime. To Gunny, it was a simple matter: first nutrition, then physical exercise, then a test, and then action.

Exercise was not going to be much of a problem. The major had a room that had been converted into a gym. There were a few free weights and a large contraption with flexing rods that allowed for resistance training up to four hundred pounds. There was also a treadmill. Rommel made leisurely use of the equipment at least four days a week. These were the basics, the tools Gunny would use to strip away the soft civilian layer that covered Rommel.

Outside, there was a stucco wall with a gate along the public sidewalk. This created a small front yard with a kidney-shaped, close-cropped lawn and a walk that meandered from the gate, by the sidewalk, to the front door. The wall made for a place to sit, quiet and restful. Gunny would bring Chesty into the yard and sit with her, as he might with a small child at a playground. The dog rolled on the grass, stared at the sky, and napped. Later, with Chesty on a leash, Gunny would wander down the road. A few blocks away, at the foot of El Camino del Mar, he discovered gravelly China Beach. Trekking up the hill in the other direction, he discovered the museum at the top of that same road. In the first days, he preferred the gentle sloping descent to the beach. Sitting in the sun with his eyes closed, Chesty sat by his side, her single eye likewise closed, and her moist black nose twitching as she sampled and classified the scents from the ocean and the small beach. As the first days became a week, and the week became two, Gunny felt better. He began taking short hikes uphill, making his way along the Lands End trail, and continuing to the side and behind the Palace of the Legion of Honor. In this way, days became weeks, weeks became a month. Rommel would remind Gunny that guests were visitors and that visitors left. Gunny would make the occasional trip downtown to Lefty O'Doul's for a plate of corned beef and cabbage, followed by an hour or two in the bar. Gunny would explain to the denizens that he had known Lefty, and that, as nice as the establishment was today, it was nothing like when Lefty ran the place. At the end of the lunch and impromptu lecture, Gunny would take a leisurely walk around Union Square, looking into shop windows, pretending that Hermès scarves, Montblanc pens, and Patek Philippe watches interested him. Gunny would then walk up and down Maiden Lane, trying to tell anyone who would listen that the alley got its name because this was where nineteenth-century prostitutes plied their trade. After all this, Gunny would sit in Union Square and watch the hippies. Technically, they weren't hippies; they were speakers and organizers loosely connected with the Occupy movement. Sometimes they would tell Gunny that America had been handed to the corporations, and that every citizen was obliged to reclaim their civil liberties. Gunny would listen patiently and explain to the young and middle-aged protesters that they were screwed unless they fought back, and that, even then, they were probably screwed anyway. As the sun began to set, Gunny would take a cab back to Sea Cliff. He would then report to Rommel that apartment vacancies were scarce, but he was certain that something would break free soon. What he didn't tell Rommel was: not having to pay rent meant that old Gunny's retirement check provided disposable income he hadn't experienced in fifteen years.

• • •

During his walks with Chesty, he began to suspect that he might not be alone. The odd feeling began with a harmless train of thought. He thought about parking. Up at the museum, there was never enough parking. Down the hill, by Rommel's house, there was less congestion. One way that San Franciscans dealt with parking was by driving smaller cars. Not everyone drove smaller cars, of course, but San Francisco has more than its share of compacts and imports. Driving in Chinatown, for instance, is much easier in a smaller car. Out by the ocean, it wasn't as big a deal, but people don't buy cars for one neighborhood, they buy them to drive, and it was easier to drive a smaller car in the city. That is, except for Rommel. Rommel drove a blue-green Cadillac Seville. It was twenty years old, but it was in mint condition. Not many people are like the major. Probably just as well. You wouldn't want to pack a city like this with SUVs. SUVs. It occurred to Gunny that he had been seeing SUVs. There was almost always a black GMC Yukon within fifty meters of the front of the house. Often, coming back from the beach, there would be a black SUV that he and Chesty would pass. Standing, now by the statue of El Cid, in front of the museum, Gunny looked out over the parking lot. There were a few, but only one was a nice shiny black SUV. Moreover, a man was sitting at the wheel, some buzz-cut blockhead wearing aviator sunglasses. No facial hair. He seemed fit enough. *Go over there and start something?* Gunny thought about it, but he hadn't come prepared. Gunny decided to walk back to the major's house. If they were following him, he could afford to pick his time. They would be there tomorrow and the day after.

☙ঞ

He and Chesty were nearly home when Gunny spotted an occupied sedan in Rommel's driveway, Crown Vic. Gunny didn't have to guess about these two. The general demeanor of fatigue, cheap suits, flatfoots.

"Good morning, officers. Can I help you?"

"Is Matt Rommel at home?" the woman said.

"I don't know. I'll have to check."

"Do you mind if we come in?"

"It's not my house. If the major's here, he can invite you in himself. If he isn't, then you won't want to come in." Gunny led Chesty through the gate and into the house. He called out. No answer. Gunny came back out. Across the street, he could see the same SUV with the same goon in a suit and tie behind the wheel. "He's not here. You could leave a message, or you could just have that jerk-off call you when he gets here."

The woman seemed surprised. "What are you talking about?"

"That guy," Gunny gestured. "That sorry bag of dicks has been camped out here for the last few days. He's not yours?"

"No."

"Makes sense. Better car. Nicer suit."

Lieutenant Carmichael stepped into the street and approached the black Yukon. Detective Garcia followed, taking up a position toward the rear of the vehicle that would allow him to radio in the plates and give him a tactical advantage in the event that such an advantage became necessary. Carmichael stared at the driver. The driver did not make eye contact. Not a good sign. Carmichael tapped on the driver's side window. The window lowered, and the driver looked at her through dark-tinted aviator sunglasses. Suit coat, white dress shirt, blue-striped necktie. Caucasian male, thirties, had to be a nineteen-inch neck, but the man did not appear overweight. Carmichael decided that he had the look of private security.

"License and registration," Lieutenant Carmichael said.

"Is there a problem, officer?"

"License and registration," Carmichael repeated. From the corner of her eye, she could see her partner, Garcia, using his portable radio to check on the vehicle's license plates. The young, white, thick-necked driver handed a card and a piece of paper out the window. A glance at the registration told Carmichael that the SUV was a rental. She looked at the driver's license.

"Mr. Tanner, would you like to tell me what you are doing here?"

The thick-necked young man remained impassive. "Not really," he said.

"Step out of the car, Mr. Tanner."

"Is there some problem, officer?" the thick-necked young man said. If the remark was intended to mimic cooperation, it was too little and too late.

"Step out of the car, Mr. Tanner. Do it now." Lieutenant Carmichael drew her service weapon and trained it in a two-handed stance on the driver. Immediately, Detective Garcia produced his .40-caliber Sig, trained it on the driver, and approached to within fifteen feet of the driver's door.

The thick-necked driver opened the door and slowly got out of the SUV. He kept his hands in plain sight.

"Turn around," Carmichael ordered in an even voice. "Place your hands on the vehicle." She glanced at Garcia, who immediately holstered his weapon and produced his handcuffs. Garcia braced the driver against the door. Garcia used his right foot to move the driver's feet farther away from the vehicle, forcing the driver to lean more heavily against the SUV. Garcia began patting the man down and froze an instant later. Swiftly, Garcia reached inside the driver's jacket and pulled out a sturdy looking black object. "Gun!" Garcia shouted.

"I have a permit for that," Tanner said.

"Don't you move!" Garcia shouted. With his right hand, Garcia took one wrist and brought it back behind the man's back. Garcia cuffed that wrist, brought the other arm back and cuffed the other wrist. Garcia stepped back, allowing the driver to turn around and face Lieutenant Carmichael.

"What's this about, officer?"

"You are required to inform law enforcement officers of the fact that you are in possession of a concealed weapon." Carmichael gestured toward the house across the street, Rommel's house. "Do you know the man who lives in that house?"

"No."

"Fine. I am in the mood to do this the hard way. You are in possession of a firearm, and you failed to advise members of law enforcement when given the chance. You are parked outside the home of a man I regard as a *person of interest* in an ongoing investigation. You are under arrest for the clandestine concealment of a firearm. You have the right to shut up and go to jail."

"We don't need to do that, officer. As you already know, my name is Bob Tanner. I am an operative in the employ of Black Horizon Security. My assignment has nothing to do with the owner of that house, but I have been assigned to maintain surveillance on his houseguest, that man right there."

Carmichael stole a glance at the old man standing on the sidewalk.

"Him? That old man right there? You are being paid to maintain surveillance on that geriatric?"

"Yes. He may not look it, but Mr. Gilhooley is a well-known crank who has created problems for our firm in the past. As luck would have it, our chief executive officer is visiting the San Francisco office. Over the last few years, Black Horizon Security has figured prominently in the news due to our contract work with the federal government in Iraq and Afghanistan."

The old man called out. "And New Orleans. Don't forget New Orleans, scumbag!"

"As the face of our corporation, our boss, Richard Cheney, is a public figure with a high profile. Our corporate-security protocols require any branch receiving company VIPs and other dignitaries to identify any local potential threats and keep them under surveillance until said VIP has left the area. This is particularly necessary with the Occupy protests that are scheduled to be held later in the month."

"Did you say, Richard Cheney?"

"Yes."

Carmichael reiterated, "You are telling me that Richard Cheney is the CEO of Black Horizon Security?"

"Yes. His name is Richard Cheney, but probably not the Richard Cheney you are thinking of. Cheney is a common name."

Detective Garcia spoke, "And the world is full of Dicks."

"Shut it," Lieutenant Carmichael said.

"What involvement does Black Horizon have with Occupy?"

"Black Horizon has the same involvement as many of the other security companies. We provide services to a number of corporate clients, many of them in the finance sector. Since part of the Occupy protests are targeted at large banks and investment firms, it's natural for our clients who operate in these industries to be concerned for the safety of their property and personnel. Later this month, Occupy intends to pack Union Square with over one-hundred-thousand protesters. Even with the support of local law enforcement, there is a chance that Occupy will attempt to swarm out of Union Square and descend on the Financial District."

"Uncuff him," Lieutenant Carmichael said. Detective Garcia turned the Black Horizon operative toward the black SUV and removed the handcuffs.

"Give him his gun," Carmichael said. Garcia looked at her. "Do it!" Carmichael said.

Tanner returned the pistol to its holster and adjusted his jacket. Carmichael spoke. "Mr. Tanner, get into your SUV and get out of here. Don't come back to this street, and don't send a replacement operative back, either. This is San Francisco. We are not going to tolerate armed thugs casing our neighborhoods at will. Any Black Horizon operative found here in Sea Cliff will be taken into custody. We have more room in our jail than you have operatives."

"I don't know, officer. We have a lot of people, some of them with very specific skill sets."

Carmichael bristled. The threat was implicit but plain. Vince Garcia moved into position to back his partner's play. "Get your mercenary ass into your shiny, black thugmobile and leave, or I will take you into custody right now."

9

Enter Sheriff Bunny

Any time not spent mixing anabolics into the major's food, or goading him during his workouts, or building up his own endurance through walks out-of-doors and trawling Union Square, Gunny spent in the den. The major had his books and his mementos; but best of all, the den was where the major kept the Balvenie PortWood and the Montecristo No. 2s—densely packed torpedoes of Cuban tobacco. The lustrous cherrywood humidor kept the cigars soft, almost spongy. The cigar's rich taste was reminiscent of a nutty chocolate. These were contraband cigars from Cuba, an enemy of democracy. Gunny knew his duty. He would set fire to these cigars. He would burn them all. He might do it one cigar at a time, but the wicked contraband would be destroyed. Gunny filled a heavy crystal tumbler with the Balvenie, over cubes of ice. He took a long, even pull on the dark, smooth scotch. Gunny knew that, if the Scots ever became enemies of democracy, he would rise to the challenge and strain that contraband through his geriatric liver and nullify the threat inherent in a contraband bottle of twenty-one-year-old scotch.

The den was also home to the 55-inch plasma television and a great reclining chair. There, from his command chair, he would watch the History Channel and the Military Channel, and the Discovery Channel, and any other channel that blew things up, tore things apart, or explained things. Gunny had little patience for fiction. Fiction was for people resolving their lives or seeking escape. With a single exception, Gunny's life was as resolved as it was going to get.

It was there, in the den, that Gunny experienced what he would come to regard as one of the last miracles of his life. He heard the outside door open. He could tell Rommel had company, two people or more. Gunny didn't care. He needed one thing from Rommel, and whoever these visitors were, they weren't likely to help Gunny get what he needed. Gunny returned his attention to monochromatic images of Leyte Gulf. Just as Admiral "Bull" Halsey was preparing to pursue a Japanese ruse, leaving the invasion force underdefended, Gunny began to sense that he was being watched. He shifted in the great leather recliner and looked back. A single eye in the square, black, furry face glowed at him. Chesty stood, just inside the doorway, staring at him. Gunny was on the verge of regaling Chesty with a few pithy comments about her canine ancestry when he saw Chesty's companion. By the great black dog's side stood a schoolgirl. Gunny hadn't been in the same room with a schoolgirl in fifty years, not since his own little girl. If she was a fourth grader, then Gunny decided, she was short. But if she was younger than that, then she was tall. The auburn-haired child had the eyes of an ordnance disposal expert, which is to say, rock-steady. He looked at her as if she were the answer to a question he had quit asking himself many years ago. She looked at him as if he were magical. It was that profound moment of affinity that the very young and the very old sometimes share. He was the storm-tossed soul struggling toward the shadow, and she was the ancient soul in a young body, come to relieve him of his tour of duty. She was *life*, going forward into the future. Gunny was *experience*, trudging back from the front lines. They looked at each other.

"Who are you?" the little girl said.

"I'm Gunny. Who are you?"

"I'm Aubrey."

"Aubrey, have you ever seen the History Channel?"

"I'd rather watch *Sheriff Bunny*."

Gunny shrugged. "How 'bout this, you answer a question and we can watch *Sheriff Bunny*. Can you tell me what enfilade is?"

"No."

"How about defilade?"

Aubrey shrugged. "No."

"OK, can you tell me why you have to control the seaways around an island if you are going to stage an amphibious assault?"

Aubrey looked Gunny straight in the eye. "Can you tell me who Sheriff Bunny's deputy is?"

Gunny thought about it for a moment and handed Aubrey the remote control. "Fair enough, *Sheriff Bunny* first, then amphibious operations."

Aubrey took the remote, sat in front of the television and leaned back against Chesty who, no stranger to the afternoon adventures of *Sheriff Bunny*, had curled herself into a crescent backrest just behind Aubrey. "OK," she said.

In that moment, a criminal conspiracy was born.

10

Sausalito

"Doing anything this morning, Gunny?"

The old man looked up from the 55-inch plasma screen.

"Aubrey coming over?"

"No."

"It's *Ancient Aliens* week on the History Channel. I like watching the nut with the wild hair. He reminds me of Professor Irwin Corey. You remember him?"

"The comedian?"

"Yeah."

"Today is moving day, Gunny. You can come and help me, or you can be the guy who's moving. Coming?"

"Since you asked nice, sure."

"Get Chesty's leash, hook her up, and meet me out front."

Gunny took the leash from its hook in the foyer. He looked down. Chesty sat at his feet, focused intently on the leash. The old man and the one-eyed dog walked out into the small courtyard and out through the gate. Parked at the curb sat an old green, blue, brown, and gold van conversion in immaculate condition. Across the van's side, an Aztec warrior in a feathered headdress knelt holding the motionless body of a lifeless Aztec maiden in a flowing white gown with a plunging neckline that just barely concealed the maiden's massive breasts. It was a Mission Street pieta. Its compelling message: The driver of this van was a man of moment, a descendant of the mighty and noble Aztecs, and a person of merit who knew of greatness, suffering, and the loss of one or more persons with massive breasts.

"Holy crap," Gunny said, surveying the rig.

Rommel was already behind the wheel. "It's a loaner from a friend down in the Mission. Put the dog in back and climb in. I have to return this thing to the body shop by four."

The van made its way down Geary to Market and, from there, into the Mission. Rommel stopped at Vince's Bar and asked around. While Diego, the bartender and majority shareholder in the enterprise, remembered having seen Annie sometime over the last day or two, neither he nor the few morning customers recalled seeing her that day. Gunny made a circuit of the bar—from the padded front doors with large embedded portholes, to the pool table and jukebox. At the rear of the establishment, Gunny encountered the narrow stairway leading to the small apartment Rommel used a few days a week.

"Nothing up there," Diego called out. Gunny sauntered to the bar.

"Storage up there?" Gunny said.

"Major's apartment."

"You're kidding me. With that big house, what the hell does he need with an apartment?" Gunny asked.

Diego shrugged. "In the old days, he used it to keep the ladies, from the museum, from getting too interested. Some of them would come down here after the major, but once they saw the neighborhood and the bar, they never came back. All except for one. Good lookin', smart, tough. I like her. She's been down here a couple of times."

"I think I know the one," Gunny said.

"I was hoping to see more of her. You wouldn't think a man like the major would be so gun shy around women, but he is. He likes 'em, but he don't like to be around 'em too much. I think he's afraid they'll take over or something."

"Every man lives in his wife's house," Gunny said.

"Where you know the major from?" Diego asked.

"Corps. Different places. How 'bout you?"

"Nam. He was my platoon leader." Diego pointed to a framed eight-by-ten photo of a German shepherd on the wall. From the photo, hung a Silver Star. "That's Vince. He saved a lot of lives, and, in the end, the major saved his. I named this place and my oldest son after that dog. We stole him, and he lived with my wife and kids and me until he was almost fourteen."

"Nice-looking dog, but dogs don't get Silver Stars."

"It's one of the major's, but don't kid yourself, Vince earned it."

"Nice place you've got here, Diego."

"Thanks."

"So why do you give Rommel a room here?"

"The major put up the seed money. I made it work and bought most of it back from him. So, the bar's part his, too, but he doesn't take any cash out of it. Besides, he puts in a couple of nights a month behind the bar. That lets me take the family out to dinner and a show sometimes."

They left the bar. Rommel began a methodical search at 14th Street. By the time they'd reached 24th and Bryant, Rommel eased the van to the curb directly behind an elderly woman pushing a large chrome shopping cart. Rommel parked the van, walked around, and opened the sliding door. He was just able to grab the leash as Chesty jumped out. The woman turned to survey them speculatively. At the sight of the great black dog, she beamed a gentle, lovely smile.

"Babe! Come here, honey! How is my big, sweet protector?" Chesty pulled straight for Annie, who was already crouched with arms outstretched to welcome Chesty, who plowed forward, head lowered to receive the gentle caresses. Chesty's stub of a tail wagged furiously.

"The last time I saw you two, Babe bit you on the heinie. I hope it didn't hurt too much. Are you all right?"

"You know, Annie, it didn't hurt too much. It hurt just the right amount. Plus, I was needing a tetanus shot anyway. Isn't that right, meathead?" Rommel looked directly at Chesty who, in the thrall of gentle adulation, was indifferent to everything else. "How are you, Annie?"

"I'm just fine, Mr. Bunyan. It's a lovely day, isn't it? A little cool, but lovely all the same. Are you here to see me?"

"As a matter of fact, I am. I saw the nicest neighborhood the other day, and I thought that you might like to see it. Can you spare fifteen minutes?"

Annie turned the proposition over in her mind. "I'm still making my rounds. I just have so much to do." She seemed lost in a moment's thought. "I can't leave my things."

"Of course not," Rommel said. "We'll take them with us."

"I suppose a little outing would be fun. What do you think, Babe?" Chesty stared at her with one adoring eye.

With a little effort, Rommel loaded the cart into the van and lashed it down. Annie climbed into the back and buckled her seat belt, Chesty on the bench seat, at her side. With that, the van headed toward the freeway and, from there, toward Highway 101 and the Golden Gate Bridge.

"My, this is wonderful," Annie said. "But we're a long way from my usual haunts."

"Just another minute or two," Rommel said, as he took the first exit into Sausalito, an upscale village just north of the Golden Gate Bridge. They drove down Bridgeway, along the water and the restaurants and the parks with their wide immaculate sidewalks. Rommel turned onto a side street. He parked in front of a beige 1940s vintage bungalow, directly across from a fire station. "Here we go," Rommel said.

Rommel unloaded the cart. Gunny held onto Chesty's leash, and Annie turned slowly in a complete circle as she took in the view. "It's gorgeous," Annie exclaimed. "It's like something out of a fairy tale."

"You got that right," Gunny said, darkly.

Annie looked at him, tilting her head. "Huh?"

"Well, you know—" Gunny said. "You know how they separate the men from the boys in Sausalito…?"

"Gunny," Rommel said.

"I'm just saying."

"Put a sock in it, Gunny."

Gunny, the essence of injured innocence, turned to look out at the stunning promenade and said to no one, "…with a crowbar."

Rommel gave Annie a short tour, letting her push her cart up one clean, broad, level sidewalk, and after crossing the street at the corner crosswalk, down the other. Annie took in the park and the bay views, San Francisco glittering like a jewel from across the bay. After a while, they were back across the street by the great Aztec van.

"This would be a lovely place to be," Annie said. "Much nicer than where I am now."

Rommel walked toward the bungalow. "And look at this." Rommel grasped the door to the single-car garage and slid it to the side. It moved easily. He walked in and turned on a light. The small garage was clean but sparse, with a single overhead light. The floor was concrete, the walls— redwood framed on the inside, stucco on the outside. "It turns out that no one is using this garage. As soon as I found that out, I thought of you. If you wanted," Rommel said, "you could bring your cart in here, close the door, and camp when you felt like it. There's nobody here to bother you."

• • •

Annie looked around the small garage. It had definite possibilities. At the rear of the garage, the door was ajar. "What's this?" she asked.

"I don't know," Rommel said. "Take a look."

Annie pushed the door open. The lights were on as she stepped into the small kitchen. A few steps beyond, facing the street, there was a small living room with a couch and a rug. Off to the side, was an archway. Beyond that, two small bedrooms and a small bathroom with a large porcelain tub. "Who lives here?" she asked. "There are linens and blankets folded on the bed."

"Nobody lives here," Rommel said.

"Nobody?"

"I happen to know for a fact, that nobody lives here," Rommel said.

"Well, if nobody lives here, I could stay *here*, if I felt like it, instead of in the garage, don't you think?"

"You know, Annie, I think you're right. If you felt like it, you could certainly do that."

Annie smiled at Rommel. "Men are so silly, so impractical."

"As it turns out, Annie, I happen to have a friend who works right across the street at the fire station. His name is Stephens. So, if, for some reason, you needed to get in touch with me or if something went wrong, you could just go across the street and he or one of his coworkers would be able to help you or contact me."

"That's nice." She opened the refrigerator. "There's food in here. Did people leave food in here?"

"I'm pretty sure it's fresh."

Annie walked into the living room and sat on the couch. She was home. "Well, you were right. This is very nice, indeed. I feel a bit like Goldilocks." She paused for a long moment as if waiting for something. "Well, I'm a bit tired. If no one lives here, I think I will take a nap. So if you gentlemen will excuse me…" She walked them to the door.

Gunny, Rommel, and Chesty walked to the van and climbed in. Gunny looked at Rommel. "What just happened here?"

"Annie's had some problems out in the Mission. She's a very nice person, and I don't want her getting hurt."

"So you gave her a house?"

"I'm hoping it's temporary. Listening to her talk, I think she has family somewhere in the Bay Area. I've got a detective trying to find some of her relatives."

"Just because a homeless person has family doesn't mean they're going to come and get her. I mean, sometimes, families just get to the point that they can't cope."

"True."

"Did she call the dog Babe? And she called you Mr. Bunyan. She thinks you're Paul Bunyan?"

"I'm not certain what she actually believes."

"And so you hire a private detective to find a family based on the recollections of a person that thinks you're Paul Bunyan?"

"A lot of stories contain grains of truth."

Gunny shook his head. "She's nuts, and Major, you're not far behind. You gave her a house?"

"I've had it for a while. I was going to move in and then things changed. I came into some serious cash and bought the place by the ocean. I wasn't sure what I wanted to do with this place. It's a great location, and Sausalito is a neat little town. Then the market tanked. Maybe, when the market recovers, I'll sell it."

Rommel could see the wheels turning in the old man's head. "That thing in the news. That was you and her. The papers think you're two gay guys. Holy crap, you're the Gay Avenger!" Gunny hollered.

"Shut up, old man."

Gunny pointed a finger into the air. "This is a job for the Gay Avenger!"

"Shut up, old man."

The old man cackled until Rommel thought Gunny might make himself sick.

"Jesus." Gunny caught his breath and rode for a while in silence. "It won't help, you know."

"What won't help?" Rommel asked.

"This bullshit. You come into some money, and you think you can make things right for people. You are going to save all the friendless bastards on the planet. Problem is, you can't protect people from the world. That sweet, old bag lady back there, those people in Bosnia, all the civilians in all the war zones you've seen, the desperately poor, the sick, the dying. Are you trying to get those people out of your head? You can't save them, not one of them. If their number is up, it's up. Life will find them and fuck them, and there's nothing you or anybody else can do. The world finds them and tears them apart, and there's nothing you can do but try to look out for yourself."

"Bold talk for someone who got thrown out of an old folk's home. Should I pull over and let your ass out?"

Gunny stared out the window as they rode in silence. They crossed the bridge, drove down Lombard, and turned on Van Ness. After a while, Gunny said, to no one in particular, "There are only one or two things I need to do in this life, Major. Once I take care of them, I don't much care what happens."

11

Saying Grace

Carolyn was on her way out the door and on her way to work, when it hit her. There had been no recurring nightmare the night before. In fact, she hadn't had a nightmare in over a week. She drove down from the Berkeley Hills, dropped Aubrey off at her school, and watched the little girl walk into the building. Carolyn decided something important. She decided that she felt pretty good, overall. She decided that the time she had spent with Matt Rommel was good for her, good for her psyche, just good in general. Aubrey thought the world of Rommel, and she adored the old man. Carolyn decided that it was an odd little extended family, but in its own way, it made sense.

A couple of times during the week and at least once over the weekend, Carolyn and Aubrey would find themselves at the house in Sea Cliff. Aubrey would invade Gunny's redoubt and commandeer the television remote. Aubrey and Gunny would share their secrets, plot their plots, and watch military documentaries and law enforcing cartoon bunnies. Carolyn would pass the time sitting and talking with Rommel in the living room. Sometimes, they would all sojourn up the hill to the Palace of the Legion of Honor. Sometimes, they would wander down the hill to the beach. On those occasions when they weren't actually going into the museum, they brought Chesty. When they were all together, they were as much of a family as Carolyn could remember.

Often, they would all eat dinner together, usually around the kitchen table. If Rommel cooked, it meant marinated round steak and vegetables. The man would buy a couple of large round steaks, cut them into portions, wrap them in aluminum foil, and store them in the freezer. It made for a nice enough meal, but there was little variety. So, more in self-defense than anything else, Carolyn would often insist on cooking, just to break up the monotony. Carolyn knew that without her, neither Rommel nor the old man would ever see a casserole.

On this particular evening, they all sat down to dinner: steak with mushrooms and onions, string beans, and corn. Carolyn turned to Aubrey.

"Honey, why don't you say grace?"

Aubrey folded her hands and lowered her head. "This is my rifle. There are many like it, but this one is mine. It is my life. I must master it as I must master my life—"

"Honey," Carolyn interrupted, "Why don't you say a different grace?" She looked at Rommel. Rommel was staring at Gunny. Carolyn looked at Gunny. Gunny beamed with pride. He practically glowed.

Carolyn waited until after grace concluded and everyone began to eat. "So Gunny, in between cartoons, what have you been teaching Aubrey?"

"Just things a young lady needs to know."

"Like the Rifleman's Creed," Rommel said. It was not a question.

"No harm in teaching a prayer to a smart little girl," Gunny replied.

The conversation lapsed as the meal commenced in earnest. Aubrey broke the silence. "The boys are hogging all the four-square balls," she said.

"What boys?" Carolyn asked.

"The boys at school. Every recess, they run to the bin and grab everybody's balls."

Gunny seemed ready to say something. Rommel leaned forward and fixed the old man with a deadly stare. Whatever comment the old man was considering, it went unuttered.

"So what's four square?" Carolyn asked.

"A game, of course. Each person gets in a square. There are four squares. You bounce the ball and hit it to the next square, and that person has to keep it going. Four square is fun, but those maggots keep grabbing our gear."

Gunny seemed ready to speak. Again, Rommel leaned forward and Gunny let the moment pass.

"You should complain to your teacher, and she will make sure everyone shares."

"Nobody likes a squealer," Aubrey said.

"Squealer, honey?"

"A rat, an informer," Aubrey said. "The Lard haytes an infarmer," Aubrey said, as if trying to imitate an Irish brogue.

"The Lord has it in for all kinds of troublemakers. Doesn't he, Gunny?" Rommel said, darkly.

"That's true," Gunny said, oozing innocence.

"I can fieldstrip a 1911!" Aubrey piped up. Rommel felt a knot tighten in his stomach.

"What is a 1911?" Carolyn asked.

"A sidearm," Rommel said, uneasily.

"Not just a sidearm," Gunny said. "The finest handgun ever made."

"A gun," Carolyn said, a sense of alarm growing. "You gave this small child a gun?"

"John Browning's gift to the pagan babies," Aubrey beamed.

"Don't say pagan babies, honey." Carolyn wheeled on Gunny. "You do NOT put a gun in the hands of my child. I won't have it."

"Technically, a gun is a large weapon system attached to the deck of a ship," Gunny offered.

"I won't have it. Do you understand?"

"There wasn't any ammo, just the weapon."

"Short or tall, they all fall to hardball." Aubrey seemed to be deliberately provoking her mother.

"Huh?" Carolyn said. She looked at Rommel.

Rommel seemed uncomfortable. "Bullets which are fully jacketed with metal, copper usually, are sometimes called ball ammunition or, in this case, hardball." Rommel looked at Gunny. "Just where did you find this firearm, Gunny."

"Downstairs," Gunny said, referring to the basement Rommel had built and fitted out as a pistol range.

"It was a mess!" Aubrey said.

"What was a mess, sweetheart?" Rommel asked.

"The g…, the pistol," Aubrey corrected herself.

"And why was it a mess, honey?" Rommel continued.

"It was all covered in thick goop and wrapped in lots of rough paper. It took a long time, but me and Gunny cleaned all that nasty goop off each and every part," Aubrey said.

Rommel leaned forward. "Gunny, are we talking about a pristine 1942 M1911A1 shipped from the factory and still in its original wrapping and Cosmoline?" Rommel modulated his voice, but his irritation was plain.

"Yes, sir. I'm pretty sure that's the one we're talking about," Gunny said. "It had all of the modifications made in 1924. If you like, I can upgrade the barrel, give it a trigger job, and you'll have a MEU(SOC)."

"Mew sock?" Carolyn said.

"A specially modified version of the M1911. Special units use them. Typically, they are assembled with after-market grip safeties, ambidextrous thumb safeties, triggers, improved high-visibility sights, match-grade stainless-steel barrels, custom grips, and improved magazines. Even with all that, it wouldn't come close to replacing the value lost."

"Value lost?" Carolyn asked.

Gunny jumped in. "If you're a collector, some people put extra value on things still in the original packaging. I never figured you for one of those guys, Major. I thought you'd want little Aubrey here to learn on a nice new weapon."

"You thought I would want you to teach a seven-year-old child how to handle a firearm? Nothing about that seems stupid and dangerous to you? Let me make it clear, Gunny. Her mother and I don't want her handling guns until she's older. I don't want you teaching her *The Manual of Arms* or how to kill with a knife. While we're on the subject, I want you to stop teaching her *The Manual of the Sword*."

"You knew about that?"

"My Mameluke is askew on the wall, and there are cuts in my leather furniture. I want you to be an old man, and I want you to let her be a little girl. Play nice, watch TV."

They ate in silence for a minute or two. Rommel put down his knife and fork. "I have to ask. Where is the pistol?"

"In the den," Gunny said. "In your desk. I put a box of 230-grain FMJ right next to it."

"FMJ? Two hundred grain?" Carolyn said.

"Full metal jacket. Two hundred and thirty grains is the weight of each bullet. That's a little over one-half ounce," Rommel said.

"Short or tall, they all fall to hardball," Aubrey said.

"That's enough, dear," Carolyn said.

"So, tell me, Gunny," Rommel said. "If I go in there, am I going to see scratches on the slide or the frame from where a certain someone inserted the slide stop during reassembly?"

"Like you never did that when you were a boot, Major. The point is that Aubrey can fieldstrip and reassemble a 1911 in under three minutes. You let me work with her, and we can get it down under a minute."

"You heard her mother. That's the end of it."

"Yes, sir."

After dinner, Rommel and Carolyn sat on the sofa in the living room. Gunny and Aubrey adjourned to the den. Chesty followed close behind. After a while, the History Channel could be heard from down the hall.

"Are you angry?" Carolyn asked.

"About what? The pistol? The furniture?"

Carolyn nodded.

"I wasn't planning on selling the pistol. I just liked having it in pristine condition, the way it was when it came from the factory. I'd think about the last person to touch those parts. Some Rosie the Riveter, maybe. Everybody working together for a common cause. Protecting a noble nation with just laws. I guess I don't need oil-soaked paper and Cosmoline for that."

"As for the rest of it, kids and dogs mean a certain amount of wear and tear. I really don't mind that at all. Gunny, on the other hand, Gunny bears watching."

"Why?"

"Gunny is a border collie with nothing to do. You take a border collie and leave him alone, and he gets into all kinds of trouble. Border collies need to work. For almost fifty years, Gunny did two things. He learned everything about weapons, tactics, and logistics that the Marine Corps had to offer. After that, he dedicated his life to teaching those skills to any marine who was placed in his charge. Learn, do, lead, and teach. That was his life, and it's obvious to me that Gunny's going to try to do that until they finally close the lid on him. I can tell you that, over the last few weeks, he's been like a damn teenager in an old man's body."

12

The Emerson Primary School Massacre

Carolyn, Aubrey, and Rommel sat in small plastic chairs before the large, heavy-metal desk of the Emerson Middle School principal, Mrs. Gladiola. From the walk into the building and down the hall, it was plain that the joint was abuzz. Something had happened, and the students and staff had still not settled down. *Even so,* Carolyn thought, *whatever it was could have nothing to do with a second grader. Whatever Aubrey had done to disturb the authorities at Emerson, it had to be something relatively minor, the sort of thing a second grader would be involved in.*

Shoes, dress, hairdo—everything about Mrs. Gladiola was sensible. A sturdy woman in her sixties, Mrs. Gladiola carried herself as though she were dealing with a matter of the highest moment.

"I called you down here because the school district has been forced, by your daughter, to deal with a very serious situation."

"Her?" Carolyn asked, looking to her side at her daughter, the little girl in the smock, seated next to her. "Aubrey is responsible for a very serious situation? Did she hurt someone?"

"No."

"Did she steal something?"

Mrs. Gladiola shook her head.

"Did she break something or damage school property."

"It isn't that simple. Something happened today that our officials unanimously agree could have resulted in a catastrophic loss of life. A hate crime, organized and perpetrated by your daughter."

Carolyn was stunned. "Oh, my God! Wait, you told me that she didn't hurt anyone, steal, or break anything. What kind of a hate crime are you talking about?"

Aubrey's voice was small and faint. "The four-square balls," she said, her stare boring a hole into the green linoleum floor.

Carolyn looked at Mrs. Gladiola. "This is about the four-square balls? Aubrey told me a while ago that, every lunch and recess, the boys hog the four-square balls and tetherball stations. Is that what this is about? And how does something like that become a hate crime? And how the hell does a tiny, little girl like this set your entire school on its ear?"

Rough language. Mrs. Gladiola was ready for this. "I'm going to have to ask you to watch your language and control your temper, Mrs. Kast."

"I'm going to have to ask you to tell me what is going on here, Mrs. Gladiola."

Mrs. Gladiola leaned forward, hands clasped on the desk—one of the massive, indestructible, metal desks that, years ago, federal, state, and local governments procured en masse. "Perhaps Aubrey can tell you what she did."

Aubrey continued to stare at the floor.

"Aubrey," Mrs. Gladiola said, with more emphasis.

"Every recess, the boys take all the stuff, and there's nothing left for the girls. So today, I went over to one of the four-square games and grabbed the ball."

"And the boys took it back?" Carolyn asked.

"No. I kept the ball and ran around the back of the school."

"So?"

"So, all the boys started yelling, and they chased me."

"Then what?"

"I ran behind the school and down to the other end. There's a gate. I ran through that."

Mrs. Gladiola interrupted, "There is a narrow access way behind the school, just wide enough for the custodian's truck to pass. At the other end of the school, at the chain-link gate, there was a large group of girls. They allowed Aubrey through the gate, trapping the boys in that space."

Carolyn shook her head. "I don't understand. Couldn't the boys just turn around and go back the way they came?"

"There were a large number of boys. They had formed something of a mob. They pressed forward, trapping the ones in front against the gate. There was a great deal of yelling and shouting."

Aubrey nodded to no one in particular, "The fog of war."

Carolyn shushed the little girl, "Honey, you're not helping yourself." Carolyn then looked back at Mrs. Gladiola, "And this is Aubrey's fault?"

"It was Aubrey's fault that there were a dozen girls on the second floor overlooking the access way. It was Aubrey's fault that they had positioned boxes of water balloons on that second-floor landing."

"It was Aubrey's fault that the group of girls at the locked chain-linked gate unraveled the emergency fire hose and sprayed cold, high-pressure water on the boys trapped at the gate."

"I had to." Aubrey's voice was tiny.

Carolyn leaned down toward her daughter. "Why did you *have to*, sweetheart?"

Aubrey looked up at her mother. "They were enfilade."

"Gunny!" Rommel said, between clenched teeth.

"Enfilade?" Carolyn asked.

"All lined up in a file, the ideal infantry target," Rommel said.

"What your daughter did here today was no less than provoke a riot. Our psychologists are very concerned about the disturbed thinking that could organize and execute something that, under more serious circumstances, could have been a massacre."

"Oh, please, it was a water balloon fight," Carolyn said.

"Only one side had water balloons. They also had a fire hose."

"Gunny says the hose is like rock and roll."

Carolyn looked at Rommel. "Rock and roll?"

Rommel shifted in his seat and looked at his shoes. "Automatic-weapons fire."

"Gunny says that, given the natural terrain, a properly executed maneuver would have every advantage, even an element of air support."

Carolyn felt the slightest bit queasy. "Air support?"

"The second floor," Aubrey said. "Gunny says that, technically, air support is just fire support from an elevated position, but that since the boys couldn't gain access without leaving the scene of battle and entering from the front of the school, we had an advantage the enemy couldn't match. If they had, a reserve unit would have caught them on the stairwell landing and fired on them with balloons while the second-floor unit and the reserve unit exfiltrated down the hall and rendezvoused outside the teacher's lounge. Gunny says boys are stupid, especially second lieutenants."

"Oh, my God." Carolyn began to feel sick. *Access, enfilade, scene of battle, reserve unit, natural terrain? What had Aubrey been learning from that old man?*

Mrs. Gladiola continued, "A water fight may seem like

a harmless event to you, but I can assure you we have parents who are very upset. Some of these children may have been traumatized."

"By water," Rommel said. It was not a question.

"I don't think we have an alternative here. Aubrey has created a major disturbance here at Emerson and we are still not done dealing with the repercussions. We have no choice but to expel Aubrey. I hope you understand."

Carolyn spoke. "I most certainly do not understand. You had what amounts to a water balloon fight started by a second grader, and, with your education, training, and years of experience, you can't deal with it."

"I am dealing with it. Aubrey has to leave."

Carolyn turned to Rommel. "This is the work of that crazy old man. Don't you have anything to say?"

"Principal Gladiola is right. Aubrey needs to leave," Rommel said.

Carolyn was nearly speechless, managing only a single word. "What?"

Rommel fixed the principal with a look. "Principal Gladiola, how long have you been a school principal?"

"Twenty-three years."

"All of it in elementary schools?"

"As principal, I have managed and administered eight schools. They have ranged from elementary and middle schools through urban high schools with more than two-thousand students."

"And it is that experience that helps you understand that you are overmatched."

"I beg your pardon?"

"Mrs. Gladiola, I'm not arguing with you. I agree with you. When it comes to dealing with Aubrey, you are always going to be outclassed."

Mrs. Gladiola visibly bristled, starting to speak before Rommel interrupted.

● ● ●

"I'm not taking anything away from you. I'm sure you are a brilliant, cultured person. You like French literature?"

"Excuse me?"

"What's your favorite Molière play?"

"The Misanthrope," Mrs. Gladiola said.

"My point exactly. A cultured, well-educated, capable person. But Aubrey has spent the last couple of months learning from one of the Marine Corps' greatest non-commissioned officers. To be honest, her mother and I thought they were just sitting in the den watching the History Channel. Instead, it looks like little Aubrey has absorbed a large portion of the Officers Candidate School curricula. You must have noticed that she uses words that children don't. She not only thinks tactically, she's demonstrated organizational and logistical skills that your entire faculty failed to identify and respond to in a timely manner. That's what Marine Corps noncommissioned officers do: They teach, and they lead. Truth be told, they run most of the service. This particular old man is one of the greats. Every generation has a handful, and, trust me, this one is more than a handful. In matters of tactics and situational awareness, this seven-year-old is always going to outclass you. She knows who, where, how many, which way in, how to get out, use of cover and concealment, and the natural topography. Apparently, she's been trained to analyze and assess the situation and seize the initiative. At the time, we didn't know that she was absorbing more than a few service-related anecdotes and traditions. Now, it's obvious. You are never going to be able to handle her, and it won't be due to insubordination, you're just going to be outclassed on a perpetual basis."

"I don't think that's the case."

"I'm just saying that you're right. Don't you wonder how seven- and eight-year-old girls were able to roam your campus at will, staging water balloons in your hallway for later use? How did that happen?"

Before Mrs. Gladiola could respond, Aubrey spoke up, "We staged from the janitor's closet. There's a sink. We used a carton that used to hold paste wax. The janitor only waxes the floors one week a month. We had a whole week." Carolyn took the child by the hand and bent down to give Aubrey her sternest look.

Rommel continued, "From now on, it's going to be like the cartoon with the roadrunner, and you are always going to be the coyote, perennially outclassed, scheming to try to keep up, buying gadgets from Acme Corporation that blow up in your face or take you over a cliff. It's not going to be pretty."

"She's just a child," Mrs. Gladiola responded.

"I think it's time to refer Aubrey to the professionals."

"I *am* a professional."

"Absolutely, but let's face it, part of being a professional is knowing when you're overmatched. I'm sure that other educators within the school district, or even the superintendent, will understand and respect your decision to cut your losses."

"I am not cutting my losses. I'm not losing at all. Personally, I think you are making way too much of this child's abilities. I don't see why corrective action taken here at Emerson won't be more than sufficient to deal with this matter."

"I stand corrected, Principal Gladiola," Rommel said.

The four of them sat there in silence, all of them aware that the course of the meeting had turned. Mrs. Gladiola looked back and forth from Carolyn to Rommel, waiting for the first intimation that she had been maneuvered. No remark was forthcoming. They continued to sit in silence. Finally, Principal Gladiola spoke. "Mr. Rommel, I don't like you."

Rommel spoke, "Yes, ma'am."

"Don't call me ma'am. In fact, I think it's better if you never speak to me again. Mrs. Kast?"

• • •

"Yes," Carolyn said.

"We are going to see how things go. My staff and I are going to keep an eye on Aubrey, a very close eye. She is going to lose some playground privileges. If she behaves herself, she'll get most of them back before she goes off to college. I look forward to meeting you again under better circumstances. Is Mr. Rommel Aubrey's father?"

Carolyn shook her head.

"Splendid. I knew there was something about Aubrey that I liked. Let's not bring Mr. Rommel to any more meetings."

Carolyn thought about it. Mrs. Gladiola did not have a say in Carolyn's selection of friends. On the other hand, what had started as a notification of expulsion had turned into a much better meeting. Carolyn was coming out ahead on this and so was Aubrey. Carolyn nodded. "Done."

Together, Carolyn and Rommel walked down the long cinder-block corridor with its many coats of paint. They stepped into the sunlight and walked toward the car. She studied him, this man who had only ever done well by her. She felt the sunshine and a gentle breeze on her face. Somewhere within, she felt a bit more. This was a good man. She looked him in the eye.

"You are a genius," she said.

"You are the first person to come to that conclusion."

"We are going to have to do something with Gunny," Carolyn said.

"It's been tried. The only thing that helps is geography."

"Geography?"

"Lots and lots of geography. I am going to put that old man on the moon."

13

Office Hours

Gunny shifted in the big leather recliner, taking care not to spill the Balvenie. Perfect cubes of ice shifted against the crystal whiskey glass with a cheerful tinkling. Today was sniper day on the History Channel—American snipers, Canadian snipers, Russian snipers, men, women, snipers all. On land or at sea, one shot, one kill. When there were interview clips of Carlos Hathcock, Gunny would sit up. He and Carlos were nearly the same age; a fact that gave Gunny pause since Carlos had passed on more than a decade earlier. For what Gunny needed, Carlos would have been perfect. But you don't always get perfect. Sometimes all you get is someone like the major. The more Gunny studied Rommel, the man, the more difficult Gunny's task seemed. The major was pretty well set. Money wasn't a problem. He had something like work to pass his time. He had a piece of that great little bar down in the Mission that even had an upstairs apartment. It even looked like the major might have wandered into a family of his own, complete with one great kid. Someone who had all of this was not likely to throw it all away. Gunny looked down at the side of the chair and Chesty looked up, mildly curious. Chesty had not chosen to fight in the ring. She had been forced. Matt Rommel wouldn't walk willingly into the ring either, but the major was going, one way or another.

Gunny felt the faint, low rumble of the garage door opener, heard the electric motor. Chesty scrambled to her feet and padded down the hallway to meet the big man. Gunny wondered if Aubrey would be coming to present an after-action report on their little operation at the school. That was one smart little kid—smart, tough, and squared away. For a moment, Gunny smiled. But Aubrey made Gunny think of Alethea, and the heartache of that strangled the glimmer of joy. Gunny heard a single set of footsteps. The major was alone. Rommel's footsteps seemed to head for the kitchen, followed by the tense staccato of canine toenails. Gunny decided that food made the dog tense. Tense with expectation and tense with food aggression once Chesty took possession of her prize. Gunny heard unaccompanied footsteps. The major was coming. The dog would remain in the kitchen.

"Patrick?"

Gunny decided this was ominous. The major never used his given name. "Yes, Major?" Gunny replied.

Rommel entered the den, walked past Gunny, and toward his desk. Since Gunny's arrival, Rommel had more or less surrendered the den and the big screen and the recliner and the cigars and the whiskey to his houseguest. A fact that Gunny appreciated. Gunny watched Rommel survey the books. They had been removed from the shelves and stacked on top of the major's desk. Gunny waited for the light to go on. It didn't take long.

"Son of a bitch," Rommel said. "You know, Patrick, the way these books are arranged—this reminds me of the layout of Aubrey's school: Main building, playground, maintenance access to the rear of the structure. Guess where I've been, Patrick."

"Well, Major, it sounds like maybe you went over to little Aubrey's school. How did she do?" Gunny said.

"Apparently she executed your plan perfectly. She demonstrated organizational and leadership skills that one doesn't typically see in a second grader."

Gunny beamed. It was official. Gunny loved that child. What a wonderful grandchild she would have been. Once again, the thought of Alethea and the grandchildren who were never to be his crushed the smile, and the old stone face returned.

"You nearly got her expelled."

"Oh, come on, Major. It was a water balloon fight."

"Where only one side was armed. The principal was describing your little operation as a hate crime. To hear the lady tell it, your operation was a crushing victory, and that makes Aubrey a threat to public safety. That's a lot to lay on a seven-year-old."

"How is little Aubrey?"

"She's tougher than George Raft. And that brings us to the point of this little counseling session. You are not here to toughen up my guests. You are not here to teach them to disassemble and assemble firearms. You are not here to teach them the Rifleman's Creed. You are not here to turn little girls into hard-charging, small-unit tacticians. I am sorry that a lifetime of dangerous duty didn't kill you, and that now, you are an old man—but that is not my fault. You are going to straighten up while you are here. You are not going to train that child for a career in Force Recon, and while we are at it, you are going to stop bugging me with this nutritional and physical training bullshit. I am retired, and I know it. I know that my country will never call me back to service, and, baby, I am just fine with that. One more thing, even though I am content to enjoy my approaching golden years, I can still pull you apart like an overcooked chicken, so you need to get off of my last nerve and find that new place to live."

Gunny took his time responding. This was as close to an opening as he had seen over the past weeks. "I'd be pleased to accommodate you, Major. I need you to do a little something for me. If you help me, I'll be gone in a heartbeat, never to return."

"Well, there's a deal too good to pass up. What is it, Gunny?"

"Help me kill a man."

Rommel stood immobile, making not a sound. Gunny waited. Rommel stared at him but said nothing. Finally, Rommel spoke. "Pack your gear, Gunny, you're gone."

"Let me explain."

"You have something to tell me that is going to make me *kill* someone? Get your gear and get out."

"You owe me."

"I owe you a goddamn murder?"

"You owe me the chance to talk to you. To tell you how things are. We've killed people, Major. You know what? Most of them were just slobs who wanted to protect their homes and their families. It was very goddamn seldom that we've actually killed someone who did anything worse than wearing the uniform of his country and standing against us. That was never murder, but I doubt if it ever did the world any damn good. Hear me out, and I'll tell you about somebody who not only has it coming, but is a bona fide enemy of the constitution, exactly the kind of maggot we both swore to defend our nation against."

Rommel walked behind his desk and settled into the chair. "This had better be good."

Gunny took a moment to organize his thoughts. "It starts with Hurricane Katrina. At least two thousand American civilians killed outright and hundreds of thousands flooded out of their homes with nowhere to go. For the first few days, the federal government was worse than useless. Tens of thousands wandered around without food or water. Instead of helping the dislocated—local communities set up barricades, armed themselves, and refused the refugees passage. In some areas, local law enforcement went door-to-door forcing people from their homes, confiscating their firearms and, in a number of cases, brutally beating the occupants without regard to gender or age.

"The rich people did what you would expect. They hired goons of their own to protect their property from looters and cops alike. Some of the firms were local security companies, but a lot of them were international mercenary groups. Major, you can look this up. There were mercs from Europe, Israel, and South Africa. There was also an American company. A company that spent the better part of the last ten years growing fat on corporate welfare, shooting up Iraq and Afghanistan, using mercenaries recruited from the American military. Black Horizon earned billions in no-bid contracts to shoot up marketplaces and other places where unarmed civilians gathered. None of them has ever been charged in these killings. When they got to New Orleans, they pretty much did the same thing but on a smaller scale. They would cruise the state highway in convoys and open fire whenever they felt like it."

Rommel shifted in his chair. "I remember some story to that effect. In one case, Black Horizon claimed that a group of young people opened fire from an overpass with AK-47s."

"Right, Major. All teenagers in Louisiana roam the countryside with AK-47s. It was bullshit. The point is that I know for a fact that the man who runs Black Horizon and a select group of his thugs used the confusion and upheaval of Katrina to murder American civilians."

"You should take that to the law."

"Major, do you really believe that I didn't start with the law? Let me finish. I am talking about one specific atrocity. Eighteen members of a church group were found drifting, facedown, in a canal just to the south of a wealthy neighborhood named Royale Oaks. Most of them were children and old people, all of them dead, all of them in their Sunday best. Investigators believe that this little group had spent one long day wandering from place to place, trying to find transportation out of the area. The local coroner classified the deaths as undetermined. Undetermined! A dozen-and-a-half people traveling together just died. That was it."

"And based on this, you want me to help you kill someone?"

"Not just someone and not for a handful of strangers. The Royale Oaks homeowners association hired their own mercs. They hired Black Horizon. This company publicized shooting at American citizens during Katrina, and these people are found dead only a few miles from a Black Horizon area of operations."

"And you know this group from Black Horizon performed these murders?"

"You're damned right, Major, and I know the individual directly responsible."

"OK…" Rommel waited for the other shoe to drop.

"Black Horizon's own publicity puts the head of the company on-site at Royale Oaks when the killings took place."

"That's your proof?" Rommel said. "Eighteen people died within a few miles of this enclave. This firm and its boss were at the enclave, and that establishes their guilt? Why would the head of a billion-dollar company be there?"

"New line of business. Same mercenary army but now in place, armed, and shooting at American civilians instead of Afghans. Cheney was there for a photo op."

"Cheney?"

"Yes, Richard Cheney, chief executive officer of Black Horizon Security."

"Are we talking about Cheney, that sick old asshole?"

"No, completely different asshole. Cheney is a common name."

"And the world is full of Dicks," Rommel said.

"That's exactly what that young cop said," Gunny blurted out.

● ● ●

"What young cop?"

"The one that works for that hardcase woman who wants to put you in jail. They came by the house."

"When?"

"Last week, maybe."

"Thanks for letting me know. Why would they mention this Cheney guy?"

"The house was under surveillance by Black Horizon Security."

"The goddamn house was under surveillance, and you didn't tell me?"

Gunny let the question pass. "That Carmichael chick jacked up the Black Horizon operative and sent him on his way. She's pretty tough. I like that in a woman," Gunny said.

"There's nothing you don't like in a woman."

Gunny said nothing.

"So let's look at the ground we've covered so far. I came in here to tell you that your arcane bullshit is making problems for a little girl who is very important to me. I tell you that you need to square yourself away or pack up your gear and get out. Your response is to tell me that the police have been to my house, but you didn't bother to tell me. Better yet, you knew that my home was under surveillance by a mercenary army with ties to black ops around the world, and you didn't bother to tell me that, either. That would be enough for your average asshole, Sergeant, but you are well above average. So, you cap it all off by telling me that you want me to help you kill a man because he was nearby when eighteen people turned up dead, even though *two thousand* people died in the same disaster. Why should I not bounce your ass out of my house right now?"

"Because you owe me."

"I owe you dick. Why do I owe you anything?"

"Because I was there when you threw everything away. I am the only fighting man in this country who knows what

Beyond the Law

you are made of, and when I die, the world will know you only as some ne'er-do-well instead of the highly trained killer who gave up everything to save two hundred of the least important people on the planet. As for that bag lady, I know about that, too, because I know you. Of course, that cop Carmichael knows, too. So does Vince and his dad, Diego, and every slob in that little bar.

"I know—" Gunny continued. "I know that Richard Cheney is a war criminal."

"That's a given. Everyone on the planet knows that."

"I know that he killed those people in New Orleans."

"And you know this how?"

"I know this because I confronted the son of a bitch. Right in his own office. And do you know what he keeps in his office? Trophies."

"Like what?"

"He's got a little bowl resting on a little counter behind his desk. In it, he's got little bits, odds and ends. While I was there, lying on the top of the heap was a Force Recon badge."

"And that means something?"

"My daughter, Alethea. When she was little, I gave one to her, that one."

Rommel sat silent, then said, "I didn't know you had a family. I guess I never thought about it."

"It was a long time ago. The marriage didn't last long. My wife was a churchy woman, and I never was. The ads used to say that Virginia is for lovers, but let me tell you, down South, it's mostly Virginia v. Loving. I guess we made every mistake that we could, except for Alethea. She was my light and my life. Now, she's dead, and Cheney's still alive. I don't want to leave this world without fixing that."

Rommel leaned forward, looking Gunny square in the eye. "I won't murder for you. Not for you, not for anyone. You take what you have to the law, and you keep after them until they do something. That's my best advice."

100

"Your best doesn't help, Major. This used to be a nation of laws. The laws are still there, but they don't apply to the Cheneys and the big corporations of this country. There was a time when a citizen had to serve this country in order to rise to a position of authority. The Romans had their *cursus honorum*. In the same way, there was an honored path in this country. A citizen had to prepare himself for public life and had to render meaningful service to the nation before that person would be allowed to advance to a more responsible position. Now, all we have are remorseless whores with Ivy League degrees they didn't earn, who will do anything for their corporate masters. Those corporations are the citizens who vote with their dollars. They choose their stooges and use the treasure of our nation to pay the uniformed thugs and goons who push us around in our airports and on our streets. We trade our rights and our liberty for the hope that the corporate government won't take even more from us. This is the world you are leaving to that little girl."

"That may be," Rommel said, "but you are done playing with little Aubrey's mind. As a matter of fact, let's just agree that you will be gone by Monday."

"What about that apartment over the bar? Lend me that for a couple of weeks, and I'll go now."

Rommel pulled out his key ring and removed a single key. "Done."

"I'm sorry if I caused any trouble for Aubrey," Gunny said. "I love that child as if she were my own. I hope you never have to live with the kind of loss that I live with every day of my life." Gunny rose from the big chair, left the den, and packed his possessions.

● ● ●

101

14

Black Horizon Security

"Gunny told me about Bosnia," Carolyn said.

"Nice of him," Rommel said.

"He said you threw away your career."

"That would be his opinion. And don't kid yourself, at the time, Gunny was aching for a fight. Besides, the Dutch were in charge. Major de Vries was in command. I was an observer attached to NATO, or as we called it at the time, IFOR."

"Gunny says you jammed the barrel of your rifle into the Serbian commander's belly, called him a bandit chief, and asked him how many men he wanted to lose."

"Gunny needs to shut the hell up." Rommel looked around as if trying to come to a decision. After a moment, he faced Carolyn. "This is what happened and there isn't any more to it than this. I was assigned to IFOR, that's the group NATO put together to deal with the Bosnian problem. I was working as an observer. My job was to observe a small Dutch contingent of about two hundred men under the command of Major Peter de Vries. 120 klicks, er kilometers down the road a Serbian force caught a contingent of Dutch peacekeepers by surprise while they were tasked to protect a Bosnian village. The Dutch were unprepared and were subdued without a shot being fired. The Dutch were bound to trees and light poles. The Bosnian population of eight-thousand men, women and children were marched into the woods and murdered."

"Why didn't the Dutch in that village fight?"

"They weren't organized or equipped for it. The Dutch at Srebrenica were a peacekeeping contingent."

"Didn't they have guns?"

Rommel shifted in his chair. "This is one of those things that civilians don't quite get. You can have troops for combat operations, and you can use troops for peacekeeping. They can be the same people, but the mission, equipment, organization, and mindset is not the same. Peacekeepers almost never have all the equipment that combat troops would have. Armor, heavy machine guns, artillery, and anti-tank weapons are often not provided to peacekeepers. Peacekeeping units typically have fewer troops than units organized for combat. The mission is also different. A combat unit keeps the good guys on one side and the enemy on the other. Their mission might be to assault and take the village. A peacekeeping unit's job is to be in the village as civilian life goes on all around them."

"OK," Carolyn said, tentatively. Rommel decided that more clarification was in order.

"I dearly hate sports analogies, but you're going to have to allow me this one. Imagine that there is a basketball game, and you are the referee. There are two teams. They play the game on the court, and they obey the referee when he makes a call, er, a ruling or decision. You as the referee have a striped shirt and a whistle, and that's it. The game can be played because both teams agree to obey the referee."

"Now, let's say that one day, you and one of the teams are at the court waiting for the game to start. What would you do if the other team showed up with guns and knives and a lot more players than their opponents had? You have a striped shirt and a whistle against dozens of guns. At that point you, the referee, are powerless. The other team is defenseless, and you can't protect them."

"The Serbs showed up with the advantage of surprise and with overwhelming force. Both the Dutch and the Bosnians were as good as defenseless. Personally, I hate peacekeeping missions; it's a crappy job. You've got crazy people on both sides, and the situation can turn deadly in a heartbeat."

"So why didn't that happen to you and the Dutch at the other village?" Carolyn asked.

"We had more warning and a slightly better tactical position. Word of the attack spread quickly. By the time a different contingent of Serbs descended on our village, the Dutch had relocated the civilians to a small commercial facility, established a perimeter, and secured it. We didn't have all the equipment you would want, but we did have some cover and decent fields of fire. When the Serbian commander presented himself, the Dutch were ready for him. The Serbians were a much larger force, and the momentum seemed to be on their side. They demanded the transfer of the civilians into their custody. The Serb commander gave Major de Vries an ultimatum: surrender the village or be massacred along with the civilians. Major de Vries refused. What we had was a standoff. The Serbian political apparatus used diplomatic channels to put pressure on the NATO politicians. They demanded the surrender of the village. We were outnumbered. The Serbs had the capability, and they had expressed the intent to overrun us. To prevent an even worse defeat and the massacre of allied forces, NATO command made a decision to withdraw from the village leaving the villagers to their fate. The Dutch commander refused to obey his orders. I also was ordered to leave. I also refused to obey. In the end, there was a hot, brief skirmish, but the Serbs withdrew under a loud, aggressive escort of A10 aircraft. We were relieved shortly thereafter."

"And that was the end of your career?"

"In a sense. I served for a few more years. I used that time trying to figure out what to do with the rest of my life. I had a line number to 0-6. Naturally, that promotion to colonel was withdrawn. Upon my retirement, the corps decided that the last grade I had completed satisfactorily was not lieutenant colonel, but major. So I retired as a major."

"Why?"

"Following orders is a big deal in the corps. It's something they insist on."

"Why didn't they court-martial you?"

"I don't think they wanted the publicity. The corps would have had to explain to the world that the honorable course of action was to allow 280 men, women and children to be murdered, and that I committed a crime by refusing to allow it to happen."

"They're cowards." Carolyn was visibly agitated.

"These men are never cowards. Vindictive, maybe"

There was silence, a look between them, a rare moment that promised Carolyn a glimpse inside the man.

"It's not just the *what*—it's the *why*," Rommel hesitated. Carolyn held her breath. "The idea of a career mixes with the individual's ego. I don't care who you are, if you are thinking career, that ambition begins to define you. If you're not careful, your personal sense of merit becomes dependent on your rank. It isn't long before career considerations influence your decision making. Let's say someone under your command screws up. You think the individual can be salvaged, but further up the food chain, they want to make an example. You could put up a fight and protect the guy, in order to see if there's anything worth saving, but you don't. That guy's not coming up for promotion, and you are. So you give him up. No big deal. He shouldn't have screwed up in the first place. You tell yourself that the further and higher you advance, the more good you can do."

"Then one day you're in a small, cold, dirty village—on the edge of what's supposed to be civilized Europe—looking at a couple hundred defenseless civilians. All these people have are their clothes and their lives, and nobody in the rest of the world gives a crap about them. I had to ask myself, 'what was that good thing that I was going to do at the next level of rank that was going to justify allowing those deaths?'

"De Vries and I looked at each other. We didn't have enough of the heavy stuff, but we had automatic weapons, lots of ammo, and thousands of murderers and rapists to shoot. On the downside, our careers were over, and we'd be lucky if we didn't end up in jail. On the upside, we were outnumbered almost ten to one. So, once the shooting started, we figured that neither of us was going to live long enough to worry about answering to headquarters."

"What happened? How did you survive?"

"The Serbs blinked. Maybe they didn't want to take that many casualties for so few Bosnians. Maybe they didn't want to be strafed by A-10s. Maybe they figured that NATO would pay them back in spades somewhere else. Anyway, I spent a couple of years stateside in backwater assignments. De Vries left the Dutch army. Now, he's a printer. I get a beautiful card from him every Christmas."

"Do you two ever talk about it?"

"Just once, a few years ago. He told me he went home to his wife and his children, and he told them what happened. His wife and kids adore him. Everyone in town respects him, and there's no one he can't look in the eye. He's satisfied."

"And you?"

Rommel looked at her. Paused. "I am content. I am never going to be the kind of man I was. No ordinary thing will ever seem as important as it once did."

"So Bosnia changed everything for you?"

"Bosnia and ten years working as a corrections officer changed everything for me. I have seen all the ugly things I want to see. I like sleeping on clean sheets and eating in restaurants with tablecloths. I am content to enjoy living in the society I spent years protecting. It's no more complicated than that."

The phone rang; Rommel answered, speaking into the phone. "Black Horizon Security, we have all the security we need." Rommel looked at Chesty, who had sauntered into the room, sat at Rommel's feet, and stared up vacuously, her large tongue lolling out the side of her mouth. "Yes, sir," Rommel said, "Topflight security. Couldn't be any better," There was a pause. "Oh, *that* Black Horizon. I don't want to be rude, but the company you work for is filled with dirtbag mercenaries who were lucky to escape justice in Afghanistan and Iraq. I certainly don't need anything from you people."

Rommel looked across at Carolyn and shrugged as if to say that the interruption was not his fault, and that he was getting off the phone as quickly as possible. And then Rommel's expression changed. "Yes, to my inconvenience and misfortune, I can say that I do know a Patrick Michael Gilhooley. The Gilhooley I know is an old man. Are you telling me that even though you work for a company of thugs, you're being bothered by an old man, and you need my help? By reputation, you guys are tough enough against unarmed civilians. Have you tried showing him to the door and asking him not to come back? You are supposed to be a security company, right? Deal with it, and don't bother me. And be careful with that old man, or I will come down there." Rommel hung up the phone and looked at Carolyn. "Apparently, Gunny's job interview is not going well. He told me he had an interview. I thought it would be something simple, you know? Retail, maybe."

"What did they want?" Carolyn asked.

"The same thing everyone wants. They want me to come and get the old gentleman, and take him far away. I could charge people for such a service. They'd pay, too. I'd make a steady living."

The phone rang again. The big man got to his feet and moved toward the phone. He did not look pleased. "Rommel," he said. "What did I just tell you people?"

Rommel paused. "Where is he? Is he hurt? He had better not be hurt. Fine. Just leave him there. Stay away from him. I'll be right down. Where are you people?" There was a pause. "OK, that works."

Rommel looked at her. "I kid you not, they say he's taken over an office and barricaded himself in. Not only that, Black Horizon Security is sending a car to pick me up."

❧❧❧

Alone in the reception area on the twenty-sixth floor of Black Horizon Security's corporate office, Rommel stood on the expanse of gray carpet and scanned the treatments mounted on the burgundy walls. The area spoke of wealth, power, stability. It was also practical, the corporate offices forming a wedge that allowed for overlapping bands of fire that looked out on one big killing zone. After the briefest of moments, Rommel was led by the receptionist to the large mahogany double doors which were alone on the right. At first, Rommel thought this might be some sort of plush auditorium. A capacious expanse, the office was both opulent and minimalist. On the far end, fifteen-foot tall floor-to-ceiling windows flooded the massive office with light. Near the windows, ten yards distant, a massive wooden desk faced the entrance with an equally massive credenza to the side. Behind the desk at the far end, a trim, young blonde-haired man sat studying him as he approached. The waste of this much space was intended to establish dominance. A visitor had to trek across the empty space to approach the *boss man* as he sat behind his fortress desk and stared. For an employee with bad news, the effect had to be doubly severe. Rommel walked toward the desk, keeping an unflinching stare leveled at the young man who seemed to be studying him. On the desk surface: a single thin file and a single gold pen, no computer, no printer, no screen of any type. Of course, it would be nothing to conceal such things in such an office. On the credenza, he could see a small brass bowl filled with miscellaneous bits. Was this the bowl of souvenirs Gunny had told him about? Were these the little trophies of a serial murderer? On the other hand, they could be the things that a man might toss onto a dresser at the end of the day: cufflinks, change, tie clips. But the contents of this bowl looked like bits of cheap jewelry, some cheap beads, buttons, and even a few military badges and insignia, a portion of which looked like gold wings. Was this intended as a Zen representation, a chaotic jumble of artifacts alone in an ordered universe? Why would a man who wasted five-thousand square feet to create an imposing environment allow a single display of modest bits? Above the credenza, a single antique rapier was mounted to the wall. To the other side of the desk and a few yards forward, an extensive breakaway area had been established with a single large couch, in dark leather, and matching modern armchairs positioned to the left. Right and opposing the couch, in the center of that area—a large glass coffee table with a single empty vase. Along the walls near the couch, antique books on fencing and the use of the rapier were enclosed and mounted in individual cases.

The man rose. He was tall, nearly as tall as Rommel. He moved with a grace that suggested superior muscular coordination. He walked toward Rommel, his hand extended, a practiced smile splitting a tanned face beneath a Nordic-blonde crew cut. Rommel shook his hand. The man's grip was strong, his technique practiced, as he twisted his wrist ever so slightly to put his guest at a disadvantage should the handshake be followed by grappling. Rommel thought about moving to counter the grip. In a comedic film, they would begin their encounter, wrestling right there in the office. Rommel let the moment pass. The grip was symbolic. This tall, confident young man was telling Rommel that he was well used to controlling situations.

"Thank you for coming. My name is Richard Cheney."

"An unfortunate coincidence?" Rommel responded.

"Coincidence, yes. Unfortunate? I wouldn't say so," the younger man responded. "Do you know of me?"

"You run a mercenary army disguised as a security company. You're an ex-Navy SEAL who used his inheritance to form Black Horizon Security just in time to make billions in fees from the federal government through a decade-long series of lucrative no-bid contracts providing security in Afghanistan and Iraq."

OK, Gunny had a point, Rommel decided. Maybe Cheney was another dirtbag in a suit. A successful, accomplished, dangerous dirtbag who built an empire out of government contracts: supplying combat-qualified military veterans to hot spots. Still, a dirtbag nonetheless.

"Thank you for coming. I wanted to meet you, Mr. Rommel. Do you prefer to be called Major?" Cheney was making another point. Cheney had looked into Rommel's history.

"Mister is just fine, Mr. Cheney. I'm here to pick up Mr. Gilhooley. Apparently, the old gentleman wandered into your offices and created a disturbance. Since you, for some reason, are not going to ask the police to take him into custody, someone in your company called me to escort him off the property."

"Believe it or not, Mr. Gilhooley has been an inter-mittent thorn in our corporate sides for a number of years. Sergeant Gilhooley—"

Rommel broke in, "If you're going to use his rank, get it right. It's master gunnery sergeant, retired."

Cheney continued, "Master gunnery sergeant, retired, has developed some sort of a grudge about something and has been pestering us, off and on, for the last few years."

"Fine. Show me where he is, and I'll take him along. Failing that, call the cops and have them take him away, and I'll go post his bail."

"Master Gunnery Sergeant Gilhooley can wait a moment longer. I wanted to meet you. You know, I was still in the teams as your career was ending. Believe it or not, you were something of a celebrity. For many young officers, your career was a cautionary tale. Strong, fearless, highly effective, highly respected, and then, one day you throw it all away. You threw your career away for nobodies—shabby, shiftless losers who mean nothing to anyone. Suddenly, *you're* the nobody, and the world moves on." Cheney studied the big man as he spoke.

• • •

"Black Horizon employs thousands of highly skilled military veterans. For those who can control their personal lives, six years of obedient service makes them independently wealthy. Meaningful compensation for those who serve in the legions of the new empire."

"Shit. New empire?"

"You must have noticed the rapier on the wall. I see that weapon as a metaphor for my firm. In the Middle Ages, swords were large, heavy, clumsy. Sword craft was restricted to the nobility and the nation's military. As metallurgy and European metal crafting improved, a new type of sword emerged. Lighter and more manageable, with the rapier, gentlemen could go about their daily lives with a sword at their sides. In fact, some scholars believe that the word rapier derives from *espada ropera*, dress sword, if you will. A man couldn't drag a clumsy broadsword through the streets, but he could go anywhere with this clever bit of hardware. Over time, dress swords became even slimmer and more compact. In my metaphor, conventional military assets are the clumsy broadsword—weighed down by expense, international relations, bothersome congressional oversight, and the rule of law. By comparison, Black Horizon is the elegant dress sword: flexible, maneuverable, and ready to go anywhere in the world at a moment's notice.

"The world is changing. America is changing. The nation is embracing privatization. Once, services like currency, education, police, and even national defense were handled by the government. Now, we see packages and letters delivered by corporations. Banks and other corporations issue credit cards, which are *de facto* currency. Moreover, employees are usually paid by direct deposit, so people can go through their days, weeks, months and even years without touching a single paper dollar. The government arrests and convicts criminals, and sends them to corporate-run prisons. In some states, there are more prisoners in private, corporate-run prisons than in state-run facilities. In New York, protesters like these Occupy Wall Street hooligans are often kept under control by a partnership between corporate security and the NYPD. Soon, the sole function of the US government will be to collect tax revenues and dispense these funds to flexible, efficient corporations that will perform the actual services traditional to government, including law enforcement, the judiciary, and prisons. These Occupy people—these howling mobs with bad mortgages and student loans they can't afford, and their sniveling about due process and the rule of law. Soon rabble like this won't even be a memory.

"I am proud to say that my firm has led the way in privatized warfare in Afghanistan and Iraq. We provide security for embassies and visiting government dignitaries, and we execute tactical operations against hostiles. Over the years, Black Horizon has engaged in hundreds, if not thousands, of firefights with indigenous populations across the globe."

"Many of whom were not armed and could not return fire," Rommel said.

"Mistakes were made." Cheney paused and allowed himself a smile. "Mistakes and billions of dollars of profit."

"So how is it that neither Black Horizon nor any of its employees were put on trial for these *mistakes*?" Rommel said.

"No one has been tried because American law does not forbid murder or torture outside of the United States," Cheney said.

"Bullshit."

Cheney smiled. "Yours is a common misconception. The reality is that American organizations, both political and private, are precluded from prosecution or even civil lawsuits by The Torture Victims Protection Act of 1991. This finding has been upheld by the US Supreme Court in *Mohamad v. Palestinian Authority*. The ruling was unanimous."

Cheney continued, "For most of history, warfare has contained an element of commerce. When the Roman legions added to the empire by conquest, the merchant class was there with them to broker-in slaves and loot. Black

Horizon Security seeks to replace the legions where possible. Our government in Washington sends private contractors like Black Horizon into areas of conflict. Where we can, Black Horizon applies deadly force and pacifies the indigenous population. At that point, we are ideally positioned to profit from the assets of the conquered people. Black Horizon can put a guard, a squad, or a heavily armed battalion anywhere in the world to enforce the will of the United States government, any of its agencies, or one of our corporate clients. If you want to be crass about it, Black Horizon can kill every man in any village in the world, rape their women, take their treasure, and be back stateside before the weekend. We are in and out before the world press even knows there's a story. And, best of all, it's legal. Private security has evolved."

"When Hurricane Katrina hit Louisiana," Cheney continued, "I'm proud to say that Black Horizon was in the vanguard of the response to the disaster, preventing the sacking of wealthy communities by taking a firm hand with looters and even keeping local law enforcement in check. That brings us to Master Gunnery Sergeant Gilhooley, USMC, Retired."

"Over the years, Gunny has created a number of disturbances targeting Black Horizon personnel. Apparently, Gilhooley had a daughter. She lived in New Orleans and was killed during Hurricane Katrina. She and a group from her church were found drowned. Gilhooley claims that our personnel are responsible, directly or indirectly, for the death of his daughter."

"And?"

"And Alethea Gilhooley's death has nothing to do with Black Horizon Security. During that period, there were numerous incidents of looting and other criminal conduct. We've looked into the matter several times, and there is nothing to suggest that Black Horizon had any involvement in her death. We would like these disturbances to stop. Mister Rommel, we would like you to help."

"Cheney, your problems have nothing to do with me.

The old gentleman was spending a few weeks with me until he got back on his feet. Now, he's in his own digs. If you have managed to put yourself on Gunny's list, my advice to you is to get on a plane." Rommel paused. "I will say this. Gunny will make the occasional mistake, but he knows a dirtbag when he sees one. If Gunny thinks you're an asshole, then you're probably an asshole."

"And what is your opinion?"

"After this little chat? I wouldn't say you're an asshole. I'd say you're a serious asshole."

Cheney's face flushed a hot scarlet. "I'm not used to being spoken to like that, Mr. Rommel."

"That's a statement that comes straight from the asshole handbook. We're done here, Mr. Cheney. I don't think that we're going to need to speak again in the future. Have someone show me where the old gentleman is, and he and I will be on our way."

At the far end of the office, the door opened and a large man entered. "Mr. Feith will escort you," Cheney said. "Do be careful."

Rommel rose and faced the door. "Feith," Rommel said. "No wonder the old man is haunting you people." Rommel surveyed the big man at the door. Feith had to be at least ten years younger than Rommel, and he looked fit enough. Feith had a body builder's physique: big shoulders, massive upper body and arms. In a fight, Feith would almost certainly wade into the fracas and bang away. He was probably quick enough, but Rommel couldn't decide if the man had the stamina for a protracted engagement.

There was an old Marine Corps saying: Be polite, be professional, but have a plan to kill everybody you meet. Rommel could see that Feith was sizing him up, just as Rommel had decided about Feith.

"I always thought we would meet again. What is it? Major? Isn't that the rank they retired you at?"

"I never expected to see you, Feith. I figured that you'd piss off a nun, and she'd break your back. Show me to the old man, and keep the chit chat to a minimum."

The door closed. Cheney stood in the cavernous office, alone with his thoughts. He thought of a young woman, years ago in New Orleans. He had broken her. There, on the bedroom carpet, she had lain as expressionless as a broken doll. Once she knew the others were dead, she disconnected from her body. There was nothing else he could do to her. Almost reverently, he relived breaking her neck. Even dead, her expression was unchanged.

15

Career Day

The elevator opened onto a sea of cubicles with waist-high partitions. Today, however, no one was sitting at their work stations. All attention was focused on a single office. The door was closed, but the wall was floor-to-ceiling glass. A round conference table and a credenza had been overturned. The large wooden desk had been dragged across the room and used to barricade the office. Rommel looked in at the wild-eyed old man inside and tapped on the glass. "Time to come out, Gunny. You're bothering everybody."

"Everything was fine until that pack of goons showed up and tried to put their hands on me."

"These people?" Rommel pointed at four large men in blue blazers. Rommel looked at Feith for an explanation. Feith spoke. "Mr. Gilhooley obtained a job interview under false pretenses. It didn't take the hiring manager long before she realized the old wreck didn't know anything about corporate finance. She called security to show him out of the building, and the old man went nuts when they showed up."

"She didn't know something was wrong when she got an application and a resume from a seventy-year-old man?"

"He didn't mention his age."

Gunny perked up. "They can't ask about my age. That's discrimination!"

"You're a crazy old man, Gunny. That's not discrimination, that's a stone-cold fact. Tell me, what's the difference between net present value and internal rate of return?" Rommel said.

Gunny paused, "Uh…"

"Come on out, Gunny. It's time to go. Another thing, you remember me telling you that I was getting tired of you involving me in your episodes? This is one of those episodes. Now, come on out."

Gunny tugged at the desk. Apparently, the desk was a lot heavier in the absence of adrenaline. As Gunny pulled, Rommel pushed at the door. Together, they made an opening, and Gunny squeezed through, stepping out of the ravaged office.

Feith stepped forward. "Just a minute," he said, as he reached out a large paw, grasping at Gunny's withered shoulder.

Rommel slapped it away. "Back off." In support of Feith, the four men in the security detail advanced on Rommel and Gunny. One guard deployed a telescoping baton. An instant later, there were three more audible clicks, and they were all holding batons. It was too late to move back into and re-barricade the office. They were more or less, in the open. To the right, there was an alcove between offices with office plants, a table, and a few chairs. Rommel pushed the old man toward the confined space. This would restrict the ability of the team to maneuver around his flank. Rommel shoved Gunny into the corner and turned to face Feith and his four-man team just as the baton blows began to rain down. Rommel stepped into one attacker on the downstroke, deflecting the baton arm toward the man at his side. The blow caught the other man on the wrist, causing him to cry out in pain and drop his telescoping baton. Rommel stepped on his attacker's foot, lowered a shoulder and pushed him to the side, forcing him to fall into his team. Rommel knelt quickly to grasp the baton on the ground. The attackers were quick to recover, and blows began to rain down on Rommel's back and shoulders as he began to rise. But, by then, Rommel had the black metallic weapon. Whipping out fiercely at his attackers, Rommel caught one man squarely on the forehead, dropping him like a stunned ox. Rommel roared, sprang forward, flailing savagely at his attackers. The small group faltered as the pain of the blows they received took the heart out of their assault. Dispirited, it became obvious that they were far more concerned about avoiding blows than dispensing them. They began to break ranks just as another team of four emerged from the elevator.

Rommel grasped at Gunny. "Keep to the wall. Follow me. Let's go." Gilhooley followed in the lee of the storm, close behind Rommel, as they moved toward the elevators. From just out of Rommel's baton range, the second team began to hose a torrent of pepper spray directly into Rommel's head and face. Keeping his head down, using his left hand to interrupt the spray while lashing blindly with the baton, Rommel continued to guide Gunny toward the elevator bank. Suddenly, Rommel changed direction and sprang toward the pepper spray, swinging wildly. The baton caught the spray can closest to him, and the security man dropped the can, screaming in pain. Rommel's lungs sucked searing pepper fumes, as tears and snot cascaded down his face. He could see only shadows, gaining only a sense of his attacker's positions. Guessing, Rommel moved toward his right, lashed out, and struck paydirt. Now, both the first and second teams were on the verge of breaking. Rommel charged blindly, swinging the metallic baton furiously. The men scattered and ran just as the third team arrived on the scene, unleashing a volley of tasers.

Rommel remained on his feet, his entire body a single massive spasm. He tried to advance on the new attackers. He willed it, but nothing happened. Rommel was a mass of clenched, useless muscle. The electric arc and crackle were deafening. Arms clenched, stiff legged, Rommel had a sense that he was falling, that he was taking forever to fall, that he was floating, face-first, onto the carpet. In the gray darkness, Rommel entered a nearly dreamlike state. He dreamed he had become an old factory. In that darkness, he sensed the presence of creatures who had come to work. They pounded on the old structure. They pushed it, twisted it. They were determined, but unhappy. From that distance, Rommel became aware that he was being beaten—volley after volley of weighted metallic blows were furrowing into his flesh and against his head as large black boots launched into his sides. Blackness washed over him.

16

The Jug

Matt Rommel felt the smooth, cold, concrete floor long before he was truly aware that it *was* a smooth, cold, concrete floor. He saw shoes, two near his head and a larger number farther away. Someone, a man, was sitting nearby, and it was that person's shoes that were closest. The other men were standing at a distance. Rommel's eyes wouldn't focus. He tried to lift his head. It seemed to be Gunny sitting on the bench. He looked up at Gunny who was studying him. He looked at the men standing at the far end of the cell. He looked at Gunny again.

"They wouldn't behave, but they're doing much better now. Right maggots? I was going to teach them some close-order drill. Give them something to do. Major, you know you're in jail, right?"

Rommel stared up at Gunny. He didn't have the energy to groan.

"You don't look so good, Major. You wanna lie on this bench?"

No response.

Gunny continued as his image came into better focus, "I wouldn't lie on that floor, Major. Can you see these guys? I mean these are filthy guys. That's gotta be a filthy floor."

Rommel groaned.

"You wanna use the toilet?"

Rommel's eyes followed the floor to the wall. Into the wall was mounted a stainless-steel toilet. In this particular case, *stainless* was a bit of a stretch. Rommel grunted, "Sure. Bring it over here."

"Man, that was some fight, Major. At least until they brought out them tasers, then it turned into more of a beating. Even so, that was some beating. They were really getting into it. After a while, I thought one of the receptionists was going to come over and put the boot to you."

Rommel rolled feebly onto his side and looked up at Gunny. The old man was sporting a black eye. Blood crusted the old man's forehead and traced a path down his face onto his shirt. "Well, the important thing is that *you* are all right, Gunny. You *are* all right, aren't you, Gunny?"

Gunny seemed happy to chat. "I think I'm all right, Major. They wailed on me a couple times with those metal club things, and I went right into the tank, took a dive almost immediately. Once they saw that I was down, they went back to you and started wailing again. Yep, that's the secret, ya gotta know when to fold 'em, or you really get your ass kicked."

Somewhere in a distant part of Rommel's mind, a dim alarm sounded. A small voice told him that something was not right. *The old man had made a religion of fighting beyond endurance. He had made a religion of it. Now, he goes into the tank in a struggle against people he despises. Why would he do that? Had this been some sort of exercise? If so, what had been the object of the exercise?* The small suspicious voice was no match for the nausea, the pain, and the overwhelming fatigue.

The cell door jangled open. Two large deputies and a smaller one stood at the opening. "Rommel. Gilhooley."

Rommel slowly dragged himself to his feet. The cell swayed. Everyone he could see seemed to be swimming, and a wave of nausea poured itself over him and settled into his stomach as an aspiring ball of acidic puke. He looked toward the not-quite-stainless steel toilet and decided against it.

The lead deputy spoke, "This way." Rommel followed the deputy, and Gilhooley followed Rommel. They were led to a cage that resembled an old-fashioned bank teller's station. Inside the cage, a sheriff's deputy waited. On the counter sat a manila envelope containing the contents of Rommel's pockets as well as his wristwatch. Rommel signed for his property and stepped through a metal door into a receiving area. Waiting for him were two women, Carolyn Kast and Lieutenant Carmichael. Behind Lieutenant Carmichael stood Detective Vince Garcia, his godson and son of his old friend Diego Garcia. Rommel walked toward Carolyn. Based on her reaction, Rommel had to assume that the beating he could still feel also affected his appearance.

"Oh, my God!" Carolyn said it loudly and flatly. "Why have you not had medical attention?" She wheeled on Lieutenant Carmichael. "Why has this man not had medical attention?"

"Not every person who gets arrested at a fight goes to the hospital," Lieutenant Carmichael said.

Carolyn stepped close to Matt Rommel and reached up with trembling hands, ever so gingerly touching at his face and scalp. As he looked down into her face, he saw her expression change into something dark and ominous. He had seen similar expressions in the faces of murderers. As she turned back toward the police lieutenant, Rommel thought he heard her growling.

"This man has open wounds on his face and scalp. He can barely stand. It's obvious that he's been beaten within an inch of his life. Nobody thought to get him medical attention? You people should be ashamed. Whoever is responsible for this is going to pay. The city is going to pay. The lard-asses who let this happen are going to pay. They are going to pay with their jobs, with their homes, with their property and livestock. Before this is over, I am going to own the fillings out of their kid's goddamn teeth."

In that moment, both Rommel and Vince Garcia moved forward to restrain and separate the women just as Gunny came through the metal door into the reception area. "Wow, what did I miss?" Gunny said.

As Rommel held Carolyn back, he could feel her hot flesh. In the tips of his fingers, he could feel the rapid pulsing of her blood as it coursed its way through her body. Even Rommel could tell that something about their relationship was changing.

Gunny spoke up, "Thanks for coming, Carolyn." He turned toward Rommel. "She was my one call. Did you bring the Caddy, sweetheart?"

So, now it was sweetheart? Rommel wanted to grit his teeth, but as loose as they felt, he thought better of it.

The three of them turned and headed through the exit with Lieutenant Carmichael close behind. Once in the parking lot, Carmichael called out, "We are going to need to talk to you, Mr. Rommel…" The lieutenant noticed that all three of them seemed focused on something else.

Across the parking lot, a huge man with a dirt-streaked face and a matted beard, bundled in at least a half-dozen layers of filthy clothes, had set aside a long, thick cardboard tube that might have been the castoff core to a roll of carpet. The behemoth was using a large rock to shatter the driver's side window of an older blue-green Cadillac, Rommel's Cadillac. The blaring horn and flashing headlights of the car alarm didn't faze the vandal in the slightest. Slowly, the giant bundled man opened the door and leaned his head and shoulders inside the Caddy as if browsing through the bargain bin at a flea market. Rommel, Gunny, and Carolyn turned as one to look at Lieutenant Carmichael. The question on their faces was obvious.

"That's Goliath," Detective Vincent Garcia said. "He does that."

"He does that?"

"Yeah," Detective Garcia said.

"He breaks into cars?"

Detective Garcia nodded. "Hundreds of them. If he sees a bag or something he wants, he smashes the window, opens the door, and takes it. Hell, he's been arrested fifty times, at least. Never prosecuted. The district attorney's office says it's pointless."

"Pointless?" Rommel asked. Rommel decided that today was destined to be one of those perfect days. "Why is it pointless?"

"Goliath doesn't have two marbles rolling around in that noggin of his. Jail time doesn't mean anything to him. As you will observe, he's also completely broke and filthy as hell. He's not competent to stand trial and the whole law enforcement cycle means nothing to him, so what's the point?"

"I don't know," Rommel said. "How about, he's breaking the law, and you two are supposed to be officers of the law."

Lieutenant Carmichael interrupted, "We have better things to do than arrest mental defectives."

"You arrested Gunny," Rommel said.

"Hey!" Gunny objected.

"Maybe the fact that you people have decided not to enforce the law has something to do with the fact that your pal Goliath is down here in the parking lot of the Hall of Justice, breaking into cars." Rommel turned toward Vince Garcia. "Do you feel like making the fifty-first arrest, Detective?"

"Are you sure? He really stinks."

"You're young, you should have no problem chasing him down," Rommel said.

"I don't have to chase him." Detective Garcia shouted at the top of his lungs, "Goliath, get over here!" Vince shrugged at his godfather. "See? He doesn't even run. I can cuff him and walk him right in. Are you sure you want to press charges?"

"Did it ever occur to you that he's trying to tell you something? Maybe he wants a little help."

"We're not social workers," Carmichael said.

"Hell, you're not cops, either." Carolyn stepped forward, still looking for that fight.

Rommel did something he had never done before. He put his hand on her shoulder. Rommel leaned his battered head down toward her. "Easy, big gun. I'll stay and bail you out if I have to, but it's not my first choice."

Carmichael spoke up, "We still want to speak with you."

Rommel moved slowly, every movement a chore. "Do you have a card?" Rommel accepted the card and tried to read it. Close up, farther away, everything was still blurry. "I'm going to see a doctor. I'll have my lawyer call and set up an appointment."

The three moved slowly toward the Cadillac, whose horn was blaring and lights flashing. As they reached halfway to the car, Goliath, sporting a thick cardboard tube— perhaps seven feet long and four inches in diameter—and layered in layer after layer of dark, dirty cloth, passed them. A shambling Don Quixote of the street, he walked slowly toward Detective Garcia and an incarceration that even Goliath, with his diminished mental capacity, knew wouldn't last more than a few hours. The atmosphere that surrounded Goliath hit the three of them at the same time. Detective Garcia hadn't lied. Goliath stank.

17

The Hall of Justice

An unhealthy excitement was brewing in the bull pen. Lieutenant Carmichael could sense it the instant she pushed the glass door open. A clutch of men surrounded a video screen, standing quietly one moment, erupting in a roar the next. "Damn! That has got to hurt!"

"He's going down. Watch."

"Not yet. Watch this."

"Whoa!!" The crowd erupted. If it was a sporting event, Carmichael decided, it must be a heck of a game. There were more scattered voices.

"The guy's a tank. Look, they're gonna break and run. Look at that. Look at that!"

"Just in time for more guys. Here they come."

"Whoa!!" The crowd erupted, yet again.

Lieutenant Carmichael reached the gathering. They were watching a security disc: one big man, one smaller old man, and multiple attackers in blazers and neckties. "Are any of you people working on this case? No? Then get back to work. Show's over." Carmichael took the disc from the

● ● ●

player and walked to her desk. "Where's Garcia?" She could see Vince across the office, just coming through the glass double doors. "Detective Garcia!" she called out. "May I speak with you?"

Detective Vincent Garcia approached his boss' desk. "There's something I want you to see." Vince walked around her desk so that he could see the monitor just as the video started. He recognized his godfather, Matt Rommel. Rommel was guiding a much older man out of an office and away from the camera. A man in a sports coat reached out toward the old man, and Rommel batted the hand away. And then, all hell broke loose. Four men with telescoping batons attacked and rained blows down on both Rommel and the old man. Rommel counter-attacked, seized one of the telescoping metal batons and drove them back. Four more men moved in with chemical mace and attacked. Rommel attacked. *No way around it*, Vince thought, *this was a hell of a fight*. He stifled an urge to cheer. At the moment, it seemed as if Uncle Matt would drive them all away. He stood silent as the last group brought Rommel down with a salvo of tasers. Detective Garcia watched as Black Horizon Security rained down kicks and blows onto a defenseless man. Garcia's jaw set. His teeth clenched.

"Well?" Carmichael asked.

"Clear case of assault and battery, if not attempted homicide. Are we going to apprehend these Black Horizon people?"

"That's not what I'm talking about. I'm talking about that near riot in the Mission. You told me you didn't know any single person who could wreak havoc on those street people. It looks like your good-old-friend-of-the-family is an excellent candidate."

Detective Vincent Garcia said nothing. Carmichael waited. Still, Garcia did not speak. "Don't you have anything to say, Detective Garcia?"

Something had changed in the demeanor of her partner. He seemed proud. "You should present the case to the district attorney. Bring this disc. Tell the DA that you think you know who broke up a gang rape in the Mission, saved an old woman, and beat the crap out of a mob of bums. Show the DA this disc. Here you have irrefutable evidence of your suspect, protecting an old man from an armed gang of mercenaries.

"All I ask is that you let me be there. It has been weeks since that melee in the Mission, you will be lucky to find three of the transients involved. You won't find two who actually remember what happened, and none of them are going to talk to the DA, let alone show up and testify in court. Show this disc. I want to be there when the DA explains to you how much a San Francisco jury loves mercenaries. In the meantime, we have real cases of real crimes perpetrated by real assholes. I don't know about you, but I would like to incarcerate a few of them." Garcia gestured at the screen and looked at his boss. "You know, my father served in combat with that man."

18

Barbecue at Vince's

Darren Feith smiled. These were his golden days. They just had to be. He had money. Not just the shipboard money-on-the-books sort of money, real money. Fifteen-hundred-dollar suit money. Downtown luxury-apartment money. Decked-out Jimmy SUV with leather seats money. Expense-account money. And the best part was that none of those things cost Feith a nickel. Month after month, most of his salary went into the bank and stayed there.

He handled a piece of Mr. Cheney's business, a piece with high-level management visibility. Well-paid, professional people worked for him, and he had gained the reputation of being a fixer. When a problem arose that couldn't be handled with the usual combination of reason, veiled threat, and money, Feith would get the call. When problem situations were left to Feith, the solution was simple. Feith had a sliding scale, and the troublemaker picked his fate: fear, pain, death. Feith preferred troublemakers with a strong survival instinct. Like the Spanish proverb observed, *a word to the wise is sufficient*. Most people want to live and retain their health, so for all practical purposes, it was free money most

• • •

of the time. Sometimes, a troublemaker would be so wrapped up in his own importance, a little work was required. Nothing cuts through the mask of importance like pain. Of course, these were the people who couldn't be reasoned with and wouldn't learn from a persuasive threat. Just pain wasn't enough for people like this. There had to be the imminent threat of death—an unpleasant, uncomfortable, and, if possible, terrifying death. You had to hurt them and scare the crap out of them at the same time.

The worst people to deal with were the duty dogs, those sad souls who felt they had some higher calling that demanded resistance to coercion. There weren't many of these, and it was best to identify these people as quickly as possible. They wouldn't scare. They wouldn't listen to reason. The best solution was to kill them quickly, lose the bodies, and move on.

Ninety percent of the time, it was free money. Nine percent of the time, you had to put in a little work and break a body part or something. Just one percent of the time, there would be a killing. This tidy formula always worked. That is, it worked unless Mr. Cheney felt the need to get personally involved. Mr. Cheney's involvement always made for a long night. A night that always involved torture, sexual humiliation, slow killing, and hours of cleanup. The thing was, you never knew what would draw Mr. Cheney's personal interest. If he felt personally challenged, that would do it. Then again, he was just as likely to be drawn by an attractive spouse or child. Those were the worst nights. Cheney called them *family nights*. Fortunately for Feith, he hadn't had to drag himself and his crew through a Family Night since New Orleans.

Feith shook off the thought. Here he was, cruising in a fine vehicle with his trusted lieutenants after a fine meal, and all of it on the expense account. Best of all, Feith was guiding the black GMC Yukon toward his pride and joy. Feith felt it was time to show off a little, and nothing is showier than a new Ferrari.

Technically, it wasn't new, but it was new to Feith and fifty-eight thousand dollars was all the retired gunnery sergeant could bring himself to part with. It was a brilliant lemon yellow, gorgeous by any standard you wanted to apply, and, incredibly for a seventeen-year-old car, the Ferrari 348 Spider was cosmetically flawless. Fourteen thousand, seven hundred and fifty-six miles of garaged perfection. There are only two reasons to own a car like this. One was the experience of performance driving in an automotive work of art. The other, a much more powerful reason, was to be seen in such a car. The Ferrari is the trophy wife that never gets tired of you, steals only the money required for maintenance and doesn't sleep with your friends. The three men riding with Feith were the closest thing he had to friends. They all had the same goals: to exchange combat operations' skills for lots of cash, to live the good life, and to get out before the odds caught up with them. These men would be impressed. They would see Ferraris in their futures, and they would work all the harder for such a tangible, rewarding future. "Gentlemen," Feith said, "I want to introduce you to the new love of my life…"

Feith rounded the corner where the Ferrari was parked. It was directly under a street lamp; he had made certain of that when he chose this spot to park the car that very afternoon. Clean, wide street, upscale neighborhood, big bright street light, Feith had thought of nearly everything. And there it was, automotive art in a brilliant lemon yellow. It was impossible to miss. The other thing that was impossible to miss was the massive, disheveled man, wearing layer after layer of obviously filthy clothes. The shambling creature parked his shopping cart against the nearest home and set a massive cardboard tube next to it. The man then turned his matted beard toward the Italian supercar and began his approach, holding by his side a rather large brick.

Feith thought his heart would stop as he watched the giant bundle of rags smash the brick into the driver's side window. "Get him," Feith roared.

"That bum? Who cares what these bums do on the street?"

"That's my goddamn car!" Feith pointed to the auto-motive confection which was being sacked before his eyes. "Don't let that asshole get away." Feith and his lieutenants bundled out of the gleaming black Yukon.

Goliath turned to face the men, all of whom were clad in black tactical fatigues, just like some San Francisco police department units. Goliath just stood there, as if waiting to be taken into custody. Feith and his three men paused, taking time to gauge Goliath's response.

"It's like he thinks we're cops," one of the men said.

Feith advanced slowly and spoke with authority. "Turn around and put your hands behind your back." Goliath hesitated and then began to turn around. "I'll be damned," Feith said, reaching on his belt for a zip tie restraint. "He *does* think we're cops."

The tallest of Feith's men spoke. "So he thinks we're cops. If you cuff him, what the hell are you going to do with him? Jesus, I can smell him from here. The guy reeks."

Feith pointed at the Ferrari and the shattered glass. "This is my car. This is what I've been waiting all night to show you guys. It was perfect. Mint condition, only fourteen thousand miles. You think he gets to walk away?"

"Fine. Cuff him and sit him on the curb. Call the cops and let them take him away."

"That's the same thing as letting him go. If the law worked, we wouldn't have jobs. Corporations would rely on law enforcement."

"Great, sir. You've got him. What are you going to do with him?"

The question stopped Feith in his tracks. His blood was up. The idea of killing the giant simpleton felt right but this was not Afghanistan. Hell, it wasn't even New Orleans. As angry as Feith was, he knew that a simple murder might lead to an investigation. God knew how many people were watching. The problem was simple, teach this simpleminded bastard a lesson he would never forget and do it in a way that wouldn't come back to him, or if it did, would be easy to deny, easy to deflect.

"Fine." Feith spoke just a little louder than necessary. "We let him go. But not in this neighborhood." That would satisfy the nosy bastards looking out of their windows. "We'll take him down to the bus terminal and turn him loose," he said, loudly for the benefit of any nosy neighbors.

Feith grabbed Goliath firmly by his wrists and guided him to the SUV. Goliath went willingly. "Open the door," Feith said.

"Jesus, chief. He stinks. Do you really want him in our ride?"

"Open the door and shut up," Feith said.

"Let's put him in the cargo area. We can have that part scrubbed."

"Oh, for Christ's sake. OK, open the hatch," Feith said.

Goliath lowered his head and two of Feith's men eased him into the cargo area.

Feith opened the driver's door and got behind the wheel. His men climbed in and immediately lowered their windows. Feith pulled away from the curb and called into the back seat. "Anderson!"

"Yes, sir."

"That gas can on the back, is that just for looks?"

"No, sir, it's full."

"Zip ties?"

"Uh, yes, sir…"

Feith smiled, two birds, so to speak. "So, where's that little bar that Rommel owns?"

19

Give Me My Killing

At Vince's, if you wanted the table farthest from the pool table and farthest from the rest rooms, that put you at the table nearest the bar. Close enough to allow Diego to join the conversation and still keep an eye on the two men quietly seated on padded stools at the bar. Carolyn sat between Matt Rommel and Gunny. It was clear that the two men were even more uncomfortable with each other than before.

Carolyn began, "So Gunny, I understand you are moving to Virginia."

"Yeah, I'm going to check in with a buddy near Quantico for a few weeks. He and I have a few ideas we're going to try out. Besides, if you're careful, retirement money goes a lot further back there."

"Aubrey's going to miss you."

"I'm gonna miss her, too." Gunny didn't have much to say. The conversation lapsed. Against the far wall, near the pool table, the jukebox played a bouncy tune sung by a perky woman with a youthful voice.

"I can't make out the lyrics," Carolyn said. "Can either of you make them out?"

Rommel looked to Gunny. Gunny had nothing to say. Rommel said, "I can't follow it all, but the refrain, *susto, pero me gusta*, means *I'm afraid, but I like it.*"

"I like it. I wonder what the name of the song is," Carolyn said.

"I'd only be guessing," Rommel shrugged.

The front windows bordered the ceiling, placed too high to see what was going on out in the street but more than adequate to let in light during the day. Gunny stared at them. "What's that?"

Rommel turned in his chair and looked back. "What?"

"That glow."

An orange glow flickered and flared outside. Rommel was on his feet through the door almost immediately. Pushing the door open, Rommel looked back and roared, "Diego, get a blanket and a fire extinguisher. Go!" Rommel stepped out onto the sidewalk as a flaming giant, arms flailing, staggered toward him. Rommel ran at the flames and hit the creature with his shoulder, driving them both to the asphalt street. Rommel rolled clear as the flaming creature grasped at him. Rommel stripped off his jacket. He was beating the flames with his jacket when Diego pushed against him.

"I found a tarp in the storeroom."

Rommel spread the tarp out with a flick and threw it over what was now, clearly a man, a huge flaming man. Rommel struggled against the giant, trying to cover him completely, trying to suffocate the flames. Gunny reached the scene with a bulky, red fire extinguisher and let fly with a billowing white flume of compressed fire retardant. The white powder caught in Rommel's lungs. For the second time, Rommel rolled free, this time coughing, hacking, trying to clear his lungs and breathe.

The fire died, but the body smoldered beneath the tarp. On his knees, Rommel approached the body, pulling the tarp free and releasing a paralyzing cloud of fetid miasma that knocked everyone back. There was the stink of the gasoline accelerant and burning human flesh, but far beyond that, there was the crippling, wretched, stinking filth of accreted human filth, sweat, feces, urine, hair, and necrotic tissue. It was Goliath. Goliath: the great, filthy, shambling, window-breaking, car-pilfering vandal.

Rommel knelt over the body, surveying the grime and burnt flesh. Rommel could see that Goliath's eyes were open, nearly starting from their sockets. Goliath was not breathing. The behemoth spasmed, as if trying to draw breath. Rommel tilted the great filth-caked cranium back to clear the airway. Nothing. Rommel decided that sticking fingers into Goliath's mouth to clear the airway was an excellent way to lose said digits. The man must be in agony but not even a groan could escape his throat. Rommel inspected the throat and neck, and found a crease of skin. He studied the deep crease with his fingers.

"Zip tie. He's strangling. A knife isn't going to do it. There's too much skin in front to get the blade between the zip tie and the neck. Going in at the back and pulling the blade against the plastic line will crush the throat even more. Diego, wire cutters? Small ones!"

Diego pushed through the crowd that had gathered around and dashed into the bar. In a moment, he was back with a pair of tin snips. "It's what we got," he said.

Rommel ran his fingers along the back of Goliath's neck, using his fingers to create a little space for the snips. Rommel positioned the zip tie between the blades and squeezed as if trying to crush the ligature. The zip tie popped free. Rommel rolled Goliath flat onto his back. Nothing had improved. Goliath still could not breathe. He bucked and thrashed against Rommel, wild terror in Goliath's eyes. Rommel fought against the arms, using his fingers to probe along the wild-man's throat.

• • •

"It feels like his throat is crushed," Rommel said. "Tequila. Big bottle. Clean towels. And a tampon. Not a peep, Gunny. Get me a goddamn tampon. And some tape."

"Where am I supposed to get...?" Gunny looked at Carolyn. Carolyn dug into her purse.

"Here," she said, handing the white oblong packet to Rommel. Diego returned with a quart of tequila.

"Añejo," Gunny said. "Jesus, not the good stuff."

Rommel knelt on Goliath's massive arm, but Goliath was fading into unconsciousness and offering far less resistance. Rommel splashed the tequila across Goliath's throat. From Rommel's trouser pocket, he removed a brass-trimmed pocket knife, opened it, laid it on a clean towel, and poured tequila over the knife.

"Somebody hold his head," Rommel ordered. Gunny started to move but Diego was already there, kneeling, bracing the dying giant's filthy, crusted head between his knees and securing Goliath's head with his hands. From a distance, a siren wailed, approaching.

Rommel surveyed the throat: through the filth, matted and scorched hair remnants, and scorched flesh—it was impossible to tell much. Rommel held the blade's tip perpendicular to the throat, pointed it over the hollow of the throat just above the breastbone and stabbed deeply, and then twisted the knife to create room for an opening. Goliath barely stirred, but his chest rose as air filled his lungs.

Rommel ripped the tampon from its wrapping, tore off the plastic applicator, and cut a larger opening in the end. Rommel shoved the tubular plastic applicator into the hole. "Tape."

Gunny pulled off a long strip of duct tape and handed it carefully to Rommel who wrapped it around the tube and then around part of Goliath's neck.

The ambulance klaxon blasted, and the crowd parted. The EMTs, accompanied by a fire crew, took over. Three black-and-whites blocked traffic and several police officers joined the EMTs. Rommel looked up at no one in particular.

"Someone set this man on fire after they used a zip tie to garrote him. He's badly burned, and his throat is crushed. We put out the fire, cut free the garrote, and inserted a tube so he can breathe."

Rommel struggled to his feet. He could feel the stench of burning flesh on his person, his hands, his clothes, even his hair and face. He took the bottle of añejo and handed it to Carolyn. "Pour a little on my hands." He meant to include the word please. It didn't happen. Perhaps she understood that it was implied. The tequila mixed with the ash and filth, forming a rivulet of thin sludge that poured off his hands and onto the street. "Thank you," Rommel said. The big man bent over, poured the remainder onto his hair, and scrubbed the alcohol into his face and onto his clothes. It didn't help. The stink of human suffering sticks to everything, and this was worse than usual. There was a shower upstairs and a change of clothes, if Gunny hadn't moved them.

Rommel could feel Carolyn staring at him. "You all right?" he asked.

"I'm more worried about you," she said.

"I'm OK, but I'd like to go upstairs for a shower and a change of clothes. That OK with you?"

"Of course." She stared into Rommel's face. "What just happened here?"

"I'm not sure. It could just be something random and terrible. It could be something else."

"Black Horizon?"

"Maybe not," Rommel said, evasively. "As hard as it is to believe, there are bad people out there that Gunny hasn't antagonized. Isn't that right, Gunny?"

Gunny shrugged. "I'm not behind every wicked thing that happens, no matter what you've heard."

Rommel walked back to the bar. Gunny caught him at the door, grabbed his sleeve, and pulled close. "OK. I get it. You're the patron saint of people nobody gives a fuck about. You know those Black Horizon people are behind this. Give me my killing!"

• • •

Rommel's eyes burned, and it wasn't just the smoke and dirt. He placed an index finger on Gunny's chest and began to push. He leaned down close to Gunny's face. His voice rumbled with menace. "I will not murder for you, old man. I have made an end. I will kill no more—not for you, not for anyone. Just remember, I may be done killing, but I still know what it means to make someone suffer. So stop screwing with me." Rommel pushed the old man away, walked into the bar and up the back stairs to the apartment.

❧

Coming down the stairs after a shower and a change of clothes, Rommel could feel it. The tone in the bar was subdued. In fact, the place was half empty. Then he saw why. Carolyn and Gunny sat at the table. Diego leaned his back against the bar. With them were the SFPD. Not just the police, but Lieutenant Carmichael and her partner, Vince Garcia. Rommel studied Diego's mannerisms. Vince was his son, and this was a first for the two of them. Diego's son was in the bar as a police officer on official business. Both men seemed uncomfortable to Rommel. Lieutenant Carmichael saw Rommel approach and spoke, "I heard the call over the COMNET. Attempted homicide, right in front of your bar. Then I find out that you are right in the middle of it. I ask myself, what are the odds? What do you think the odds are, Mr. Rommel?"

"That's *major* to you, toots," Gunny said.

"Gunny, don't make up names for the police. While we're at it, don't make passes at the police, either."

Carmichael stared at Rommel as if stunned by a profoundly stupid idea. "You're kidding."

"I've known this man, off and on, for a long time. If there's alcohol and Gunny's handing out pet names, an amorous advance is not far behind," Rommel said.

Gunny regarded Lieutenant Carmichael with a snaggletoothed grin set in a face full of coarse gray stubble. "For a woman with a gun, you're kind of attractive, Lieutenant."

Carmichael stared at Rommel. "Get rid of your monkey, Mr. Rommel."

"Gunny is not my monkey. He is his own monkey." Rommel turned his head. "Gunny, why don't you get a bottle from Diego and pour some shots for your friends in the back."

"Here," Diego said, reaching back over the bar and grabbing a bottle of mescal by the neck. "We've wasted enough of the expensive stuff."

Gunny gathered some shot glasses with his free hand and tottered toward the back.

"Who started feeding Gunny booze?" Rommel asked.

"He was upset," Diego said. "I hate to see the old gentleman unhappy."

"Enough," Carmichael said. "What do you people know about what happened here tonight?"

"What you've already been told," Rommel said. "We were sitting in the bar. We saw an unusual light. When we looked outside, we saw a man in flames standing in the street."

"We? Just tell me what you saw Mr. Rommel."

"I saw a light. I looked outside and saw a man standing in the street. The man was burning. I pushed him to the ground and covered him with a tarp. I saw Gunny use an extinguisher on the remaining flames. I saw the man could not breathe. I examined his neck and found that a zip tie was blocking his airway. I cut the zip tie and removed it. The man still couldn't breathe. I cut an opening in his throat and put in a plastic tube that I secured with tape. That's what I saw, and that's all I know."

"Do you know the victim?"

"I believe he is the man who broke into my car at the Hall of Justice. The man who was arrested, on that occasion, by Detective Garcia."

"See, here's my problem, Mr. Rommel. I already know that you are a violent man. I have the proof on disc, courtesy of Black Horizon Security. I can't prove it, but I know that you prowl around, looking for the opportunity to beat on people who are smaller than you. Protecting some random person is just a pretext."

"Now, the man who broke into your car turns up in flames and on your doorstep. I know that's not coincidental. I know that, somehow, you are behind it. I know all about you, Mr. Rommel. You had a reputation as a brutal prison guard, and I am certain that reputation was well deserved. You are a bully and a coward, which is probably why your military career was mediocre at best. We don't need you in our city. You have a guilty role in this attempted murder, and I am going to prove it."

Rommel fixed the lieutenant with a level stare. "We're done talking, Lieutenant."

Lieutenant Carmichael called out in the direction of the other bar patrons. "Does anyone have any information on what happened here today?"

"The major saved some poor bastard's life, and now, everyone on the street knows what burning human flesh smells like." Gunny was slurring his words.

"Does anyone know who might have done this?"

"Gee, I don't know," Gunny called out. "You show up at the major's house, and Black Horizon is there casing the joint. Black Horizon beats the hell out of me and the major, and you turkeys put us in jail. Who could it be, Colombo? How about the Salvation goddamn Army? You find that little prick Feith and squeeze his little raisin balls and make him talk. He's either in on this, or he knows who is, and it's probably being done for that murdering bastard Dick Cheney. In case everyone was just too polite to mention it, Dick Cheney is a fucking war criminal." Gunny approached Lieutenant Carmichael, bumping into chairs along the way until he was within inches of her face. She could smell the booze on him. She saw the fine sweat beading on his forehead and the wiry, gray stubble on his lined muzzle. And, for the first time, she saw the sorrow and the pain and the crazy hatred in the old man's raw, red eyes. "I'll talk to them if you like. You just get us all together. That's all you need to do. I'll solve your little case."

20

Just Between Us

The ambulance had long since left. The fire department eventually followed. The police were the last to leave and Vince's once again became a reasonably quiet neighborhood bar. Gunny had gone upstairs to the apartment. Diego tended to his patrons, and Rommel sat in silence at the same table he had been at when all the excitement began. Carolyn sat with him, sharing the añejo, the fine aged tequila.

"She's dead wrong. Everyone knows that. Even Lieutenant Carmichael knows she's wrong," Carolyn said.

"Huh?"

"She had no right to talk to you like that. She was way out of line, and she knows it."

"I expect she does. It's an old cop trick."

"What?"

"Accusations. They unsettle people. Sometimes, in an investigation, it's easier and quicker to make a bunch of accusations. You look someone in the eye, and you tell them that you know they either did it or that they are involved. It nearly always unsettles the target, they blab everything they know or suspect, hoping to convince the cop that they are innocent. Every once in a while, you even get a confession or some useful nugget of information," Rommel said. "That technique is one of the reasons why a lot of people think cops are dumb. Your average citizen thinks that the cop is actually talking to them. They aren't. They look at a group like this, like you would look at livestock. The cop probes; the citizen makes moo noises; the cop files it away and moves on. Emotionally, few cops can manage more than half a dozen human relationships, so everyone else in the city is a meat puppet, and the cop is just trying to get through the day. I'll tell you something about Carmichael. Tonight, as she's falling asleep, she's going to see Goliath. She's going to see the burned flesh. The man's stench and fear and helplessness are going to come back to her. She's going to remember tonight for a while."

"I don't care," Carolyn said. "She had no right to talk to you like that."

Rommel smiled. "I like having you on my side."

"You are no coward. That was plain stupid."

"See, you're doing it."

"Doing what?"

"You are responding to her as if she's doing something more than just stirring the pot, probing for an emotional response. Cops have their own agenda, and they seldom care about yours."

"I just want you to know, that I know, that you are a good man. You are not brutal, and you are no coward."

Rommel smiled into his glass. "A good lie always has a little truth in it."

"And what truth are we talking about?" Carolyn asked.

"Brutality. Prisons are controlled by gangs."

"I know that much," Carolyn said.

"Most people have some idea. They know there are black gangs and Hispanic gangs and white gangs. There's one gang people generally don't think about."

"Which one?"

"The guards." Rommel looked across the table at Carolyn. "Prisons don't run on good intentions. All laws and regulations are enforced. Enforced. Do you understand what I mean?"

"I think so," Carolyn said.

"The lawyers, and the civilian workers, and the visitors come and go, but a prison is a big locked box filled with unlucky bastards, and losers, and defectives, and some really, really dangerous people. The state locks that box up, and they put corrections officers inside and outside and along the walls to protect everyone on the outside.

"What nobody will admit is that, just to stay alive, the corrections officers become just another gang. They have to control turf and command respect. If the guards are credible, prison is relatively safe for the petty thieves and drug offenders and the nice lady who works in the clinic. If the guards don't command the respect of the people they need to control, people get hurt.

"When I worked in the system, if a guard got hurt by convicts, we paid the convicts back. A convict who attacked a guard ended up falling down a lot of stairs. We paid them back in spades." Rommel took a pull on the añejo, trying to decide how much to share. *Nobody wants to be around an ogre*, he decided. He wanted to stop. But he wanted her to understand more.

"You know *Shawshank Redemption*?"

Carolyn nodded. "The movie?"

"And the brutal prison guard?"

Carolyn nodded again.

"That character is one of the bad guys. But who kept the convict hero from being raped and beaten to death by one of the gangs?"

Carolyn said nothing.

"The brutal guard. The captain of the guards. One of the bad guys. A bad man who also kept order and protected

• • •

the inmates and the other guards." Rommel took another drink. "Well, it's just a movie. As for Carmichael, like I said, the best lies have a little truth mixed in."

Rommel smiled. *Two people in a bar, sharing a bottle of tequila and talking about the nature of truth.* "Fine. Have you ever thought about the nature of cowardice?" Rommel leaned back in his chair. "It's getting late, and you don't want to hear this crap. Wanna call it a night?"

"Tell me what you want me to hear."

"I was a corrections officer for about ten years. I thought I'd seen it all in the corps, but those years surrounded by convicts completely changed the way I looked at the world. I kept everything and everyone at arm's length, where I could keep an eye on them. Mean, cynical, suspicious, nobody wants to be married to someone like that. That's just common sense. But when my marriage was over, it never occurred to me that I was the one who destroyed it. I didn't have to think about it much because I could put in seventy hours a week in prison, protecting my fellow officers and keeping my boot on the neck of any convict I saw as a threat. I had my job and the support and respect of the other guards. So, one day I'm in the prison yard watching the knuckleheads lifting weights. There were these cell mates. Friends from childhood. At the request of their families, we put them in the same cell. One of the two had been in prison before. The other was a new fish. It turns out that the night before, these two had whipped up a batch of pruno."

"Pruno?"

"Inmates save their juice boxes, dump the fruit juice into a plastic bag and hide it, usually by lining the inside of the toilet with the bag. The juice ferments, and the result is an alcoholic beverage called pruno."

"How do they get away with that?"

"Two things you need to know. Convicts can hide anything, and they have nothing but time to plot. Plot a scam. Plot sex—consensual or otherwise. Plot revenge."

"So the experienced con gets his childhood buddy drunk. When the new fish passes out, the con sodomizes him. New fish wakes up the next day, and he knows what's happened."

"How does he know?"

"He knows because his ass is raw, and because his childhood pal has told everyone on the cell block, and now, some of them are lining up to take a run at the new fish. New fish knows he has to do something to save his reputation and keep from becoming the belle of the ball. When he gets out to the exercise yard, he sees his pal lying on the bench. Romeo doesn't see new fish coming because he is on the bench, pressing two hundred and fifty pounds."

"None of the guards know there's a problem until New Fish takes a twenty-five-pound iron plate and crashes it down on his pal's head, breaking his skull open." Rommel shifted in his chair. "So, we've got a stretcher. We load the guy on it, but we know he's dying because his brains and associated fluids are leaking everywhere. I've got the end of the stretcher next to this oozing mess and we lift and I said to this dying man, 'don't you dare get that shit on my uniform'. For a moment, everything just stopped, and everyone is staring at me. Not just the cons. My brother and sister officers are staring at me, and they are stunned, and then they are disgusted. It was only then that I understood what I had done to myself. I thought I was protecting the part of the world I cared about, but I had just made myself into something cruel and terrible."

"That was my last day on the job. I thought about my uncle's funeral, and the museum in Saint Louis, and the museum guards, and their conversation about art shaping the relationship between man and God. I bought a membership to the Palace of the Legion of Honor, and I was there every day from the moment they opened until closing time. After a few months, I met people and started working as a docent."

"That's it," Rommel said. "That is how I became the sweet and sensitive soul that earned the respect and admiration of the SFPD."

• • •

Carolyn put her hand over his. "You have my respect and admiration." She stood up. "I'm going to call a cab. Then I'm calling Denni, who will be watching Aubrey for a bit longer than she expected. And then I'm taking you home to bed."

Rommel looked up at Carolyn. He decided her hair had a special magic when it was backlit by neon. He started to say something and stopped himself. Rommel decided that this would be a good time for him to shut up.

21

Operation Goodwill

Since he had to wait, Feith spent his time studying Curtis, the wunderkind. Not yet thirty, Daniel Curtis was Black Horizon's vice president of Strategic Planning. And because Black Horizon's strategic plans had consistently become lucrative exercises, Curtis was considered by some to be second only to Cheney in the corporate hierarchy. However, this was not the way Feith saw it. There was no second in command at Black Horizon, and there never would be. This was Cheney's brainchild, his bloody little baby. At Black Horizon, there was Cheney and the employee base. Everyone was supposed to be useful, but everyone was disposable. Everyone except Cheney. When the pharaoh died, all the Black Horizon slaves and priests would be buried with Cheney, the man-god. *Everyone but Feith*, he mused. Even as a marine and the NCOIC of the Marine Corps Logistics' Base in Barstow, Feith had been useful. Feith had made a bundle for the firm and for himself. He had funneled enough materiel through Barstow for several small wars. The Metal Storm technology waiting at the Embarcadero had just been the icing on the cake.

• • •

Feith had carried a weapon for Black Horizon in Iraq, Afghanistan, and even New Orleans. Feith could leave now and never need to work another day. He could leave now, climb into that sweet, little, yellow Ferrari, and drive down the coast. But he wouldn't, not with the big payday just around the corner.

Through all this, Daniel Curtis had been Cheney's own personal Liddell Hart, a strategic visionary. Cheney had gotten Black Horizon into Iraq, but it was Curtis who had seen that, with the US military and political machinery embroiled in two wars, American defense and intelligence services would run unchecked for the next decade. It was Curtis who saw that, in addition to thousands of well-paid, armed mercenaries with carte blanche to shoot at anything that moved, these agencies each had their own dirty work they wanted done, and best of all, hidden from other US agencies. For ten years, Black Horizon roamed the Middle East. The firm could kill, kidnap, and torture without consequence. Any local was fair game, and even the occasional troublemaking ally could be dispatched, if the deed was done discreetly.

What made Curtis a genius was that, somehow, he understood that whatever you could do overseas, you could do in America. New Orleans was his masterstroke. Curtis proved that mercenary forces could wander a US city with impunity and kill at will. In the face of disaster, the rule of law broke down and Black Horizon, wherever it went, became the law and took what it wanted: property, lives, whatever. Of course, New Orleans hadn't been as profitable as Iraq or Afghanistan, but that contract proved to the entire company that, if you were connected to the powers that be, you could do whatever you wanted.

Feith thought about that church group. They had been so tired, so subdued, all of them but the one young woman trying to lead them to safety. They had gotten into the SUVs so quietly. It was as if they knew. Personally, Feith wouldn't have done it. If he had, he wouldn't have made a show of it. But Cheney had to have his way. Cheney even had to be watched, so they all watched and one victim at a time, Cheney put on a show. Cheney had to control everything, except body disposal. Once they were dead, Cheney didn't want to touch them anymore. So, they took the bodies downstream, and with that act they all became accomplices. And Cheney's message? Feith had thought about that every day since Katrina. It was simple: Cheney could do whatever he wanted, anywhere in the world. Cheney could do it to pagan babies overseas. Cheney could do it to Americans. And, if you crossed him, Cheney could do it to you or your wife or your kids. And when it was over: he would take a souvenir, put it in the little bowl on his desk, move on, and not think twice about it.

Here, sitting on the couch in Cheney's office, Feith looked at the bowl and thought about his future. *The money was good, but the risk was high. The trick was to make your money and get out without becoming a trinket in Cheney's bowl.*

The door opened quickly, startling Feith. He looked at Curtis. Curtis seemed surprised as well. No one who knew Cheney could be comfortable waiting for him. There was nothing the man would not do if it suited him.

Cheney was in rare form today, his secretary two steps behind, trying to keep up and take notes at the same time.

"Make certain he understands. We've provided brigades of non-Moslems for other Middle Eastern leaders. We can do it discreetly so that leadership has a safety valve in case their own troops should rise up or be reluctant to suppress their own people. We can create a presence that will provide a concrete, undeniable understanding that an Arab Spring or some similar nonsense is impossible in any nation that employs us. Black Horizon is committed to peace and stability for our clients. Tell him I'll be checking on his progress myself. Make certain that he understands this. Thank you, that's all." The secretary turned and left. Rumor was, even she was a millionaire.

As if reading Feith's mind, Cheney spoke. "I would say that, financially, she does very well indeed. No one who has worked for me for five good years has failed to become a millionaire unless they developed personal problems that prevented it. Anyone who doesn't abuse drugs or alcohol and keeps his nose clean does just fine. So what do you have for me?"

Curtis spoke up, "Pending approval, we're calling it Project Goodwill. The last of the deliveries from Barstow arrived last night. All the equipment seems to be in good condition. Sound equipment and staging have already been erected for the big rally in Union Square. Metal Storm, dressed to look like additional equipment will be positioned with the amps and speakers, giving us complete coverage of the square."

"Any problems?"

"Nothing important. If you do this, you're going to kill a lot of cops, as well as protesters."

"Classic shock doctrine. America will mourn its brave first responders, and Black Horizon can expect to receive sustained funding for the global war on terror for the next decade. Additionally, Black Horizon will be free to trade in weapons and incidentals with impunity."

"Incidentals?" Feith said.

"Incidentals," Curtis responded. "Pharmaceuticals, displaced persons, financial services."

"That sounds better than drugs, slavery, and money laundering." Cheney turned to Feith. "What's the situation with our old nemesis?"

"About the same. He hates you. He would kill you if he could, but he's an old man, and he can't quite manage it."

"I've enjoyed Gilhooley's focused admiration. If we could get him someplace quiet, it would be exquisite to tell him just how his daughter died, but Operation Goodwill is going to take our firm to a whole new level. I think it's time to put an end to this sideshow. I don't see Master Gunnery Sergeant Gilhooley quitting while he lives. Do you understand?"

"He blames you for his daughter's death."

"Well, he should have had more daughters. What about this other fellow?"

"Rommel. Get rid of Gilhooley, and I don't think Rommel will be any trouble."

"Are you certain? Are we talking about the same man that you needed three teams to subdue? Perhaps a warning is in order."

"Tactically, there were mistakes. The mix of tools and personnel could have been better. But Gilhooley is the one with the mission, not Rommel. Rommel has wealth and comfort. What he wants is to enjoy the years he has left. Kill Gilhooley in a way that makes it look random, and you won't have any more trouble with Rommel."

Cheney turned to Curtis. "Dan, take a couple of men and explain things to Mr. Rommel. What do you think, *plata o plomo?*"

Against his better judgment, Feith spoke. "Silver or lead. Usually that works, but you don't want to use that with Rommel. He has money. More money won't motivate him. Threatening him physically isn't a good idea, either. You mentioned the security disc. You've seen what he can be like when he's confronted. Kill Gilhooley; make it look like street crime. Leave Rommel alone. That's all you need to do."

Cheney looked at Feith. "Darren, you know I value your opinion and your tremendous expertise. It's safe to say that without your help marshalling our supplies through Barstow, Goodwill would not be going forward. That being said, don't interrupt me, not ever again. You will know when I am speaking to you because I will be looking at you. Understood?"

Feith nodded.

"Good, I want you to concentrate your attention on our supplies at the Embarcadero. This is San Francisco, and there just isn't enough privacy. Make certain Metal Storm makes it onto the tractor-trailers and into position on the square in time. I think that's all, Darryl. You can go. I want to iron out a few more details with Dan."

Dismissed, Feith made the long trek to the door. Cheney waited patiently. Whatever the topic was, Cheney wanted privacy. Feith left the office, gently closing the door to Cheney's office behind him.

❧

"I want you to put Feith front-and-center when you execute."

Curtis nodded again. "Understood."

"Feith has been useful, but he has been involved in operations above his pay grade for far too long. Normally, that wouldn't be a problem, but Feith isn't an intelligent man." Cheney looked at Curtis.

Curtis knew this was his cue. "I agree. I think everyone knows that Feith is a knuckle-dragger who somehow found himself too close to the decision-making apparatus of the firm for far too long. We'll put him front-and-center for the false flag. When Metal Storm is activated, the carnage will be absolute and some of the gobbets of flesh will belong to Mr. Feith."

Cheney leaned back into the couch, smiled, and let his eyes fix upon some imagined point far into the future. "I love this plan, Dan. Losing one of our own gives us skin in the game to come as America makes war on whatever dimwitted group of extremists we pin this on."

Daniel Curtis took up Cheney's train of thought. He was, after all, Cheney's master strategist. It did no harm to review his brilliant plan. Every corporation thinks it has a plan that will remake the world and enrich the firm. How many plans operate on such a scale and offer so much? "Feith understands the mechanics of Goodwill. Black Horizon will execute an atrocity against the locals and law enforcement and blame Moslem terrorists. What Feith doesn't grasp is that, from the perspective of the American public, there is no war fervor without American casualties. The press will have a sensational story, and the mercenary industry will have the incident needed to enflame the American public and force the military's hand."

"We have the press lined up for this operation, yes?"

"Of course. We even have a couple news crews who will be on-site when Goodwill is executed. I can promise you some incendiary footage, some horrific atrocities, perfect photo ops. A few dead media figures are not going to hurt."

"Make certain Feith's body is front-and-center. I think we owe him that."

"Absolutely."

"Now, this Rommel thing, what do you think?"

"I hate to say it, but Feith has a point. If Gilhooley was dead and there was nothing to tie it to Black Horizon, everyone would go about their business, Rommel included," Curtis said.

Cheney shifted his position slightly. "Maybe you're right, but I don't want Mr. Rommel to overlook me. Send someone after Gilhooley, when he's alone. Make it look like a break-in gone wrong."

"Too many people at the bar in the Mission, can't do it there."

"Then do it when the old fart is padding around Rommel's house, that's even better. I want Mr. Rommel to fear me. After you get Gilhooley at the house, take a couple of men and warn Rommel off. There's that nice mother and daughter who he dotes on. There's also that bag lady." Cheney shook his head at the idea of the odd assortment of people that Matt Rommel had gathered into his life. "Find a countervalue target, something that is so important to him that he will bow down. Make your point. Don't be afraid to make a splash. I want Mr. Rommel to understand that he and the people who are important to him live only with my permission. I've broken better men, much better men. See to it."

Curtis left Cheney's office and wandered the short distance to his own office, lost in thought. Cheney was wrong, but there was no talking to the man once he had made up his mind. Curtis would have to obey Cheney, but he could always take things further. Without fear, warnings were meaningless. It was unrealistic to hope that Mr. Rommel had much concern for his own well-being, and there weren't many people in Rommel's little world. Curtis would have to find something that Rommel was afraid to lose, something that was precious to the man. If there was to be a threat, it had to be a big one, and that threat had to be credible, even tangible. Curtis turned it over in his mind. Curtis knew he could afford a little flamboyance. If necessary, he could *go big*. With Cheney, there was seldom a penalty for initiative.

22

Big or Tall, They All Fall to Hardball

Carolyn cruised down Vista del Mar, made a U-turn and parked the SLK at the curb in front of Matt Rommel's house. Aubrey scrambled out of the car and made a dash for the gate. Carolyn reminded herself that they weren't early, because they weren't expected at all. They were dropping by without notice and not for the first time. No doubt about it, the relationship was changing. She rang the doorbell. Gunny opened the door. He was holding Chesty on a leash. Carolyn marveled at the old man's resourcefulness. Somehow, he had managed to retain a key to Rommel's house.

"It's nice to see you, Gunny. Is Matt here?"

Gunny smiled and looked down at Chesty who, tail wagging furiously, was nuzzling her great head against Aubrey as the little girl tried to put the muscular beast in a headlock. "This time of day, he's up the hill, at the museum. He's almost always there till closing."

"Well," Carolyn ventured, "perhaps you and Aubrey can watch Sheriff Bunny for a while, and I'll drop in on Matt." *Matt.* Carolyn smiled. *This was a man who might be worth the risk.*

● ● ●

"I promised Chesty a walk down to the beach," Gunny said. "If you two charming ladies can wait until we return, I promise the old girl and I will be back before the second Sheriff Bunny cartoon."

With that, Aubrey turned and ran down the hall. The little girl didn't object to parting pleasantries, but the cartoon people were not so tolerant. Sheriff Bunny would start on the dot, whether she was there to see it or not. Carolyn and Gunny said their good-byes. Gunny headed out the front gate, and Carolyn went into the house and closed and locked the solid oak front door. Carolyn sat on the sofa in the living room and picked up a magazine. Aubrey knew more about operating the big TV in the den than any other person in the house, and Carolyn decided that a few minutes of peace and quiet with a magazine, even a car magazine, was better than listening to a running commentary on the allies and enemies that Sheriff Bunny routinely faced in his two-dimensional, animated world.

Within just a few minutes, Carolyn heard the front gate open and close. She sensed someone at the door. Apparently, the old gentleman and the dog decided to cut their little walk short. She heard someone try the doorknob and then scratch at the bolt. Was the old rascal having trouble fitting the key into the lock? Carolyn got up and walked toward the door to open it for him.

Just a few feet short of the great oak front door, Carolyn felt a concussive boom. Someone was trying to break down the door, and it wasn't a little old man. Again, someone crashed their body against the door. Carolyn ran down the hall to collect Aubrey. She would have to grab the little girl, run back down the hallway, and escape the house through the garage.

"Honey! Come on! We have to get out of here right now!" Carolyn yelled. In that instant, Carolyn heard the frame splinter as the heavy front door slammed against the inside wall. Carolyn closed the door to the den behind her and looked around. The room was a rectangular cave with the big-screen TV against the side wall and a large wooden desk at the end of the room. The room had no windows. They could hide, but they couldn't run. Carolyn grabbed Aubrey and pushed her toward the desk. They would have to hide behind the desk, hold their collective breath, and hope for the best.

"Down here, honey," Carolyn whispered.

"What about this?" Aubrey pulled at the upper right-hand desk drawer. The drawer slid easily. From a kneeling position, Carolyn looked down into the drawer, down at the glistening blue-steel Colt M1911A1 and a red box of ammunition.

"No." It was all Carolyn could manage. She could barely speak above the pounding of her heart.

"What if he comes in here?" Aubrey said.

Carolyn hesitated. She wanted to say no. She wanted an alternative. She couldn't think of one. She extended a shaking arm over the drawer and reached in for the gun. It felt heavy and cold and very hard.

"You have to load it," Aubrey said.

Carolyn said nothing.

"Push the button. Here." A small finger snaked along the handle and pushed at the round button. The empty, oiled magazine slid from the gun, falling on the carpet. Carolyn picked up the clip. Aubrey opened the box of ammunition and slid out the plastic tray. Rows of copper-headed bullets glistened up at Carolyn.

"Take the bullet out and put it in the clip," Aubrey said. Carolyn's hands shook. Aubrey took the magazine in her right hand and picked a shiny bullet from the box. "Like this," she said.

Someone was moving down the hall. Someone kicked open the door to the hall bathroom. Automatic gunfire shook the house. Carolyn and Aubrey looked up from behind the desk, trembling.

Aubrey paused, took a breath, and loaded another five rounds. She maneuvered the clip into the base of the handle

• • •

and pushed the magazine home. She handed the gun to her mother. Carolyn held the heavy gun with her two shaking hands.

"You have to load it."

"Huh?"

"The slide. Pull the slide."

Carolyn understood. All those years of action television. The top of the pistol was the slide. You had to slide it back and then let it move back forward. The action was smooth. She could hear things clicking. The pistol was loaded and the big hammer was back, poised to make a disastrous, loud explosion. From now on, Carolyn knew she would have to keep the gun pointed away.

They hunkered down behind the big desk, blood pounding in Carolyn's ears. She tried desperately to remain silent, but she could not control her breathing. She had to be calm. She had to reassure her daughter. But, when she looked into Aubrey's eyes, Carolyn was shocked. Aubrey's gaze was rock-steady. It occurred to Carolyn that Aubrey was not hiding. Aubrey was lying in wait, the seven-year-old hunter awaiting the prey. Aubrey's gaze steadied Carolyn; her breathing slowed a bit. She could still feel her heart beating, but there was a semblance of control. Carolyn adjusted the great pistol in her sweating hands and kept the barrel pointed toward the floor. She kept her trembling finger outside of the trigger guard. If they were to live, she had to strike. She could provide no warning. She thought of her dreams. It was the mausoleum all over again.

The door to the den splintered and flew open. A concussive spray of gunfire tattooed the side wall. Someone entered the den. Carolyn could smell the gunpowder as another thunderous spray of gunfire hit the wall behind them and rocked into the great desk. There was a pause. Carolyn sprang to her feet, raising the big gun at the man standing against the far wall. Carolyn's first round fired into the desk itself. Her trigger finger twitched and the .45 roared again, striking the olive clad ghost in the boot. The man fell backward against the far wall; his hand rose up for balance. The .45 had ridden too high from the recoil, but her finger and the trigger had minds of their own. Carolyn fired again, the big bullet tearing through the gunman's upraised palm. The next two rounds slammed into the far wall. Carolyn's last round crashed into the wall, just to the side of the home-invader's neck. The pistol's slide locked in the back position. The weapon was empty. The smoke-filled room fell silent.

Carolyn watched the gunman. This was no house-robbing punk. The man was clad in what amounted to a uniform—a dusky-green canvas. The home invader paused, raised his goggles, and seemed to be taking inventory. He was alive. Six rounds from a .45 at close range, and he was alive. His target was in front of him. He had a loaded rifle. She had nothing, and he was alive. He smiled as he trained his weapon on Carolyn, who stood, frozen.

She knew she was going to die, but she stood trans-fixed. She had never seen anything like it. Even above her pounding heart, she thought she could hear the spray. How could he not notice? Carolyn nodded her head to the right. The gunman paused as if trying to decide whether she was telling him something or trying some stupid trick. He glanced to his right. The bookcase was covered in deep-crimson spray. Reflexively, the gunman raised his hand; the arterial spray coursed against his hand. The gunman clasped his bloody hand to his neck. He tottered and slumped to the floor.

Carolyn dropped to the floor, pistol in hand. "Show me how to remove the clip," she said. Aubrey pushed the button again. This time, Carolyn caught the clip. Her hands were shaking wildly. She grabbed a handful of bullets from the tray. Half of them fell to the floor. She pushed them against the clip without success at first. Then the first one slid in. Carolyn loaded bullets into the clip until no more would fit. She picked up the pistol, pointed it away, and pushed the clip home. The slide slammed forward, chambering the first round. Carolyn held the pistol before

• • •

her and jumped to her feet. The man just lay there, breathing heavily. In spite of wildly trembling hands, she held her fire.

Carolyn sensed movement at the doorway. She trained the pistol at the entrance. A head appeared. She fired. Two quick shots went wide.

"Whoa, goddamnit. Stop shooting. It's me and the dog. Is that you, Carolyn?"

Carolyn said nothing. She lowered the pistol. Gunny entered the room, holding Chesty on the shortest leash he could manage. Chesty, canine mohawk bristling up her spine, pulled against the leash in a state of agitation. The blood seemed to excite the dog, but she seemed unclear as to what she should be doing. "Easy, baby," the old man said.

The downed man stirred. Gunny took the man's weapon from him. The old man surveyed the scene. Gunny looked at Carolyn by the far wall. Then he surveyed the nearby bullet marks in the wall. He saw the gunman's bleeding foot and hand. He saw that at least one round had just nicked the would-be killer's neck, severing an artery. The man was bleeding out.

"Nice grouping of your shots," Gunny said.

The downed man stirred. "Help me," he said, in a thin distant voice.

"Sure," Gunny said. "You broke in here to murder a woman and a child. Gunny's gonna help you out." Gunny gestured to Carolyn. "Honey, time to get Aubrey out of here. Why don't you two go down the hall and wait for the police." Carolyn seemed distant, as if obeying by remote control. In one hand, she held the Colt. In the other, she held Aubrey's hand. Aubrey's eyes were fixed on the downed attacker, his breathing shallow, his lifeblood slipping away.

"Maybe you should give the gun to me," Gunny said.

"I think I'll keep it," Carolyn said, as if from a far-off place.

"Look at me, Carolyn," Gunny said.

Carolyn looked at him.

• • •

166

"You keep that thing pointed down and away. You keep your finger off that trigger, and you don't point that weapon at anything you don't intend to kill. Do you understand?" he said.

Carolyn said, "I understand." At that moment, her hand began to shake and then her whole arm. She held the weapon out, barrel pointed downward. Gunny took it quickly and gently.

"Your mommy did good," Gunny said to Aubrey, trying to smile. "Just like Sheriff Bunny."

From the hallway, Aubrey looked back at Gunny, her eyes rock-steady. The last time Gunny had seen that kind of poise under fire, a staff sergeant was calmly walking from a burning armored personnel carrier, having just evacuated all of his people—living, dead, and wounded—from the smoking vehicle.

"Sheriff Bunny doesn't miss," she said. Gunny watched them walk down the hall.

"Jesus," the old man said, under his breath.

❧

The home invader bled out. The ambulance came and went. The forensics team and nearly half a dozen cops took much longer. The fact that none of them knew anything was a highly unsatisfactory circumstance for the police. A man carrying an assault rifle and no identification stormed the house, searched the premises room by room, and was killed by a woman who got off six rounds from an antique pistol while under fire. That was all that anyone knew. So the police asked again in a slightly different way and got the same basic facts. They questioned the little girl separately and again the facts were unchanged. When the police ran out of things to look at and questions to ask, they left.

Gunny was sitting outside with Aubrey and Chesty. Carolyn and Rommel sat in the living room. Between them, there was an uncomfortable silence.

• • •

"I can't do this, *us*, I mean," Carolyn said. "You and the dog and even that old man are very dear to me, but I can't do this. I can't stand waiting for the next disaster."

Rommel looked directly into her eyes. "I understand. I'm sorry this happened to you."

"These things only seem to happen to you and that old man. You two are a nonstop disaster area. People live their whole lives without this kind of endless deadly tumult. What if something happens to Aubrey? She and I only have each other. I have to protect her. I am so sorry, I really am, but you two are going to have to have your war without us." For a moment, Carolyn thought she might cry, but there was nothing left. *No one can live with this kind of random mayhem. No one.*

"You are a fine and a dear man. I don't know anyone even remotely like you. But the simple truth is, I don't want to die, and I don't want to bury my daughter, and that's all there is to it."

Rommel leaned forward. "Everything you say makes perfect sense. I want you to know that I think you are absolutely right. I really wish I could explain all of this. Don't get me wrong; when I look at that old man, I know in my bones that he is up to his teeth in this, somehow. I don't think there's much doubt that the killer expected to find Gunny here alone. I just don't understand what is driving this. Black Horizon is behind this, but they could have killed Gunny anytime over the years. There's some urgency driving them. Black Horizon does a billion dollars' worth of business a year. San Francisco is not a large city. I can't imagine what is keeping their CEO in town. He should have gotten on a plane and left a week ago. Without Cheney, Gunny dries up and blows away. Without Gunny, Cheney has no interest in us."

Rommel stood. "Would you like me to drive you and Aubrey home?"

"That's sweet," Carolyn said, "but I'm fine. I think we should just quietly go our separate ways." She moved toward the door.

It occurred to Rommel that he should give her a gentle embrace and kiss her on the cheek, a gesture of farewell. Then it occurred to Rommel that he was an idiot. In a moment, she was through the door and gone.

Gunny wandered in, found a glass and a bottle of Balvenie, and sat in the lounge chair oblique to Rommel on the couch. Gunny took a long pull on the bottle.

"What's the glass for?" Rommel said.

"Huh?"

"If you're going to drink straight from the bottle, what's the glass for?"

Gunny stared at the glass. "Huh." He then filled the glass and took a long pull. "Better?"

"Yeah. Now, we can entertain. You invite everyone, besides me, who wants you dead, and we'll have the affair catered."

"You don't have to get like that."

Rommel looked at Gunny. "Two people were almost killed tonight. Two terribly important people. If they had died…"

"She'll be back," Gunny said.

"I don't see it," Rommel said.

"Sure," Gunny said. "A person kills for the first time, it takes a toll. She'll get past it. We all do."

"No," Rommel said. "She's not afraid. Well, no more than a sane person would be. What she is, is smart. Things have gotten out of control, and it's only a matter of time before we all end up in a bag. Besides, this is not her first killing."

"No shit? She killed a guy before?"

"It wasn't one guy. It was two guys. Practically hand to hand."

"That part makes sense, 'cause she can't shoot." Gunny mused and shook his head. "What a woman."

• • •

169

They sat in silence. Chesty climbed up on the couch, placing her head in Rommel's lap. Rommel stared at the broken front door.

"They'll be back."

"Your pals?"

Gunny nodded.

"Not for a while," Rommel said. "Carmichael's got a black-and-white outside. This is a rich neighborhood and *los ricos* are not used to gunplay. I wouldn't be surprised if the SFPD doesn't end up having to build a police station across the street."

23

Battery

Richmond P. Davis

Carolyn didn't need to look at the clock. A good week was one that demanded only seventy or so hours of work, much of it performed at her desk. She could see and feel the transit of the sun on its way beyond the Pacific. Shadows grew long. The light itself took on a sepia tint. Today was a good day. She was going to leave before nightfall. Of course, it was Sunday, so it really wasn't much of a concession. She looked at her desk, thought about stuffing a few things into a satchel and bringing them home. She decided against it. The time she had at home was Aubrey's time. It could be spent on homework or just in front of the TV, but it was time for just the two of them. From here on out, it would always be just the two of them.

Carolyn looked away from the satchel, got up from her desk, and grabbed her suit jacket as she walked out of her office. She took a quick circuit around the common office area to see if anyone was still in the office. There was no overtime for salaried employees, so it was little compensation enough to stop by and acknowledge the extra time that people put in on the job. No one.

Carolyn looked at the phone on one of the empty desks. She'd thought of him for most of the day. She wondered how he was. She no longer felt like a young impressionable soul. Not all relationships work out. Of all the reasons for a clean and definite break, few were better than being attacked by a gunman. All relationships involve a little tolerance, some give, and some take. But sudden violent death was not something to be worked around. Matt Rommel understood that, didn't he?

Carolyn sat at the vacant desk and reached for the phone. She dialed the number from memory.

"Hello."

"Matt?" Carolyn said.

"Hello, Carolyn. How are you feeling?" Matt Rommel's voice seemed genuinely glad to hear her, but there also seemed to be a little sadness.

"I'm all right. How are you?"

"I'm well. We're all good on this end. Lots of cleanup, and we're still getting regular visits from the police. They're still trying to make sense of last night's episode, and they don't seem to be eager to go and talk with the people at Black Horizon. So, they drop by, probably in hopes that they will surprise us doing something nefarious," Rommel said.

There was a pause in the conversation. The pause lingered. Finally, Carolyn said, "I feel guilty."

"Guilty?" Rommel said. "Why?"

"I feel like I'm running away," Carolyn said.

"Well, of all the things to get away from, I'd have to put gunfire way up on the list," Rommel said, gently.

Carolyn smiled into the phone, she nearly laughed. "That's amazing, just a moment ago, I was just thinking almost exactly the same thing."

There was another pause.

"I feel like a coward," she said.

"We both know better than that, don't we? You have responsibilities. Not just to yourself. You have a responsibility to protect Aubrey," Rommel said.

"I know. I still feel like a coward. How do I know?"

"Know what?"

"How do I know if I'm a coward? I mean, really, what is cowardice? Have you ever thought about that?" Carolyn asked.

"Since you bring the matter up, yes, in my former profession, I have considered the nature of cowardice."

"And?"

"And I think you need to cut yourself a little slack," Rommel said.

"No, really, I want to know."

"Fine, let's make it easy and say that there are three types of cowardice. There's physical cowardice. It's the most ordinary reaction in the world. People fear injury and death. Overcoming physical fear is just a matter of conditioning. When Aristotle spoke of his time as a young man in the Athenian army, he said, 'We became brave by doing brave things'."

Rommel continued, "You overcame your fear when you needed to. The word coward doesn't apply to you, OK?"

Carolyn couldn't let go. "What about the other two types of cowardice?"

"There's moral cowardice. That's much more difficult to deal with, and it says everything about a person's character. To tolerate wickedness and injustice for fear of running afoul of authority or public ostracism is a tragic and shameful act. Again, it doesn't apply to you."

"And the last one," Carolyn continued. "It seems like physical and moral cowardice would cover everything. What's the last one?"

"The last one is really just my opinion. I wouldn't worry about it."

"Tell me. I want to know," Carolyn said.

"The last type of cowardice is cruelty. Like I said, that's just my opinion. When you look at ancient civilizations like Rome, they believed that the gladiatorial games kept their civilization strong. Fact is, that was just wishful thinking. Strength comes from within. It comes with struggle and discipline, and a morality that doesn't come from a talking head on the television."

"I think I understand," Carolyn said. "Cruel people are trying to appear strong."

"Sometimes," Rommel said. "Just remember that there are people whose viciousness has nothing to do with internal conflict. There really is such a thing as wickedness."

"I'm going to miss you," Carolyn said. "I really am sorry."

"Again," Rommel said, "you don't need to apologize. I understand and so does Gunny. You are doing the right thing by protecting your family. When it comes to you and Aubrey, you will never know how important your safety and well-being are to me." Rommel said the words gently. Carolyn could feel herself beginning to cry.

"I have to go," she said, and hung up the phone.

Carolyn locked the door to the office and waited for the elevator. Wiping away the tears, she tried to focus on something more upbeat. She admired the bronze elevator doors that were part of the building's art deco charm. For the first time, it occurred to her that there was a funereal quality to bronze. Not these highly burnished doors that shone their antique resplendence. *Still*, Carolyn thought, *if these doors were to dim, to tarnish, they would take on a more sinister quality. Snap out of it.* She couldn't allow herself to wander down a path where she became afraid of everything. She couldn't afford to be terrified by the past. The past was dead. She knew. She had killed, and dead was something she understood.

She rode the elevator down from the fifteenth floor, down through the lobby, and into the garage. The doors opened on the lower floor of the garage. Carolyn looked out at the fluorescent-blue casting of the silent garage and the powerful sense of stillness. There were few cars on this level, at this time of day, on a Sunday. She could see her car, maybe a hundred feet away. There were a few stray sedans, company cars probably. There was a large black SUV, not too far from her own car—the burnished copper SLK AMG. In the light, her car looked a little sickly, as if it were afraid, wanted to warn her, and couldn't because it was paralyzed with terror.

Carolyn shook it off as she stepped out of the elevator and walked to her car. Monthly parking here was expensive. She paid for it because the building was secure. There were security guards and video cameras to monitor activity in the garage. Unconsciously, she looked up toward the camera. At first, she didn't see it. It wasn't quite where she remembered it. Then she spotted it. Spotted it. Had someone spray-painted over the security camera? Carolyn turned and started walking back toward the elevator. It might be nothing. She might be a chicken. Screw it. If she wanted to, she could take a taxi all the way home to Berkeley. She heard shuffling behind her. She didn't need to look. She didn't care what it was. She ran for the elevator, reached it in an instant, and started slapping at the button. Only then did she turn around.

Monsters. No, men, huge men. Four of them, dressed in black, balaclavas covering their faces, running at her, full speed. This was a good time to scream and scream Carolyn did. Adrenaline shot through her body. She screamed again and fumbled in her purse for her pepper spray. Four dark yetis, one small can of pepper spray. She thought about her keys. She could gouge them with her keys, but pepper spray first. *Screaming, then pepper spray, then keys.* For an instant, she fumbled with the small aerosol can. Carolyn raised it, spraying as she did so. *Spray, then aim the stream into their eyes. Scream, spray, and then gouge with the keys.* It all happened in an instant before the first massive, gloved fist crashed against Carolyn's temple. Her whole body shuddered, like a wooden ship run-up on the rocks. She went sideways, falling, floating,

● ● ●

something like that. It didn't occur to her that she could avoid falling. It just wasn't her decision, and when she hit the pavement, it didn't seem all that important. She felt rough hands under her arms. She shot up, buoyant in a sea of slaps and punches. She heard it and felt a little breeze. Her blouse ripped. *Is that what this was about?* She would have given them the blouse if they'd asked for it. Carolyn thought to speak as she wobbled on her feet, strong hands clutching at her. *No speaking*, she decided. *Punch. Punch, kick, punch, kick, scream. Yeah*, she thought, *screaming was just fine.* Again, these were the thoughts of a single moment. She balled up her fist and tried to launch it. They had her by the arms, the fist would not fly. One big goon stepped in and crashed another massive fist into her belly. The belly gave. Air rushed out of her. Carolyn struggled to breathe but could not. She couldn't fall, either. They held her up. Another fist into the gut. She was suffocating. Someone yanked at her hair, forcing her face up to look at her attacker. The great gloved fist eclipsed everything, crashing itself into her face. Sparks splintered into the gathering darkness. Warmth, sticky wetness. Carolyn opened her mouth but still couldn't breathe. Blood filled her mouth. Her nostrils would not serve. Her nose was crushed. Weakly, she spat out the blood, spat it at her attacker. Another crushing blow. Another. Another. Nothing.

؏ؖ؏

Rommel answered the phone. He heard Denni del Grecco's voice. "Is Carolyn with you?"

"No, she isn't."

"Have you seen her today?"

"No. Is there a problem?"

"Aubrey is with me, and Carolyn hasn't stopped by to pick her up, and she hasn't called. I tried the office. I tried her cell phone. I called the building security people at work. There's no one in the office, but her car is still parked in the garage."

Rommel's heart beat faster. He could feel something unwelcome in the pit of his stomach. "Have you called the police?"

"Do you think I should?"

"I don't see why not. Tell them Lieutenant Carmichael wants to be informed. She spends enough time bothering me. She can do something constructive. Do you have my cell phone number?"

"Yes."

Rommel stood. "Good. I'm going to get dressed and drive over to your offices. It's probably something silly. She could have gotten locked out of the building without her purse." Rommel could feel the sickness in his stomach robbing him of strength. Fear for others is still fear, and, uncontrolled, fear can kill you. "Try not to worry. I'll call as soon as I know something." Rommel walked to the closet. *Outdoor wear*, he thought, *steel-toed boots, denim, wool—and a holster*. He reached into the back of the closet.

Rommel was halfway down the stairs when the phone rang again. He moved swiftly toward the living room phone and the good news he hoped for. "Rommel." He tried not to sound too gruff, or too anxious, or too much like he cared, which he did.

"Maah Wah thah, Maah!" It sounded like a woman.

"Carolyn?" Rommel repeated the word. "Carolyn!"

There was a jostling noise, as if the phone was being passed to another person, a person with a deeper, more deliberate voice. "Isn't that sweet? I think she's trying to warn you. Mrs. Kast is not feeling well. You should come and collect her. I hate to belabor the obvious, but you should come alone. I want to speak with you on a matter of some importance. Come alone. Come unarmed. Listen to what I have to tell you, and then you and Mrs. Kast can go home."

"Where?" Rommel said.

"Fort Funston, Battery Richmond P. Davis. It's along the Great Highway, look it up. You're wasting time." The line went dead.

San Francisco's Great Highway is a four-lane boulevard that runs four miles along the seaward edge of the peninsula from the Cliff House, near the outer entrance of the Golden Gate to Lake Merced, where it leads eventually into Highway 1 and meanders down the length of the state.

● ● ●

As the Second World War approached, the army built its largest San Francisco gun emplacement: Battery Richmond P. Davis. At just over five hundred feet in length, Battery Davis was roughly boomerang shaped with the curved ends closest to the Pacific Ocean. With a sixteen-inch gun placed in hardened concrete and steel casemates at each end, Battery Davis could match even the largest battleship guns in use at the time. The gun emplacements at each end were connected by a single corridor. After the Second World War, Fort Funston housed a Nike antiaircraft missile battery. Eventually, even that was abandoned, and the entire fort fell into decay. Fort Funston was ceded to the National Park Service. Along the San Francisco peninsula, the defensive bunkers decomposed. Great steel and concrete ruins were buried into the dunes along the beach. Battery Davis was no exception. If anything, given its size, Battery Davis had the eerie quality of a great land-locked shipwreck. During the day, the area was a leash-free dog run along the sand dunes and cliffs. Above the cliffs, it was the city's most popular location for hang gliding. But at night, dogs and citizens, hang gliders, park rangers, and police went home, and the gangs moved in. Typically, they would build a fire and sit and drink, laugh, and roughhouse. Tonight was different. Five jet-black SUVs deployed before Battery Davis, with one vehicle driving to the north gun emplacement and one vehicle driving to the south gun. Three parked before the breezeway in the center. Big men with big guns and vests bristling with gear tumbled out and the lounging gangs, like urban jackals, scattered into the darkness, some forgetting to rescue their beer and ale. Within five minutes, Battery Richmond P. Davis and its perimeter was secured for the first time in forty years.

An hour later, Rommel turned the Seville onto Fort Funston Road. The meandering blacktop lanes represented the remains of the artillery emplacements that had been part of the West Coast defenses during the two world wars. Rommel slowed the sedan to a crawl as he approached. This was the only reconnaissance he was going to be able to perform. Three SUVs were parked in the center. Their headlights were on. To the south, Rommel saw a boxy outline, probably another vehicle.

As he parked behind the SUVs, three large men advanced toward him. All wore tactical vests with MOLLE harnesses that allowed for the addition of modular units of gear, ammo clips, holsters strapped low on the thigh, comm gear, rations, canteens, whatever was desired. Two of the men were carrying FN P90 automatic rifles, the other an M4 carbine. Dressed all in black canvas or denim, the outfits gave the impression of uniforms, but as these men were apparently allowed to use and carry whatever gear suited them, the term uniform did not seem entirely appropriate to Rommel. Supplies that an entire unit have in common are supplies that an entire unit can share. This is particularly true for ammunition.

The leader of the three gestured with his automatic. "Hands." Rommel raised them. Two men provided security, keeping their weapons trained, while the lead searched Rommel. The Colt was in its holster. It was easy to find. Lead took it. The rest of the search produced no additional weapons.

Lead gestured toward the breezeway. "This way."

"I'm going to want that back," Rommel said, looking at his Colt.

"This way."

Rommel followed the lead; the other two men followed Rommel. As they passed into the breezeway, Rommel could see that one of the hatches had been pried open. Within, shop lights shone on the moist walls and floor of the corridor. Halfway down the corridor, another light shone from an open doorway.

Lead gestured. "In there."

Rommel entered the corridor; the team leader and the other two were now behind him. That meant that there were reinforcements at the end of the corridor in case he ran that way and certainly more men in the lit room that seemed to be waiting for him. Rommel moved deliberately. His best

• • •

option was to attack the armed men behind him. Not much of an option. Following would lead him to Carolyn. She was almost certainly here. She was almost certainly hurt.

Rommel reached the doorway. Construction lights blazed against the gray concrete walls and floor-to-ceiling graffiti. Water seeped from the top corners and oozed toward the bunker floor. The facility was an abandoned relic, and years of abuse did nothing to diminish that fact. Rommel scanned the room. Not a large room, maybe fourteen-by-twelve feet. Once, this had been the battery plotting room, the nerve center that received sightings from the spotters at each end, near the gun emplacements, and turned the info into targeting data. Two ancient metallic tables were joined to form a conference table of sorts. The steel chairs, also relics, ringed the table. The remaining space was taken up by half a dozen big men—big beefy men with short haircuts, black fatigues, and modular lightweight load-carrying equipment or MOLLE harnesses and gear. Even here, it seemed that each man had managed to carry a different weapon, M16, M4, FN P90, an SKS, an AK-47, and an AK-74. Each had attached an absurd number of ammo magazine pouches onto their MOLLE gear. One had even attached a holster for an M48 Tomahawk onto the chest strap of his harness. These were mercenaries. They carried the weapons *they* chose: various types, various calibers. In the absurd context of the undisciplined mind, they wore uniforms, but they were allowed to make each one different. In a firefight, most of them couldn't share ammunition with a comrade due to the variability of the weapons. Rommel decided the spectacle looked like Dress-up Day at a school for soldier wannabes. They were intimidating in their display of muscle and armor but to Rommel, they did not seem to be the sort of men to think things through. The MOLLE gear, for instance.

The purpose of modular lightweight load-carrying equipment carrying gear is to allow the fighting man to have everything he needs for combat operations readily available. The straps and vests were infinitely flexible in what they could hold: ammunition, rations, a seventy-two-ounce bladder for carrying water, additional weapons, and attachments. It could be a lot to wear and could easily weigh sixty pounds or more. *These men*, Rommel noted, *were loaded to the tits*. That was great for the field, not so great in a small room. In a small room, that much gear could restrain them, make them clumsy, and interfere with the movement of the men next to them. *Whenever you meet a man, be civil, but figure out how you are going to kill him*. Rommel would stay as close as he could to Tomahawk Boy. Rommel would also stay close to the door for a different reason.

Rommel looked for Carolyn. She sat, curled in upon herself, on a steel chair against the far wall between two thugs, as though she were their trophy. Blouse sleeve torn away, hair matted with blood, her nose splattered across her swollen face. She seemed to recognize him, but she did not appear to be glad to see him. Carolyn seemed to be waiting for death. At the far end of the table, also flanked by two over-equipped mercs, sat a youngish man with fine brown hair and delicate features. He wore a dark wool suit with a lavender silk tie against a brilliantly white linen shirt. This man alone seemed immaculate sitting there in this dark, seeping, graffiti-tagged wreck of a bunker. Unlike Carolyn, the man seemed glad to see Rommel. He also seemed completely at ease.

"Mr. Rommel, come join me."

Rommel, his back to the now closed and secured steel door, sat down. "Here's good for me. Why don't you come over here?"

"Please don't be stubborn. This isn't really as bad as it looks for you and Mrs. Kast."

"Fine. Bring your ass over here and sit next to me." Rommel gestured at a chair occupied by one of the six mercenaries. "Get up, big boy, and let your boss have a seat by me."

The man glowered at Rommel, looked at his boss, and stood. The delicate man in the tailored suit got up, made his way to the other end of the table, and sat down on

Rommel's left. To Rommel's right sat the great blonde man who had attached the tomahawk and sheath to his MOLLE harness. The muscular, blonde man needed only to pull the war ax down from its holster-sheath and wreak havoc.

"Mr. Rommel, my name is Dan Curtis. I work for Mr. Cheney as I'm sure you've surmised. Mr. Cheney is concerned about you, but he wants you to have the chance to make good decisions, decisions that will be in the best interest of those who are close to you. Decisions that will not cause Mr. Cheney unanticipated inconvenience."

"Here's where we are, Mr. Rommel. After years of being unreasonable, the annoying Mr. Gilhooley has to die. Mr. Gilhooley doesn't really know anything, can't prove anything, and cannot really threaten our operations. But he is loud, offensive, and irritating. After years of trying to reason with him, a decision has been taken. Mr. Gilhooley is going to die. He's been asking for it, and, now, he's going to get it. When Gilhooley dies, Mr. Cheney wants that death to be the end of the matter. He wants you to know that this death is necessary just for the sake of peace and quiet. Mr. Cheney wants to give you the opportunity to act in your best interests, do nothing, and make no trouble afterward. That's all you have to do, nothing. Live your life. Mind your own business, and you and everyone you know will be allowed to live in peace."

"Allowed," Rommel said.

"I think allowed is a fair way to put it. If it weren't for our tolerance and goodwill, Mrs. Kast could be dead right now. Instead, despite her uncalled-for resistance, Mrs. Kast can get what's left of her nose fixed and live to see her daughter grow up."

Rommel bristled ever so slightly.

"I've hit a nerve. Aubrey. Sweet child. Right now, her world makes sense. Right now, she's safe. But make no mistake. Black Horizon makes war on a level you cannot imagine. We can make war an incredibly intimate experience. I know that you were a warrior,"

"American fighting man."

"Not a true warrior? That is a shame, because all of these men and all the operatives that Black Horizon employs are true warriors. They understand and have practiced war on a level too primitive for you to understand. War on the tribal level using techniques we have learned and practiced in Africa. They worked in Africa. They worked in Iraq. They worked in Afghanistan. They even worked in New Orleans during Katrina. If pushed to it, we can make retribution incredibly personal."

Rommel studied Curtis, watching his eyes.

"As I mentioned, Africa really is the key to this. It is the oldest continent, seat of Man's genesis. To understand us, you have to understand how factions wage war in Africa. There are no civilians in those conflicts."

"That's nothing new," Rommel said.

"Yes, but the sheer terror of it is like nothing you can understand. Everything is a weapon. Case in point, on one occasion, rebel soldiers attacked and occupied a government-aligned village. As the carnage died down, the mayor was dragged into the center of the village and raped repeatedly. The mayor was a man. Those rebels made an example of him by raping him relentlessly over a period of four hours. As the saying goes, he begged for death. Most people can't imagine that being done to a man as an act of war. Certainly, that would be a horrific thing to do to a woman."

Curtis looked into Rommel's gray eyes and spoke softly, in low moderated tones. Rommel could sense the mercenaries in the room leaning forward, listening. "Can you imagine such a terrible thing being done to a child? To an innocent, auburn-haired little girl?"

The room had been deathly still as the mercenaries strained to hear one of the top officers in their corporation speak. The effect was almost hypnotic. Perhaps that was why they hesitated in that crucial millisecond as Matt Rommel took Dan Curtis by the head and chin, snapping his neck and leaving his head to collide lifelessly onto the table. In that next instant, Rommel had seized the handle of the blonde's tomahawk, yanked it free, and planted the blade into the big man's skull.

The bunkered room exploded in pandemonium as half a dozen large men simultaneously pushed and struggled to stand in a room packed with steel chairs and tables. They tore at their harnesses, trying to break loose their firearms as Rommel flung blood and hair and bone off the end of the M48 Tomahawk claiming one victim after another. They struggled to stand, struggled with their weapons, and, in a panic, scrambled madly over each other as they saw their comrades murdered before their eyes, saw a raging Matt Rommel trampling over the bodies of the armed, dying men who had stood next to the survivors only an instant before. One mercenary's Glock cleared its holster just as Rommel struck the war ax down against and through the forearm, rending cloth and flesh and bone. The Glock clattered against the table and one of the chairs as it tumbled uselessly to the floor.

ووو

Carolyn dived under the table as the mad scramble began. She could see thick, black, denim-clad legs push against each other, surging in one direction for a few seconds only to change direction and try to scramble the opposite way. The din was incredible. They roared. They cursed over the screams of other men. Some of them seemed to collapse toward the floor, but they could not fall because there was no room. Some of them sagged. Some of them slumped. The room was filled with the smell of fresh cut copper. Blood. She could see blood dripping down legs and arms, puddling in some places on the concrete floor. But the smell was so strong. The room must be awash in blood. At any moment, Carolyn knew that these men would flip the steel table she was hiding under and hack her to bits. A moment later, there was a pause in the bedlam, a heartbeat of silence. She heard a single panicked voice roar, "I surrender!" followed by a strangled scream, then nothing. Silence. Carolyn waited. She heard nothing. After a moment, Carolyn heard a voice. It seemed familiar, as if someone she had known in life had met her in hell and struck up a conversation.

"We should go."

Carolyn ventured a peek above the table. Rommel among the gore. On the tables, over some of the chairs, and along the floor lay draped a collection of men and parts of men. On the furniture, across the walls, everywhere, the splash of dark blood streaked its accents. She could smell it baking on the hot work lights.

Carolyn felt stupid with terror. No scream would come. She could not will her body to try to flee in panic. She could only look at this man she thought she knew.

◈◈

Rommel took inventory, examining the bodies and equipment. He selected a short black assault rifle, an FN P90, some flashbang grenades, and two long magazines. Rommel still clutched the tomahawk in his left hand. He looked at Carolyn, the stare of a butcher standing in his shop.

"Too much gear," Rommel said, quietly as if he were criticizing a construction crew from the comfort of the sidewalk. "Yer in the field, bring yer gear. In a crowded room like this, you have your weapon at hand so you can use it immediately," he said. "And this goofball." Rommel shook the tomahawk. "He put this weapon right within my reach, as if I would be too afraid to touch it. I hope the rest of them are just that stupid."

"The rest of them?"

"You heard the guy in the suit. Nobody hurts Aubrey. Nobody who talks, or thinks like that, gets to live. We have to assume that they all think that way. That means they all die. Tonight. Right now." Rommel reached for the steel door. "There are men at each end of this facility. We need to go down the corridor to the north. There's one vehicle and one or two men at or near the north gun emplacement. You come with me."

Carolyn demurred. "I want to leave," she managed weakly.

"I want to live in peace," Rommel responded. "But it's not happening tonight. Come with me. I'll get you out of this alive. You and your daughter get to live in peace. Everybody else dies." Rommel eased the steel door open, looking cautiously, north and then south.

"The door," Carolyn said. "You insisted on sitting by the door."

"The only way out," he said. "They figured their problem would be keeping me confined, but when I got here, after I saw what they did to you, I didn't know if I was going to let any of them leave." Rommel stared at her, brushed her cheek and blood-matted hair gently. "Then they told me what I needed to know."

"What did they tell you?"

"They told me that dead men don't hurt children. Come along." They moved swiftly, quietly toward the northern end of the corridor. Rommel surveyed the steel door. It was welded shut. Rommel and Carolyn hurried back toward the breezeway entrance. Rommel pulled the charging handle on the FN P90. Rommel leaned down toward Carolyn, his forehead touching hers.

"This is going to go quickly. There are at least two men out there. First, the flashbangs, and then, if I can, I'll do it without gunfire. After that, I have to hustle to the south and then the north emplacements from the ocean side. As soon as I move, you go out the door after me. Hide in the brush on the hill by the beach. If I don't come for you in ten minutes, burrow in and wait another thirty minutes. No one is going to stick around looking for you. Here are the keys to the Caddy." Rommel pushed the keys into her hand. "Don't worry, I'll finish this and be back for you in no time."

Rommel eased the door, pulled the pin, and rolled out the first grenade. He had no idea where they might be. Seconds later, a brilliant light streamed through the opening, and a concussive boom rattled the door. Rommel sprinted out, rifle up. They were both near the entranceway near the SUVs. Rommel charged forward as quickly as he could. He was too slow to take them with the tomahawk. He trained the FN P90 on the man who had managed the best response. Rommel assumed body armor and let out a short burst that shattered the man's skull. Rommel directed a longer burst at the second man who fell to the ground. Rommel struck the man twice in the forehead with the tomahawk and sprinted south into the darkness.

✦✦✦

Carolyn ran toward the beach and hid along the hillside. She heard two short bursts of gunfire. She waited. She heard nothing. She had no idea how much time had passed. *Was that it? Was Rommel even alive?* In the distance, she heard an engine start. *Who was that?* Carolyn scrambled up the sandy bank, clutching at the tall wild grass, trying to keep her balance. She reached the breezeway and saw two men lying dead, their faces obliterated. They didn't seem like Rommel. From the north, a black SUV spun its wheels in the dirt as it roared toward the access road. Approaching at a run from the south, Carolyn saw a single figure running toward the SUV, firing long bursts into the engine grille and front tires. The tires blew, and the whole SUV seemed to hunker down as it dug through the dirt on flat rims. The running man paused, hunched momentarily over his gun, and came up firing into the grille again. In a moment, the assailant was by the passenger side of the SUV firing into the window. The dark figure flailed at the window with a hatchet or an ax, pulling savagely against the broken glass as he yanked the door open, fired into the vehicle, reached in and dragged two bodies out onto the sand and dirt. Immediately, the attacker used the tomahawk, raining down savage blows onto the two men. The two figures ceased to move. The dark assailant continued to strike and then stopped. Carolyn looked across the darkness. The figure looked up, faced her, and began to walk toward her. Carolyn felt no fear. She knew this man.

Matt Rommel held his hand out. Carolyn took his hand in hers. "That's nice," Rommel said, "but I need the car keys. It's time to go."

Rommel turned the Cadillac north onto The Great Highway. He dug his cell phone from his jacket, trying to manage the keypad.

Carolyn heard herself saying, "You shouldn't do that."

Rommel paused. "You're right. It's dangerous and stupid." Rommel pulled to the curb, put the car in park, and then dialed the phone. "Diego, how is the bar tonight? Good. You remember Carolyn? That's her. I need you to get someone else to close up tonight. Carolyn needs someone to drive her home to Berkeley. On the way, she's going to want to make a stop at an emergency room for treatment."

"No," Carolyn said. "No emergency room."

❧❧

Rommel pulled up to the front of Vince's Bar to find that a parking space had been cleared for him, the space being held in reserve by two of the bar's burly regulars. Rommel climbed out of the Seville, moved swiftly to Carolyn's side, and opened the door for her.

"You should go inside," one of the regulars said. "Before the cops come by."

"You guys should have gone around the back," the other patron observed. Only then did Rommel realize that, even in dark clothes, it was obvious that he was covered in blood, hair, and bits of organic material. His massive hands were smeared a rusty brown; his face and hair were bloodied as well. Worse, he was clutching the M48 Tomahawk. Rommel held onto Carolyn's upper arm and guided her, as quickly as he dared, into the bar. As soon as he and Carolyn entered the bar, two other customers locked and guarded the red leather padded doors.

The place was nearly packed. Business had picked up since the days of the Gay Avenger. Vince's had become a clubhouse for stocky working men who had somehow regained the illusion of youth and adventure. In this clubhouse, the strong protected the weak, and every regular was, in his own mind, a knight errant. Diego came from behind the bar and met them.

• • •

Rommel spoke, "Are you ready? Carolyn needs to go to Berkeley and collect her daughter, and then she needs to leave the area."

Carolyn looked at Rommel but did not speak. Leaving town seemed like a good idea.

"We're an hour or so ahead of them," Rommel said. "Soon, Black Horizon is going to know that something is wrong. They'll send someone to Fort Funston to check. After that, they will mobilize, and they will start to gain the advantage that goes with being a large organization." Rommel looked at Carolyn. "Get cash. Borrow Denni's credit card. Leave the state. Take Aubrey to Orlando to one of the big resorts. They have good security for their guests." Rommel turned to the denizens of the bar. "I need three guys. Who wants to go to Disney World for a week?"

They all stood.

"No drinking for the week. You have to stay sober," Rommel said.

Half of them sat back down.

Rommel picked three big men who looked like family men. "You three share a room next to her and her daughter. Where they go, one or two of you guys go. The other one sleeps. Diego will pay for your tickets and front you the cash. Three hundred a day in cash to make up for work lost. Fair?"

The three new uncle-guardians nodded. Diego stared at Rommel in appreciation of this ad hoc largesse.

"Don't get jumpy, you guys," Rommel said. "Nothing is going to happen. They won't even be looking for her. They are going to have other things to worry about. I promise."

Rommel turned toward Diego. "She doesn't want to go to the emergency room for the nose."

"Well," Diego said, "she has a few days before the bones set. She can go to a clinic there." Diego inspected Carolyn's face with a practiced eye. "In the meantime, we can set the nose here."

• • •

"You can do that?" Carolyn asked.

Diego smiled. "This is the Mission. A broken nose is nothing." Diego looked toward the back and called out, "*Guajolotes!* Clear the pool table. Get out of the way!" Diego, Rommel and Carolyn walked to the pool table. "Up you go," Diego said. "Cesar, get the kit." Another man walked over with a cigar box, a bottle of tequila, and a water glass. Lying on the pool table, Carolyn looked at the cigar box, then she looked at Diego with questioning eyes.

"Don't worry," Diego said. "You're in good hands."

Diego opened the box and removed two slender ballpoint pens. He filled the glass with tequila and set the pens, points up, into the glass. He then removed a roll of white surgical tape.

After drying the pens, Diego instructed Carolyn to remain still. Tenderly, he felt around the shattered nasal bones, getting a sense of the number of pieces he was working with. Diego took the first pen and began, slowly and gently, to guide the pen into her nostril. He did the same with the other pen and nostril.

"Breathe through your mouth," he said. It was an unnecessary instruction.

Diego worked the pens up the nostrils and stopped. With his fingertips, he began to gently work the bones into position around the nasal passages he had shaped with the pens. When he was satisfied that things were generally in order, Diego taped the nostrils in place. Diego gently removed the bloody pens and threw them back into the box along with the tape, closed the lid, took the drinking glass of tequila, and swallowed the contents in four large gulps.

Rommel studied Carolyn's face. "Nice work."

"Thanks," Diego said. "You are paying the traveling and incidental costs for those three. After a couple of days, don't be surprised if they start knocking back the *cerveza*."

"That's not bad news," Diego said to Carolyn. "They're good, decent men, and, with a few drinks in them, they would die for you." Carolyn eased herself off the table, touched Diego's cheek and gently kissed it. The bar roared. This was adventure.

Rommel spoke to Carolyn, "Can you do this for me?"

She nodded.

"Thanks. I'll talk to you in a day or two."

৵৽

Rommel walked to the back of the bar and climbed the stairway. With a single fist, he beat at the little apartments' back door.

"Gunny, you awake?"

"I am now."

"You asked me for something. You still want it?"

"Damn right."

"You told me that you followed some of these people around. Do you remember where they went?"

"They drove by your place a couple of times. They stopped at their corporate offices, Union Square, and the Embarcadero. Except for the occasional chow break, those were the only places they went."

"Union Square?"

"Yes, sir."

"What did they do at Union Square?"

"Nothing. Best case, basic reconnoiter. They walked the square, looked at poles, scaffolds, and structures. Then they left."

"What about the Embarcadero?"

"They have people and equipment at Pier 29. Could be some kind of a staging area. Could be a place for the gorillas to sit, to keep them away from the suits in the corporate offices."

"That's where we go. Tomorrow we find Cheney and settle up. When this is over, it's prison or the grave. You all right with that?"

• • •

191

"What happened?" Gunny asked.

"Shit-talkers or killers, which are we tonight, Gunny?" Gilhooley smiled. "Gear up."

24

Pier 29

The direct route would have been Mission to Market to the Embarcadero, but Rommel saw no point in pushing luck that was probably already gone. Rommel drove up Telegraph Hill and parked. Better than a century ago, San Francisco's preeminent fire department groupie, Lillian Hitchcock Coit bequeathed funds to build a tower. The tower was to resemble a fire nozzle. If there was one thing that Lillian liked, it was a good fire. From the parking lot beneath that tower, high above the Embarcadero, Rommel and Gunny squatted in the tree line and studied the piers. Pier 29 was nearly directly below them.

Long before airports, the Embarcadero was the transit point for travelers and the loading and unloading point for the city's commerce. If the San Francisco peninsula could be thought of as a thumb, the Embarcadero was the tip of the thumbnail, jutting into the bay. Its piers were large warehouses that sat atop the pier and alongside the moored cargo ships. In a world of containerized cargo, the piers of the Embarcadero were the functionally obsolescent monuments to the age of the longshoreman. These massive warehouse-piers lined the outer edge of the wide avenue known as the Embarcadero. Today, the piers are largely ignored by tourists as they make their way to Fisherman's Wharf and Ghirardelli Square.

"Opposition," Rommel said.

"Unknown," Gunny replied. Rommel looked at Gunny. "I followed them a few times. The people I followed went here, or Union Square, or their corporate offices. When did this location become a target?"

"Tonight."

"Any reason?" Gunny asked.

"You and Aubrey getting along?"

"Sure. What a great kid."

"What would you do to keep her safe?"

"For starters, turn that warehouse into a graveyard," Gunny said, his voice quiet and even.

"So, what do you know about the opposition?"

"I never saw more than four targets. No guard set. No perimeter established."

"Electronics?"

"Unknown," Gunny said. "We can stage from the foot of Sansome and cross the Embarcadero. Front door's too public. We defeat the side gate, walk to the end of the pier, and enter the building from the side. Good?"

Rommel nodded. "Reasonable plan. But if we go in from the back, some of them may go out the front door. Since none of them are leaving, we go in the front door."

"None of them leave?"

"You see a nun or a fat old security guard, let them go. Nobody else."

᯽

Rommel parked the old Cadillac curbside at the foot of Sansome Street. The Embarcadero was a short block away. Across the Embarcadero, the great concrete façade of Pier 29 abutted the six-lane avenue. The bluff face of the pier had two front entrances: a huge retracting steel door, fifty feet tall and wide enough for two big rigs to pass each other in opposite directions, and to the right of that, a traditional steel door with a door knob and two steel hinges. Rommel spoke.

"Weapon?"

"Yes, please," Gunny said.

Rommel grimaced. "What kind? Courtesy of Black Horizon, we have a 7.62 AK-47, a 5.56 M4, a P90 with three hundred rounds of 5.7 by 28mm, and a Saiga semiauto shotgun with quadrangle shot."

"Five point seven is a little light for me. I'll take the AK," Gunny said. Rommel handed him the wood and stamped-metal rifle and a MOLLE harness fitted with magazine pouches.

"Hello, Pancho Villa," Gunny said. "Were they all decked out like this?"

"Pretty much."

"Slowed 'em down, did it?"

"Enough," Rommel said. "I'll take the P90 and six fifty-round cartridges, more than a full combat load and less total weight. Also, the Saiga comes with me."

"For the door hinges," Gunny said, to no one.

It was nearly three thirty in the morning as the two men moved through the wet morning chill, quickly across the six lanes of the Embarcadero. Traffic was practically nonexistent. This was as quiet as the city gets. Rommel stood by the smaller door and trained the Saiga on the lower of the door hinges.

At that moment, a great electric motor kicked into life, and the massive rolling steel door rumbled upward. Rommel and Gunny pressed their backs against the pier's façade and waited. A moment later, the diesel of a tractor-trailer roared to life and then stuttered briefly as the big rig shifted into first gear.

• • •

Rommel moved quickly in front of the truck, looking up past the massive truck grille, through the windshield, and into the cab. Rommel saw the man in black fatigues, saw the short haircut. Good enough. Rommel leveled the Saiga. The shotgun bucked and roared three times in quick succession. Sharp cubes of steel spewed from the barrel and tore through the big truck's radiator and into the engine itself. The great truck choked to a halt. Rommel raised the barrel. The fourth round tore through the windshield and into the cab, exploding into a pink mist that covered the inside of the remaining glass.

The steel door started rolling downward but jammed on the top of the truck. Rommel ran forward along the right side of the rig, a long flatbed with four large crates strapped to the truck bed. Rommel reasoned that the first targets might not know they were in a firefight. Why should they? Black Horizon targets were usually unarmed civilians. The first targets might still be in the problem-solving mode: trying to figure out what had gone wrong. They would be relatively close. Rommel kept the shotgun trained ahead of him. A set of black fatigues walked out from behind a packing crate. The Saiga roared; the metal cubes spattered the target and tore through the packing crate. Rommel heard men calling out. He heard the panicked cascade of boot steps forming a skirmish line. The warehouse erupted with automatic-weapons fire and Rommel and Gunny tried to hunker down behind the rear trailer wheels.

"They catch on pretty quick," Rommel said.

Gunny hunched as close to the tire and wheel as he could. "Yeah, who knew that a highly trained and heavily armed mercenary army would put up a goddamn fight." Gunny paused, catching his breath and added, "Sir."

Concrete and wood splinters filled the air. In a few seconds, Gunny and Rommel were peppered with bits of shrapnel. Rommel reached the Saiga around the outside rubber tire, tilted the barrel slightly upward, and released five quick rounds, unaimed, into the warehouse. The storm of automatic-weapons fire paused for an instant and resumed with diminished intensity.

"They'll be flanking us any minute," Gunny said. "We need to do it first. I'll fire; you move to your right." Rommel nodded. Gunny set the select switch on the AK to auto and let out a burst. Rommel sprinted for the nearest crates only to meet three riflemen coming around the other side of the containers. Rommel lowered the P90 and laid down a sustained burst. The men fell, but behind them a larger group advanced—every gun blazing. *Textbook fire suppression,* Rommel thought. Under the heavy fire, the advanced position became unsustainable. Rommel fled back to the trailer under a hail of weapons fire.

"What are you doing back here?" Gunny roared.

"It seemed like a good idea, what's with all the god-damn gunfire," Rommel said.

"Shit, what part of fire and maneuver do you not understand?"

"The part where half a dozen heavily armed assholes kill me," Rommel roared back.

From the opposite side of the trailer, rounds began to break wood and packing from the crates that had been loaded and strapped onto the flatbed. From across the warehouse a voice boomed out, "Not the cargo! For Chrissakes, don't shoot at the cargo. I want suppressive fire, low and along the floor and wheels."

Rommel and Gunny looked at each other. "Up on the flatbed and behind the crates?" Rommel said.

"Sounds good," Gunny said, reaching up, trying to pull himself up. Rommel lowered his weapon, grabbed the old man's belt, and hurled him up behind a crate. Then he leveled bursts of fire into the warehouse at places Rommel figured he would be if he were playing their hand. There was a single cry from the far side. Gunny spent thirty rounds of automatic fire as Rommel climbed behind a different crate. Gunny was looking at him. "You're bleeding, Major."

"Bad?"

Gunny paused. "Not when you consider that in another minute, we'll both be dead," he roared.

Rommel looked at the crate, partially opened by gunfire. He put his big fingers in a crevice and ripped. The panel gave way. Rommel was staring at the back of the unit. He read the nomenclature printed on a control box. He called out to Gunny. "Metal Storm. That mean anything to you?"

Through the haze of sawdust and cordite, Gunny smiled. "Can you pull the backs off these other crates?"

"Can you keep their heads down?" Rommel roared back.

Gunny laid the remaining loaded magazines in a line. "OK, GO," the old man yelled as he leveled the Kalashnikov at one section, emptied the magazine, dropped the old magazine, slapped home a new one, and peppered another section.

Rommel moved behind the next crate, tearing at the wood. His fingers bled. He moved to the next crate and pulled the back away. Now, both hands bled. Rommel called back to the old man, "Now what?"

"Cabling. You are looking for cable and a separate control box."

"Center crate," Rommel yelled.

Gunny ducked behind the center crate, tucked his head inside, and waved a brownish-gray plug at Rommel. Rommel fired a burst and scuttled over to Gunny.

"Take this. Bottom of the next unit. There's an outlet. Plug this into it. Here," Gunny said. "While you're at it, take this one to the next crate over. After that, don't come back. Keep your head down and stay behind that end crate. If it pushes you off the truck, try not to break your neck."

"If what pushes me off the truck?"

"Go, Go, Go." Gunny roared.

Rommel clutched at the two plugs and ran to the next crate. He looked at the back of the unit and saw a plastic hatch. He picked at it, but couldn't get a grip with his bloody hands. Rommel reached behind his back and gripped the handle of his Ka-Bar, popped the snap on the sheath, and drew the utility knife. Digging and twisting with the tip of the blade, the plastic hatch popped free. Rommel grabbed one of the plugs in his hand, shoving it at the opening without success. The receptacle would only receive the plug if the geometry was right. Rommel took a breath and approached the hatch with the plug with forced deliberation. The plug lined up and began to enter the housing. Rommel felt the prongs line in and pushed smoothly. The plug seated. One more cord in hand, Rommel scooted to the next crate, stabbed at the crack running along the crate and ripped the wooden side back. This time the hatch opened and the plug seated easily. Rommel looked back to signal Gunny, but the old man was already watching him, his reptilian hand on a bank of toggle switches.

The large crates erupted, forcing splintered wood spewing from the other side as a metallic scream, like a massive high-speed drill, filled the pier warehouse with smoking cordite. The crates bucked and jumped back. Rommel's crate was a screaming red-hot mass of wood, plastic, and steel. The unit shot back by half a foot, shoving him off the edge of the flatbed. Rommel tried to jump free. Instead, he fell hard upon the timber flooring. A single thought filled Rommel's mind: The jumping, whining, red-hot smoking crate might fall from the flatbed onto him. Rommel rolled left, hesitated, and then rolled right to use the cover of the rear wheels. Rommel's hands followed the strap of the P90 around his neck. The strap led his hands to the weapon. Rommel crouched, popped up behind the flatbed, and fired. He scanned through the smoke for targets.

The great crates fell silent. Rommel heard nothing but the sound of his own firing. He paused, listened. The warehouse was still. Had he lost his hearing? Rommel coughed. He could hear that cough well enough, so his hearing was not completely compromised. Rommel looked up at Gunny. Gunny remained crouched behind his crate but seemed slightly relaxed.

Gunny scanned the warehouse. "Opposing forces appear to have succumbed to suppressive fire, sir. No movement."

Rommel stood, still crouched, and moved toward Gunny's position. Cautiously, he used the forward wheels to cover his legs and hips. "Just what was that, Gunny?"

"Metal Storm, sir. High-tech terrain denial technology. Each unit is honeycombed with stainless-steel tubes. Each tube contains dozens of individual rounds. Each unit contains thousands of tubes. The firing mechanism is electronic, allowing the operator to set the rate of fire from a hundred rounds per minute up to a rate of a million rounds per minute."

"And you know this how?" Rommel said.

"Discovery Channel."

"And the Discovery Channel taught you to configure and operate this unit?"

"No, sir. Forty-eight years of hard service taught me to adapt, improvise, and overcome. The major *is* aware that master gunnery sergeant is not an honorary title?"

Rommel surveyed the carnage. "The major is a hell of a lot more aware now." Rommel sniffed. Smoke still filled the warehouse, but the nature of that smoke had changed. The tang of cordite was joined by the smell of wood and dust and plastic conduit. Rommel trained the P90 in front of him and began to walk through the enemy positions. All dead.

"Sir, the warehouse is on fire."

"Just checking for survivors."

"Can't kill them twice, sir. Might be time to exfiltrate."

"None of them get out alive," Rommel called out, but by then, Gunny was at his side.

Gunny grabbed and held Rommel's arm. After a lifetime of working with officers, nothing had changed. You had to get them to the scene of battle. You had to keep them alive. And, when it was over, sometimes you had to remind them that it was time to leave. "They're as dead as they're going to get, sir. Time to go. When Cheney gets to the office tomorrow, he is not going to know what hit him. We have time to go home, pick out the splinters, clean up, and maybe catch an hour's sleep. Then we settle up with Cheney."

• • •

Rommel continued to look around. Nothing moved, but the firelight began to flicker. Pier 29 was beginning to burn in earnest. The fire department would arrive any moment. "Fine. We go."

They crossed Embarcadero and climbed into the Cadillac.

"Major?" Gunny said.

"Yes?"

"That cargo was leaving the pier via truck. They were not exporting that weapon. They were going to deploy it."

"And you know that how?" Rommel asked.

"That's a developmental weapon. You can't buy it, no company can. That means it was almost certainly stolen and hidden. It was probably hidden at MCLB Barstow."

"Barstow is a big base, but you can't just hide something like that. Someone is going to notice."

"Not if you've got a man on the inside. Feith, for instance. Do you know how inventory is usually taken, sir?" Gunny said.

"Sure, you print a list and check everything against the list."

"That's right, sir. If something is stolen, the corps knows it quick. The list is thousands of items long—it gets split up between a dozen people, and they go around checking off the listed inventory. But, if there were a few extra boxes, no one would notice that. Everyone's focused on finding all the items listed, not on an item present but not on the list."

"You're probably right, Gunny."

"Forty-eight years of service, you can goddamn bet on it…sir."

Gunny looked out the window, saying nothing as the car pulled from the curb.

"Big protest in Union Square today," Gunny ventured.

"Yeah."

"So, maybe we did something good."

"If we live, when we go to prison, maybe they'll put us in the cell block of honor."

"Yer shittin' me. Do they have that?"

"Jesus."

"Major?"

"Yes."

"Feith wasn't in there."

"I didn't see him."

"And earlier tonight?"

"I didn't see him at the gun battery."

"You're sure?" Gunny asked.

"I was up close and personal with each and every person there. If Feith had been there, I would have noticed," Rommel said.

"Well, Feith is one of Cheney's butt-boys. If Cheney is doing something important, then he's given a piece of it to Feith."

"And?" Rommel said.

"If Feith just had this thing at Union Square, then he would have been here to make sure everything went right."

"Well, he wasn't here, and he wasn't at Battery Davis, and he wasn't with the asshole who shot up my house. Maybe he just had the night off."

Gunny looked out the window. "Maybe."

25

Gunfight at Annie's Bungalow

$\mathcal{A}$nderson sat in the back of the black Yukon and studied the back of Darren Feith's head. There were four of them, none of them speaking. They had worked forty straight days on this op, moving materiel from Barstow, one small lot at a time to avoid suspicion. They had established a depot, damn near in the middle of Fisherman's Wharf, and they had reconnoitered the delivery site on Union Square. They had run local threat analysis and only come up with one crazy old man and another retiree who all but lived at a museum. As far as Anderson could tell, there was no opposition. Whatever it was, this operation was supposed to be important, history in the making. Whatever it was, it should have been a cakewalk. After forty straight days, they'd had a single day off, time to sleep in and do laundry, maybe watch a little tube. And in that single day, the whole world exploded.

Anderson didn't know what was going on. As he studied the back of Feith's head, he didn't think Feith knew, either. Black Horizon people were dead. Had he been on duty instead of lying on his bed watching television, he could

• • •

have been one of them. The mission had cratered. Feith's call had been brief and clear. They were under attack. Gear up with full combat load under concealment and wait in front of the hotel for a ride.

So, this was some kind of counteroffensive. That made sense. What didn't make sense was the target.

The black SUV rolled smoothly to the curb in the cool, breathless Sunday morning that had wrapped itself around the Sausalito bungalow. No signs of movement in the fire station across the street. Only the mildest of breezes and distant birdsong, the stillness was nearly complete. The four men approached the house with unhurried deliberation—three to the front door while the fourth moved toward the side gate leading to the backyard. It would be a walk-through. The target would soon be dead, and they would be gone before the coffee shops saw their first customers.

As the lead man, Anderson moved to the front door. Using two slender probes, he defeated the door lock easily. His assignment was the bag lady; the purpose of this assignment eluded him. *For the first time since he had come to work for Black Horizon, they were the one's taking casualties, so somehow, her death was necessary.* The thought registered without disturbing him. He resolved to find her swiftly and kill her mercifully, if possible, without waking her. Passing through the front door, he reached for and drew the slender two-edged dagger that would quickly and quietly end her days. Feith, the team leader, was last through the door, closing it gently behind him. The tiny living room was empty. There was a simple coffee table facing the door, and behind that a couch. Behind the couch, an archway with the kitchen just beyond, the bedrooms and shared bath down a short hallway to the side. The entry team moved silently around the couch, looking toward the short hallway.

A metallic click punctuated the silence. The three men froze, ears straining. Another metallic click followed. From the kitchen, a cold, gravelly voice.

"Three of you, plus guns. What would you people have done if there had been *two* bag ladies?" Gunny stepped into the archway. The two .45-caliber MEU(SOC)s commanding the room, trained on the men at eye level. Behind him, light from the backyard streamed in through the kitchen window.

"Hands where I can see them, ladies." Gunny smiled, a genuinely happy man because Gunny knew when the gunfight was going to begin. Now, was a good time. His hands independently targeted Feith's two men, firing simultaneously. They collapsed to the floor.

Gunny looked at Feith. "Hello, dickhead." He smiled. "What's inside the coat? Slowly, now."

Feith slowly opened the black duster to reveal a combat harness on which were suspended all the grenades you would need to kill a harmless old woman.

Gunny's eyes sparkled. "Yer shittin' me." Gunny observed. *Two in the chest for this clown and then out the back*, he thought.

Gunny stumbled forward and then heard two pops. He could see the blood coming from his shirt as the force pushed him forward half a step. An old rule, he mused, *if your attack is going really well, look behind you*. Rommel's rules. Someone was in the back with a .223. If the entry team had waited for the man at the rear of the house to set up, they wouldn't have lost two men. Morons. Hessians. Better off dead. All Gunny had to do was shoot Feith. It would still be a good day, even with the dying and all. Shoot Feith, but his arms weren't listening. His knees gave way. Gunny fell, looking up at the beige ceiling. *Stucco, very 1940s*, Gunny mused.

Feith knelt over him, crowding out Gunny's view of the ceiling. "Game over, old man. How do you like those sucking chest wounds? Nothing to say, smart-ass? No shit about the Hittites?" Feith shook the old man and pulled him close. Feith hated the old man. This was a death worth savoring. "Come on tough guy, tell me something smart." He shook the dying man again.

Gunny clutched a bloody hand on Feith's black duster, pulling himself close. Smiling at Feith with a mouth full of blood, Gunny looked into Feith's eyes. "Once the pin is removed," Gunny coughed, "Mr. Grenade is no longer our friend." Gunny's trembling fist held the grenade pin before Feith's face just as Feith heard the spoon clatter across the floor.

Feith jumped to his feet, madly brushing at his weapon's harness. The grenade fell away into an interior pocket of his duster. Feith fell backward over the couch and detonated.

26

Mind over Matter

It had been a fitful hour's sleep. It would have to be enough. Rommel showered and dressed—gray slacks, charcoal turtleneck, and a dark wool blazer with red silk lining. Rommel paused, took off the jacket and reached back into the closet for the shoulder holster. There was an antique Colt 1911 on one side of the holster and two clips of .45-caliber, 230-grain ball ammo in the pouch on the other side. "They all fall to hardball," Rommel said, to no one. It was a slogan that was nearly as old as the weapon itself. Rommel walked down the stairs. Chesty followed. He took a moment to sit at the bottom of the staircase. Chesty nuzzled against him. Rommel held her square head in his big hands and caressed her.

"You are a sweet baby. I want you to know that I love you very much. As God is my judge, I intended to be here with you and to care for you for the remainder of your days. That's not going to happen. I have to protect Aubrey and her mother. To do that, I have to let everything else go. I know you would do the same because you are a brave girl. Diego's coming by if things don't work out. He is a good man, and he knows how to care for a good dog like you. You be a good girl and care for his home and his family just like you have here." Rommel kissed her gently and Chesty, studying the big man's face with her single burning eye, licked him once, tenderly. "If I had learned to talk to people the same way, maybe things would have been different," Rommel said.

Rommel stood up and walked into the kitchen, expecting to see Gunny sitting at the counter. No Gunny. Rommel made a quick circuit of the kitchen. On the counter, Rommel saw a Ka-Bar, the Marine Corps utility knife in a weathered leather sheath. The Ka-Bar rested on top of a scrap of paper. He moved the knife and picked up the note. The scrawl was scarcely legible. Rommel read.

If there's one thing I know, it's officers. I have worked with them for nearly fifty years. I know which ones are for real and which ones live for chickenshit. I know which ones will fold under pressure and which ones are the kind you'd be proud to have your kids serve with.

The way I figure it, there's only one place Cheney can hurt you. Hurting people is all that prick knows or cares about. I'm going to take care of that detail. I will see you when I get back.

No matter what else happens, make sure Cheney gets his.

Rommel set the note down. Only then did he understand. He knew where Gunny was going. He should have thought of it himself, but, even knowing what he now knew, it just didn't make sense. It wasn't an option that a rational person would consider. The doorbell chimed. Chesty gave a single deep bark. Both Rommel and Chesty walked to the door. Rommel held the dog's collar and opened the door cautiously.

"Lieutenant."

Lieutenant Carmichael stood, badge in hand. Rommel noticed that, this time, her right hand was resting on her service weapon. "This time, we are going to talk. Open the door."

Rommel opened the door and stood back, still holding Chesty by the collar. Lieutenant Carmichael eyed the dog.

"Does that dog bite?" she asked.

"That's up to her, Lieutenant."

"We are no longer playing games, Mr. Rommel. Half of the Embarcadero is still burning. Out at Fort Funston, there are a dozen dead mercenaries and evidence of a battle. I know this is about you and that old man and Black Horizon, and this time I am taking all of you into custody. There will be no more epic battles. The taxpayers don't like it." She looked around. "Where is that old man?" she said.

Rommel walked back into the kitchen as if looking for something. "He's not here," Rommel said.

"That's not what I asked you. I want to know where he is."

"I'm sorry. I can't help you."

"I don't need your help, Mr. Rommel. Today, the SFPD is helping itself. You and that old man and Richard Cheney and his people are all being taken into custody until we sort this out."

"I don't think Mr. Cheney's lawyers are going to appreciate that," Rommel said.

Carmichael changed the subject. "Where were you last night?"

"Here."

"Can anyone corroborate that?"

"Gunny and the dog."

"Were you anywhere near Fort Funston last night? Were you down by the Embarcadero?" she asked.

"No." It occurred to Rommel that part of being a good person was telling the truth. *Maybe that's why good people nearly always get screwed*, he thought.

"I don't believe you. There were reports of gunfire at Fort Funston in one of the old gun emplacements. Lots of dead men. Lots of forensic evidence. We are all over it. There was also a major fire at Pier 29. Explosions. The whole place went up in flames. The fire burned so hot, the fire department couldn't get close to the structure for almost two hours. Again, there is going to be a mountain of forensic evidence. If that evidence proves that you are involved, you will never live to see another day as a free man."

"Sounds serious."

"Is that charm? Half the city was a battleground last night. Is this your charm offensive?"

Rommel said nothing.

Lieutenant Carmichael looked down. "What happened to your fingers?"

"Belt sander got away from me."

"So where is this belt sander?"

"Like I said, it got away from me."

"No one is amused, Mr. Rommel. I, least of all. It appears that there were weapons being stored in Pier 29. High-tech weapons. Classified weapons and ammunition and explosives. Department of Homeland Security is down there right now. Do you know anything about that?"

"No. I have nothing to do with high-tech weaponry."

"There were more dead men at the pier. We think they were Black Horizon personnel. Do you know anything about that?"

"Lieutenant," Rommel said, "I don't know anything, but I will tell you what I think. I think Richard Cheney and Black Horizon are doing the same things here, in your city, that they did in Iraq, Afghanistan, and New Orleans. I believe there is money and power tied to just about everything they do. I don't believe they give a crap about you or your laws."

Carmichael looked at him. "That may be the most I have ever heard you say. As it so happens, you and I are going to visit Mr. Cheney. From there, we will all proceed to the Hall of Justice, and nobody will leave until I have answers."

Rommel knew it was an empty threat. It would be a major win for law enforcement if Cheney's lawyers didn't spring him in under thirty minutes.

Lieutenant Carmichael took out her cell phone and chose a number.

"Detective Garcia, meet me in front of the Swann building in twenty minutes." She pocketed the phone. "You're coming with me," she said to Rommel. "Just a minute, hands up." Carmichael reached into Rommel's jacket and extracted a black pistol.

"What's this?"

"I have a permit."

"Not when you're riding with me, you don't. I am in charge. We're going to talk to Cheney. If he doesn't have all the right answers, I am taking both of you into custody. I won't have you creating a situation."

Lieutenant Carmichael set the pistol on a counter and turned toward the door. Rommel leaned against the other counter, slid the Ka-Bar and sheath off the counter, tucked it—Argentine style, under his jacket, across the small of his back, and followed Carmichael out the door.

It was a short drive down Geary Street and over the hills into the Financial District. Carmichael parked the blue Crown Victoria directly in front of the Swann building. Detective Vincent Garcia was waiting. Together, she, Garcia, and Rommel rode the elevator to the twenty-sixth floor. The door opened, and the three stepped out into the spacious receiving area and onto the soft gray carpet. The reception desk was unoccupied. Carmichael looked around. No one. The floor seemed deserted. Carmichael turned to Detective Garcia. "Go that way and see if you can find anyone. Mr. Rommel and I will see if Cheney is in his office."

Rommel spoke, "An abandoned floor during the middle of a workday, that seems all right to you?"

"Just because the receptionist is not waiting for us doesn't mean the floor is abandoned," Carmichael responded. She looked at Detective Garcia. "Go," she said. "We'll be in Cheney's office."

"One more time: high-tech weapons, explosives, mercenaries—these are your words, not mine. You asked me if Black Horizon was involved. Now, you're in a secure building, their secure building, on a vacant floor, looking for the head of a mercenary army. If it was me, I would get back in the elevator and come back with more people and better equipment and tactics."

"You, thank God, are not me. This is the heart of the Financial District in the middle of the day. Mr. Cheney doesn't need to use force. He owns politicians and lawyers. He is going to tell me what I want to know, or I will take him into custody," Carmichael said. Carmichael walked into the reception area that served Cheney's suite of offices. Again, there was no secretary or receptionist. Carmichael knocked boldly on Cheney's door. On the other side, as if from a great distance, there was a muffled response. Lieutenant Carmichael opened the door. "San Francisco police department," she said.

"Come in."

Rommel followed Lieutenant Carmichael into Cheney's office. Dick Cheney sat behind his desk at the far end of the room.

"There's no one out front," Lieutenant Carmichael said, presumably by way of an explanation for the intrusion. "Mr. Cheney, I wonder if you can answer some questions for me."

Cheney glanced toward Rommel. His lean face tensed. "Is that man armed?"

"No, he isn't. I searched him myself."

Cheney smiled. "Splendid, please come in."

As Lieutenant Carmichael walked across the room, Cheney rose to greet them. The first thing Carmichael noticed was the flesh-colored latex gloves. She was already reaching for her service weapon when Cheney picked up the antique .45 from his desk and fired a round that struck her full in the chest, knocking her off her feet and onto her back. She lie motionless. Cheney leveled the pistol at Rommel as he walked around the desk. "Oh, she's all right. At least she is if she's wearing her protective vest. You are wearing your vest, aren't you, Lieutenant? Under that tasteful, understated blouse? I don't see any blood. These vests are marvelous. They can stop a .45-caliber slug from point blank. Isn't that so, Lieutenant?"

Standing over Carmichael, Cheney pointed the pistol down at her chest. The weapon bucked and roared. Carmichael's torso seemed to bounce from the floor. "Of course, while the vest prevents bullet penetration, it doesn't do much about the trauma of impact. Kinetic energy transfers to the target. Ribs break." Cheney fired again, the slug pounded into the other side of her chest. Carmichael's eyes rolled slightly as her body was concussed. "Makes an interesting interrogation tool," Cheney said.

"You mean torture."

"I mean recreation," Cheney responded, keeping the weapon trained on Rommel's torso. "You don't control people by killing them. If you take their lives, you have nothing. If you take their will, you have everything. If you can beat and rape and terrorize at will, you have everything. You take their spirit and their dignity, then you have everything."

"Gilhooley was right."

"Was, is the correct tense. He surprised my people in Sausalito, but he did not survive the encounter. Just like you're not going to survive this encounter. And, when this is over, Mr. Rommel, I am going to find that old lady and have her torn apart."

Unconsciously, Rommel braced himself for the bullet. Instead, Cheney retreated slowly toward his desk. "No bullet for you. This is one of your guns. You killed the good lieutenant. I have her partner restrained in the next office. You're going to kill him, too. Truly terrible, considering he's your godson. Crazed and having exhausted your ammunition, you attacked me with your bare hands. Fortunately, I had this…" Cheney set the pistol on the credenza and picked up the antique Venetian rapier.

• • •

Cheney held the blade at arm's length and rolled his wrist, moving the steel point in a lazy-eight pattern. "Exquisite balance." Cheney smiled. "A gentleman's weapon, much more elegant than Metal Storm. Can you imagine a firing rate of a million rounds a minute? No moving parts, remote control. I first saw it and thought it perfect for area defense against ground forces. Our clients saw it, and they were thinking market day in Jerusalem. A waste, but it's their money."

"So you're an arms peddler."

"I am a force of nature." Cheney slid his leg smoothly forward in a lunge. The blade caught Rommel high on the left side of his chest, penetrating easily. By the time Rommel understood what had happened, Cheney had withdrawn the blade and reassumed his *garde*.

"You spoiled quite a show in Union Square today. No matter. Six months from now, we will put on an even better show, perhaps Grant Park in Chicago."

Rommel looked around the office. Beyond a few items of bric-a-brac, there were no weapons. Against this weapon at this range, Rommel was unarmed and outclassed, and he knew it.

"As I said, a force of nature. I have my pick of the trained killers that our nation casts off from its military. For those who will do as they are told, I pay very well. I contract them to intelligence agencies, foreign nations, and now to those who can afford to pay, right here in America. Black Horizon is the only law enforcement the wealthy need or need fear. Every oligarch an emperor and for every emperor, Black Horizon as their Praetorian Guard. For Katrina, I had a light brigade in locations of affluence across Louisiana. It was an excellent opportunity to certify my newer people."

"Certify?"

"To ensure obedience. To find out who will torture or kill without hesitation, even when there is no discernible cause." Cheney slid into another lunge. Rommel dodged to his left, but the blade fixed itself into his thigh. Rommel grabbed at the blade with his bare hand, but the blade was gone before the bleeding could begin.

"It appears you have no defense, no final plan. I don't know why, but I expected much better from you, old man."

"Mind over matter," Rommel said, his eyes trying to follow the rapier's deadly steel tip.

Cheney circled to his right, maneuvering his prey against the coffee table in the center of the room. Rommel bumped against the table, momentarily losing his balance. He leaned back, as if to steady himself. Rommel grasped the single white vase on the table, straightened himself, and wheeling the vase overhead, flung it toward Cheney's head. Cheney parried the rapier against the vase, shattering it across the office. Rommel stormed forward as Cheney stumbled back, recovered, and aimed the deadly blade at Rommel's chest. As Rommel closed, Cheney's rapier thrust forward. Rommel swatted the steel down and away to his left using his right hand. The diamond-shaped blade bit into Rommel's abdomen, into the lower left quadrant of the big man's torso. Rommel stormed forward driving Cheney and the long blade backward. The blade was fixed and shafting deeper into Rommel's body, but he had guided it away from his heart and liver. Cheney braced himself, and the blade thrust savagely into Rommel.

Rommel roared. Sweat burst out across his face. *Jesus, God, that must be the kidney.* The pain blinded Rommel. He was transfixed like a large bug on an antique Venetian needle. For a moment, the pain paralyzed the big man. He faltered. Fading from consciousness, his mind drifted and took him back to a place nearly as dreadful, back to the last day of Force Recon training. Exhausted, the remaining candidates were paralyzed as the instructors, wearing gas masks, rained CX gas down on them. Their lungs burned as the instructors roared, "Move! What's the matter with you people? Nobody's shooting at you! Get up! Move, Move!" They had to reach deep inside, will themselves to breathe the powerful tear gas and overcome.

From that distant place, Rommel clawed back to the present, back to the office of a murderer, back to the last thing he would do on this planet. Without him, they would all die. Vince, Carmichael, Carolyn, Aubrey, they would all die. Gunny was gone. There was no law, no honored course, only a world of unbridled mercenary interests.

Cheney stepped back. He needed to withdraw the blade in order to stab again with more deadly effect, but Rommel matched Cheney's steps and charged forward. The big man grasped Cheney's jacket and drove forward, closing the distance between them and driving the blade completely through Rommel's body. As the blade ran him through, Rommel shoved Cheney against the wall. Cheney stared into Rommel's fevered eyes, twisting the blade, but the big man would not release his grasp.

"This is it? Mind over matter?" Cheney said.

Rommel reached into his jacket, behind his back, grasped the Ka-Bar, popped the snap and drew the blade from the sheath. He held it briefly before Cheney's face. "If you don't mind, it don't matter," Rommel grunted and shoved the black blade under Cheney's ribs, twisting the blade, fishing for the pericardial sac. As the sac punctured, the Ka-Bar found the heart. Cheney all but collapsed. His head rolled back, and, from a far-off place, Cheney whispered, "Oh, God."

Rommel clutched Cheney's throat in a giant fist, crushing the dying man's windpipe. Rommel thrust his face before Cheney's. "God don't want to hear you bellyache." They were the last words Cheney heard as his lifeless body slid down the wall.

Rommel transferred the Ka-Bar to his left hand and shuffled toward the credenza and the blue-steel .45. Rommel grasped the weapon and struggled toward the door. In the anteroom, Vince was kneeling, cuffed and gagged. The carpet was covered in thick plastic sheeting intended to catch the spatter of Vince's impending execution. Two men stood over Vince, guns in hand. They looked up to see Rommel: pistol in one hand, knife in the other, and a long sword running completely through him. They hesitated. The taller of the two men dropped his pistol. The second man hesitated an instant longer and dropped his as well.

Rommel could feel himself fading. He wouldn't be effective much longer. "Now, you believe in the law. Now, you're ready to face a judge and a jury." Rommel shot each man in a matter of an instant. Rommel wobbled. "The praetor says, '*fuck you*'."

Rommel knelt next to Vincent, fumbled through his sport coat and grasped Vince's radio. "Ten thirty-three, Ten thirty-three. Shots fired, officer down, 26th floor of the Swann Building. Hostiles on-site." The radio fell from his hand. Rommel fished Vince's keys from his pocket and unlocked the cuffs. Vince tore the gag from his face.

"You shouldn't let the other boys push you around like this. They won't respect you," Rommel said, drifting between worlds. "Your boss is hurt. No one in this building is a good guy. Watch yer ass." Rommel pulled at the plastic and eased himself down onto the thick wool carpet. "I think I'll bleed here."

Vince reached for the rapier handle. "Leave it," Rommel said. "I'll just bleed faster. An ambulance would be nice."

Vince moved to the door and his boss. As he was leaving, he thought he heard the big man say, "This is not the country I grew up in."

27

Mission Emergency

Matt Rommel floated in the blackness, consciousness without a body. He listened for the beat of the choppers. If he could hear helicopters, that would be familiar territory. It would mean life. He'd been medevaced before. He'd been deep under, floating to the beat of the chopper en route to life.

No chopper.

Hovering in the blackness, Rommel had a sense of others. A sense of space, a great dark space filled with others. At first, it seemed as if he felt it, and then became dimly aware that he could hear. He could hear wailing. This was a place of suffering. This was hell. He wondered where Cheney was. He wondered if he could kill Cheney again. If he could spend eternity finding and killing Cheney, would that really be hell?

Rommel drifted in the darkness on a slow-moving wave of pain that he was only aware of in a general way.

Black became gray. Gray became an unfocused sepia. Rommel saw a wall, against it, cabinets of metal and glass.

Controlled pandemonium surrounded him but did not touch him. Nothing touched him. Rommel found he couldn't shift. His arms wouldn't serve him. He looked. His left wrist was tethered by a beige velcro strap. He looked to his right and saw the same thing. Under the blue fluorescent light, Rommel breached into consciousness. He wasn't in hell. This was Mission Emergency Hospital, an understandable mistake.

Rommel came to sense that someone was standing at his side, Detective Vince Garcia.

"I can't move my arms," Rommel said.

"You're in custody, Uncle Matt." It was the first time Vince had acknowledged that honorary status while on duty.

"For what?"

"Three people are dead, Uncle Matt."

"You mean the guy who shot your boss three times and the two who were going to execute you?"

"It's a formality."

"It's bullshit."

"You had a concealed weapon."

"The Ka-Bar? Good thing. Besides, I have a permit. I don't see why it wouldn't apply to knives. I'd like to scratch my ... nose."

"Leave your nose alone. You've been under for two days. You were in surgery for more than seven hours."

"Mission Emergency?"

"If you've been shot or stabbed, this is the best place in the Bay Area. They get lots of practice. Some people from the federal government want to talk to you."

"Who?"

"FBI, ATF."

"Just in the nick of time."

"The feds are tearing Black Horizon apart. They're searching every facility the company owns or rents. They've already found a mountain of experimental weaponry and classified material. Even the Department of State is involved."

"I'll bet," Rommel said.

"What does that mean?"

"It means, who do you think put these murderers in business in the first place? The federal government paid billions to these people to shoot up Iraq and Afghanistan. They made this company exempt from the law: looting, murder, rape, torture. US contractors were above the law, free to do whatever the feds didn't want to dirty their hands with. Now, these same companies are in America doing the same things. They were above the law in New Orleans. How many of those dead bodies floating in the filthy water were courtesy of Black Horizon? Why shouldn't they do the same things here? Maybe there is no law. Maybe Gunny was right." Rommel tried to turn, tried to get a better look at Detective Garcia. "Where's Gunny?"

"Gunny's dead."

Rommel paused a long minute. "I didn't ask you how he was. I asked you where he was."

"Gunny's at Marin General in the morgue. They found him in a bungalow in Sausalito. There were three dead Black Horizon operatives with him."

"Somebody get away?"

"At least one. We don't know how many. It appears Gunny was shot by someone behind the bungalow looking in through the kitchen window."

Rommel fixed detective Garcia with a stare. "Are you going to find him?"

"The guy in the backyard?"

"The guy in the backyard."

"He took off in a black SUV. As soon as we have the vehicle, we'll have his prints or DNA. We will find him."

"Your word?"

• • •

"My word."

Rommel felt very tired. "I have to make arrangements for Gunny."

"You're badly injured. I don't think you will be going anywhere for a while."

"Undo these restraints."

"I can't. I'm sorry."

"Come a little closer, Vince. I need to tell you something." Detective Vince Garcia stood closer to the bed. Rommel looked at him, searching the face of the young man he'd known for his entire life.

"Vincent, don't spend your life being the guy who just follows orders. Don't be that guy. Stupid and cowardly people give orders just as wise, decent, and brave people do. Know who you are obeying and know why. If you can remember this you are gonna like yourself a lot better thirty years from now." Rommel smiled and closed his eyes. He could feel sleep washing over him like a great, cool, gentle, fog bank.

Rommel felt a tugging at his wrists. The restraints fell away. Rommel opened his eyes. Vince was still standing there. "I'm going to take a nap, but you need to know two things: When you talk to your superiors, make certain they understand that if I am some sort of suspect, then my story is that the SFPD is the group that led a civilian into an ambush, and nearly got everyone killed. If I am not a suspect, then this was all a tragic development that no one could have foreseen.

"The second thing has to do with these feds. Be careful. Half of the agencies you are going to talk to put Black Horizon in business. They spent billions on these mercenary companies—gave them access to sophisticated weapons and technology. They commissioned violent acts that the government didn't want to be associated with. They turned a blind eye to the murder of unarmed Americans in New Orleans after the hurricane. These people aren't looking for the truth. They know the truth. They're trying to figure out who they have to silence." Rommel smiled as he drifted back into the fog bank of sleep. "Good Luck."

28

Zippy and Bob

As quiet as a morgue. No, as quiet as a tomb, Bob thought. *That's the expression. Still, a morgue can be a pretty quiet place. Huh, a pun. Still and quiet, get it?* It was a defense mechanism—bad puns, random thoughts. Being a morgue attendant was not a bad job. Pay was OK. Sometimes, there was work. Sometimes, there was quiet. At Marin General, things were often quiet in the morgue. It wasn't a large hospital, and it served a wealthy community. People didn't die here all that often. They died quietly at home. If there was to be a struggle against death, there was money enough to do it at a sophisticated medical center. Best of all, violent death was the exception rather than the rule.

Being a morgue attendant, Bob thought. *I am a being; they are not. I think and feel and breathe, and they do not. Some day, I will be like them, and someone else will be and I will not.* Essere. Etre. Being. How many ways were there to say it and how few ways to understand?

I knew him, Horatio, Bob thought. "Goddamn job."

"What?" It was the trainee, a referral from the junior college work-study program. Not an intern, in Bob's book.

An intern was a doctor, a doctor in training. Bob couldn't pronounce the kid's name. After some negotiation, they settled on Rog, but, in the end, when Bob spoke to him at all, he called him Zippy. Maybe someday, Zippy would *be* and Bob would lie here, inert matter, pausing briefly in the hospital morgue before final disposition.

"Nothing."

Today was a big day for Zippy. In the room just outside the office, there were four body bags on four gurneys. In the entire morgue, there were only six bodies: two octogenarians and these four bad boys. A real shoot-out! Three killed by gunfire and one killed by an explosion. Incredible! This was the big time, just like those police labs on TV. This was an opportunity, and Zippy was going to learn in spite of lazy old Bob. Zippy had unzipped the bags and pulled the sides apart in order to see as much as he could. He didn't touch any of the bodies. That was the rule. "Touch a body without my permission and you're out on your ass," Bob had said. Still, so much to learn: lividity, rigor, the gaseous onset of decay. Zippy had the feeling that a mysterious, complex process was at work. A sonorous blat startled Zippy, followed by a sickening smell.

"Whoa, one of these guys farted! Do they do that?"

"Yeah, Zippy," Bob said, "They do that. It's one of the reasons I don't go around unzipping the bags." Bob wondered if the kid would ever figure out that it was Zippy's powerful curiosity, the need to unzip the bag and see what the dead were up to that earned Zippy his nickname.

Zippy had all four bags open. Three big, tough-looking guys and one skinny old man. Zippy's eyes were drawn to the biggest man, partially because he was the biggest man, also because his wounds were the most catastrophic. The jaw was broken away, and what was left of the right eye had fallen out of its orbit. So this is what a grenade does. A flinch caught the corner of Zippy's eye.

"One of these guys just twitched," Zippy called out.

"What part?"

"Huh?" Zippy replied.

"What part of the body twitched?" Bob said.

"The leg. From the knee."

"Yeah," Bob said through the office door, "that happens."

This was just amazing, Zippy thought, *the human body unwinding itself. And these guys! Four dead men, one violent act. What had happened? Was it the three young guys against the little old guy? How old was the old gentleman, anyway? What chain of events had brought him here to this gurney?* Even besides his age and stature, he seemed different from the other men on a fundamental level, somehow. Zippy moved so he could study the old man's face. Character lines spilled from the closed eyes, prominent nose, and jawline, strong even in death. What had this man been like?

Drawn toward the closed eyes, Zippy looked toward the office door. The door was closed. There was something about the old man. Something about him made Zippy want to know more. Zippy made a decision. He would break the one rule. His hand trembled as he reached toward the old man, gently lifting an eyelid. Zippy called out.

"So the eyes? The eyes twitch, too?"

Bob hesitated, stood up, the chair skittering back toward the wall. Storming out of the office, Bob advanced on Zippy who jumped back from the old man's gurney. "Did you say eyes?"

"I'm sorry. I'm sorry," Zippy called out.

"Show me," Bob roared. "Show me right now."

Zippy pointed at the old man's eye. Bob lifted the lid, watching closely. Ever so faintly, the eye flickered.

Bob pushed away from the gurney, running toward the wall phone.

"I'm sorry," Zippy repeated, still apologizing for touching the old man.

"Shut up, Zippy, you done good." Bob grasped the receiver and punched at the phone buttons. The call clicked through.

"This is the morgue. I need a team and a crash cart down here stat. We got a live one."

29

On Monsters

The arctic wind slammed the double doors against their steel frames. Rommel's mukluks shuffled along the highly waxed linoleum. The yellow walls carried a greenish tinge, courtesy of the bluish cast from the fluorescent lights. A PFC stepped out of the reception office. "Colonel Lorca wants to see you, sir."

Rommel nodded and continued along the highly glossed corridor. By Rommel's reckoning, it was a meeting that was nearly three months in the making. Rommel had spent the better part of the first month in sick bay. Alone, he had lain there, in the only occupied rack in the entire sick bay. At first there was an attending physician, and then, after a few weeks, only a corpsman. One dreary day led to the next, and, always, there was the driving rain and the howling of the wind. Eventually, as he began to move about, Rommel learned that he was being held on an island in the Aleutian chain, in a facility that had initially been constructed to support a campaign against the Japanese on Attu and Kiska. The facility had been abandoned for nearly twenty years and only recently reactivated.

After the first month, Rommel came to understand that he was not technically in custody. This was not to be Gitmo North. Uniforms were provided: fatigues, class A's, a pair of boots, and a pair of low quarters. Rommel wore the fatigues and parka when he journeyed out. This was a sizeable island. There was a snowcapped mountain and a lagoon, ideal for digging clams. There was even a sort of a forest. Trees not being native to the island, Adak National Forest had been planted seventy years ago to bolster morale. It consisted of about thirty trees. The tiny forest was next to an abandoned pet cemetery. Rommel visited often and read the bleached headstones: "We love you, Bandit. We miss you." "Pooch, Best dog in the world." Rommel thought about Chesty. Diego would care for her.

One day, an unmarked envelope arrived from Diego's lawyer. It contained a limited power of attorney. Presumably, this would allow his lawyer to maintain Rommel's household in his absence. It occurred to Rommel that, whatever the reason for his detention, they might not kill him. The thought grew stronger when he was issued a nameplate, major's insignia, and copies of the ribbons he had earned over the course of his long concluded career. He wore them. They made him feel like an old man in a uniform from another life.

But the uniform and the name badge and the ribbons began to have an effect on him. He had no assigned duties, but he had to do something. From a discreet distance, he watched the NCO and the young troops. Eventually, when they fell out for PT, Rommel fell out. The NCO added martial arts drills to the regimen, and Rommel lined up for that, too. During those drills, Rommel relearned a number of lessons. The chief lesson was that, every year, marines got younger, faster, and tougher. Knee and elbow strikes tattooed Rommel with deep-purple bruises from his calves to his neck. More often than anyone expected, Rommel would defeat his opponent, but they made him suffer every time.

Over the weeks, the young troops all seemed to know something that Rommel did not. It was almost as if they were all watching him, studying him. Once or twice, he had overheard comments regarding his ribbons. Some of the troops had never seen the one for a Silver Star. None had ever seen one with an oak leaf cluster. One of them observed the clusters on his Purple Heart ribbon. "How do you get hurt that many fucking times? They didn't teach those guys to duck?"

There were the remnants of an old woodworking shop: jigsaw, plywood. Rommel resolved to show them something come the next series of hand-to-hand combat drills.

It was after these months attached to this facility, months without understanding the overall situation, that Rommel was finally summoned. Rommel walked down fifty years of buffed and waxed hallway. To his left, a single plastic sign announced *Commanding Officer*. Rommel rapped out two firm knocks.

"Come."

Rommel walked into the room and stood squarely in front of the massive gray metal desk, but did not salute. Behind the desk, a Marine Corps colonel, ten years Rommel's junior, looked up, eyes quizzical.

"You don't salute, Major?"

"I'm retired. Have been for years." Rommel looked at the other two men in the room: one a navy commander, and the other a civilian—an expressionless man in a black suit, white shirt, and black tie. He was the faceless government official, straight out of central casting.

"No, Major. As has been explained to you, like every other retiree, the terms of your retirement state that you are subject to recall. It pleases the Department of the Navy to recall you, so here you are."

"From a hospital bed in San Francisco to a sickbay in a reactivated facility on Adak."

"Whatever happened, you were going to be taken into custody. The San Francisco police wanted you. Certain organizations within the Department of Homeland Security wanted you. We wanted you. DHS sent officials like Mr. Smith here. Very few of the people interrogated by Mr. Smith are ever heard from again. We sent marines and a chopper. Consider yourself lucky."

Rommel looked to his right. In the steel chair, with arm rests and deep-green seat and back cushions, sat a man who was no longer young, but not quite middle aged. He wore the company uniform: black suit, black tie, white shirt. The nondescript uniform was intended to create a sense of dread. Rommel smiled at the man as he would a lobster in a tank in an expensive restaurant. The man did not respond.

"Before we get started on the real reason for this drawn-out exercise, I have to ask you: What is the purpose of these wooden tomahawks? I see them in the rec room and every other damned place. I've got young troops with scratches on their faces and hands, and some with divots in their scalps."

"One man, any weapon, sir," Rommel said. "Truth is, these kids were routinely kicking my ass in the hand-to-hand drills. I needed a way to distract them and get them using a mock weapon that I had an advantage with. They learn quickly, and when they get out to the fleet, they'll have a skill that others don't."

"You understand that, at your age, no one expects you to drill with the troops."

"I understand. Believe it or not, sir, I knew a man that did just that for forty-eight solid years."

Colonel Lorca glanced into a folder. "Yes, Gunny Gilhooley, right? I never met him."

"He's gone now, sir."

"Wrong, Major. Master Gunnery Sergeant Gilhooley, USMC, Retired has only recently been released from the San Francisco VA Medical Hospital. Thanks to the power of attorney you signed and the cooperation of your attorney, we've moved him into your home. Apparently, he has a friend. A nice woman and her seven-year-old daughter look in on him and his dog almost every day."

"One-eyed?"

"The woman? I don't know. I assume she has two eyes."

"The dog. One eye, black coat with a white patch on her chest. That's my dog."

"Major, I honestly don't care. Not about the dog or the woman or any of it. I do care about you and that old goblin rolling through an American city like the Red Army."

Colonel Lorca continued, "There has been some disagreement regarding your custody. Mr. Smith and his colleagues would like to take you somewhere discreet and debrief you. They want to debrief you until they are satisfied that they know everything you know."

"And?" Rommel said.

Mr. Smith stood and approached Rommel. "And there are people of some importance who are concerned that you represent a threat to the security of this nation."

Rommel darkened and leaned, ever so slightly, toward Mr. Smith. "By doing what, exactly?"

"For one thing, killing a large number of men who, only years earlier, would have been your brothers-in-arms."

Rommel looked at Smith as if he were the only man in the room. Involuntarily, Rommel began to glower. Rommel said nothing. Killing him was no problem for Rommel, but he would not speak to this man.

Lorca spoke, "Apparently, Major Rommel does not respect you enough to speak to you. What you need to understand is that, to Major Rommel, no man who takes up arms against the American people is his brother-in-arms. In this regard, Major Rommel is not alone."

"That's not good enough," Smith said.

Lorca smiled. "I understand your position. You need to impress your will on your subject. You should threaten him. Why don't I leave you two alone for ten…"

"Five," Rommel said.

"...five minutes, and you can terrorize Major Rommel, throw a good scare into him."

"I need to know what this man's intentions are," Smith said.

"Major?" Lorca said.

"I have no further targets."

"The major is out of targets. Is that sufficient?"

Smith spoke, "You don't fear me. I don't care. Understand that the next time you go mad-dog, will be your last."

Rommel said nothing.

Lorca spoke up, "Major, you are a lucky man. You are lucky because you are free to choose. You can go back to your life. All you have to do is keep your piehole shut. Your other option is a CIA prison in Eastern Europe for weeks of enhanced interrogation and a shallow grave in a toxic waste dump on the outskirts of Gdańsk."

"Why am I getting a choice?" Rommel asked.

"There was a lot of conversation about that," Lorca said. "Communication at the highest levels. Our first objective in bringing you here was to keep you out of the custody of America's burgeoning secret-police infrastructure. You can choose to believe this or not, but you have a single friend near the top of the food chain."

"I don't have any friends like that."

"Really? This station was reactivated, supposedly as a training exercise, but it's really so that the Department of the Navy could keep you out of the hands of the DHS black-ops' people. There are sixty marines on this rock just to feed you and keep you safe. A first lieutenant or a marine captain would have been sufficient to command a facility like this. They used an O-6. Nothing about this is usual. The fact that you are still alive is unusual."

"I don't know anyone with that kind of juice."

"He knows you. He compares you with Smedley Butler."

"Nobody compares to Smedley Butler."

"I don't see it either, but he does. It seems that, years ago, he was on NATO HQ staff when the decision was made to abandon a village in Bosnia to the Serbs. He said that, at the time, he thought the shame of such an act would kill him. Then you and the Dutch contingent disobeyed direct orders; the Serbs backed down after a brief, sharp action. Psychologically, the momentum shifted for IFOR. It became clear that the Serbs might be crazy, but they were not suicidal. Your lone, highly placed friend has instructed me to give you this." The colonel held out a stiff white linen envelope. Rommel took it. The envelope was sealed but was not addressed to anyone. Rommel opened it. Inside was a single square of stiff cardstock with three engraved lines:

"Whoever fights monsters should see to it that,
In the process,
He does not become a monster."

Nietzsche

Rommel looked up and studied the colonel's face. No explanation was forthcoming.

"The next objective of your tour at this facility was to determine just how out of control you were. You and your geriatric pal broke a lot of furniture, Major. We had to know just how crazy you were."

"And?"

"About average for a retired marine. We really would like to know what it was that set you off."

"Something I heard," Rommel said.

"Something that was said directly to you by another person?"

"Yes."

"That's it?"

"That's all I have to say."

"OK, then explain this to me, because none of our forensics people can. An autopsy has determined that Richard Cheney died as the result of a stab wound to the heart."

"That's the way I remember it," Rommel said.

"Yes, but his larynx was also crushed. That wound would have been sufficient to cause death, but our people believe that *this* wound occurred after the fatal wound."

"Your people are correct."

"It doesn't really matter, but we want to know why you inflicted the second wound."

"I didn't want him making peace with God."

"What?"

"Colonel, I don't know everything. There are a few things that I believe I can't prove. I believe that God is capable of forgiving anything. Personally, I'm counting on it. Mr. Cheney ruined a lot of lives, and he literally made me kill him. In those last moments on earth, I didn't want him reaching out to God."

"And you think you can prevent that?"

"Probably not. It was a reflex."

"So you killed a man. And as he lay dying, you crushed his throat as a reflex."

"Something like that."

"Our beloved corps created quite a specimen."

Lorca closed the file. "Your one highly placed friend wants you to know that Gilhooley is alive and living in your house, and that you are out of whiskey and contraband cigars."

"What about Black Horizon? What about the government use of armed mercenaries against American citizens?"

"I wouldn't worry about Black Horizon. They may be the only security firm to go out of business due to attrition. That's not our doing. That's your work. Mercenaries like to get paid, not take casualties. Too much violent death makes a mercenary seek work with other firms. The IRS, FBI, DHS, and CIA are dismantling Black Horizon's corporate structure and taking every dollar and stick of furniture they had. That was our doing. Black Horizon is gone."

"And the other firms like it?"

"Every generation has its secrets."

"Not every generation has set armed thugs on the American people."

"Really? The Pullman Strike? The Bonus Marchers? Rouge River? Go home, Major. The loss of Pier 29 has officially been determined to be accidental, a single unlucky piece of lost ordinance from the Korean War and frayed insulation on an electrical circuit. As for Battery Richmond P. Davis, that's an urban legend, possibly started when a low-budget film company commandeered the facility for a single night of filming without getting a permit to film. What the San Francisco police believed to be a mountain of forensic evidence was determined by DHS to be bogus, and the entire lot was unfortunately lost. There is one police lieutenant who is having trouble letting go. Unfortunately, she finds herself without evidence or official support."

"What am I supposed to do with Gilhooley?"

Lorca smiled. "You're on your own, Major. The corps had him for forty-eight years. Now, he's your problem."

About the Author

F.M. Kahren is the author of *Brand Loyalty*, his debut novel and Matt Rommel's first adventure.

A graduate of UC Berkeley with a degree in English, Dr. Kahren also has a masters and doctorate in business administration from the University of North Dakota and Golden Gate University respectively.

He has published a number of technical articles for industry journals and is the author of *Strategic Planning: The Practices of PCS Companies and the Academic Literature.*

In addition to serving as a Minuteman missile crew commander and missile operations staff officer, Dr. Kahren has worked extensively in the telecommunications and rail transportation industries. The latter experience allowed him to perform a number of studies in Latin America regarding privatized rail concessions for prospective concessionaires.

As he sums it up: "I've had some interesting jobs, been fortunate in my friends and family, and managed to educate myself. I've traveled the miles and read the books. Now, I want to bring interesting stories to people and entertain them. The Matt Rommel adventures are just such stories.

On the lighter side, he was awarded a "Dishonorable Mention" for Vile Puns in the 2007 Bulwer-Lytton contest, a venue in which the purple prose is deliberate.

He lives with his family in Northern California.

• • •